LOOKING

TOWARD

EDEN

Revised Second Edition

by

Terry Pellman

Also by Terry Pellman

Eden's Dawn – The sequel to Looking Toward Eden

Weston Road

Mating For Life

Averton

When I Was Young

Revisiting Dreams: Eclectic Tales

October, 2021

"Omaha for the capital?" Nina Burton gazed down at the large uniformed bodies swarming over the green field at Memorial Stadium with little actual interest. She was a lifelong Nebraska resident, but if the Ohio State Buckeyes defeated the Cornhuskers on this rainy October Saturday afternoon, it would have proven to be of little consequence to her.

Without looking at Bryce Hamilton, she sat back in the plush seat in the sky box and took a sip of her Budweiser while relishing her good fortune in being shielded from the weather. Nina Burton was fifty-eight, with shoulder length black hair and a figure that had changed little since she had been a student at the large Lincoln campus, leaping and twirling on the sidelines and capturing more male attention than any of the other cheerleaders on the University of Nebraska squad.

Nina finally broke the tense silence: "Tell me again… why you'd want to make Omaha the capital of this Frankenstein monster. Don't get me wrong… being a native Nebraskan, I'm flattered by the proposition."

Hamilton sighed and shook his head in frustration at her skepticism. "Omaha has infrastructure, a feasible location within the group, and it would somewhat placate those who fear total dominance by Texas."

Nina lit a forbidden cigarette, looked out upon the field and shook her head once again. "Give it up Bryce."

Hamilton turned his head slowly, took the glasses off his wrinkled face and ran his fingers through the gray hair that remained around the rim of the skull. "It's not a Frankenstein monster, Nina. You will see next week."

Nina rested her elbow on the arm of her chair and leaned her head down. She began to rub her forehead as if to alleviate a headache. "And what is this thing going to be called?"

"This thing, as you call it, does not yet have a formal name. However I tend to like what was suggested by Congressman Bridger from Montana. He suggested the Constitutional States of America."

Nina released a heavy sigh. "Explain it to me the way you will to the general public, please."

"The new nation would be based upon the original Constitution of the United States of America. The proposal is that all the participating states adopt nearly all of the original Constitution and all the amendments. Special emphasis will be placed on the 10th amendment, so that we would never drift away from the founders' intent ever again."

Nina shook her head. "Has anyone noticed that you end up with the same initials… CSA… as in the Confederate States of America? The left and the media will have a field day with that."

"Nina my dear, that's a perfect example of the kinds of criticism we will have to learn to pay no attention to."

Nina began to laugh derisively. "Bryce, you know I love you like a brother. But this whole thing is a fairytale. Once you get all those separatist geniuses together in a room, the egos will come out of the woodwork, and all you're going to hear are the bright ideas on how things could have been even better. States will start maneuvering for privileges, and it will be one little turf battle after another."

"Nina, all the study groups are pretty much finished. Two years of work, research and debate are coming together."

"Okay Bryce, I'm ready for you to ask me the question."

Hamilton stood and stretched, his aging but still muscular six foot eight frame a reminder of why he had been such a force on the basketball floor for Creighton University in the mid-1960s. He turned and peered down at his law partner, a close friend in spite of their age differences and disparate personalities.

"Okay, here I go. Are you going to join us in this?"

Nina took another drawl on her cigarette, closed her eyes and leaned backward. "Heaven help me… I'm going to go along with you. I'm not with you because I think this is a good idea. And I'm sure as hell not with you because I think this is going to work. But I'm with you because I don't know what else to do. If it works, America will be forever changed. Of course, America is already being changed forever before our eyes… so why not join you in being a part of history?" She arched an eyebrow at him and laughed. "Of course, the place in history may be a mere footnote to be derided in future college sociology and political science classes. On the other hand, if it becomes a substantial movement, and actually results in changing the makeup of America, we will someday be looked upon either as heroic or traitorous."

Nina seemed to look off in the distance for a moment. "Ever since this subject came up, I have been haunted by that line from John F. Kennedy's inauguration speech."

Hamilton chuckled. "Okay, which line was that?"

Nina once again closed her eyes and leaned her head back: "United there is little we cannot do in a host of cooperative ventures. Divided there is little we can do – for we dare not meet a powerful challenge at odds and split asunder."

"And when did you start quoting Democrats?"

Nina took a deep puff. "When they are right." She pointed toward the scoreboard. She looked around to reassure herself that no one else was present in the cozy reserved confines. "The fourth quarter is just starting. Would you like to rehearse your speech? Monday morning is rapidly approaching."

Hamilton gazed at his longtime friend and smiled. "Your tone of voice seems to imply that Monday morning will be a moment of doom."

She looked up at him and sighed deeply. "And what do you expect, Bryce?"

Hamilton began to laugh. "Less than forty-eight hours left before I will be savaged by the press and members of both parties tripping over themselves to see who can appear the most reasonable in contrast to my extremism. All the talking heads should send me gifts, because I will be giving them so much to talk about they won't be forced to come up with an original idea for two months."

"You are so correct. That's what you get for being a former United States Senator. When someone like you makes a speech like you're going to make, everything takes on a whole new level of gravity. Having a bunch of state legislators popping off alongside a few failed candidates for governorships is one thing. Most of the newspaper coverage of the movement has been relegated to inside pages of major newspapers.

"Your involvement, sir, brings a new level of seriousness to this. I suppose that's why this whole effort has gotten so little media attention on the national level until this week. Your organization was just being written off as another fringe group, like a Tea Party chapter on steroids. Then a former Senator emerges as the spokesperson…".

Hamilton shook his head. "I see no choice. The Swamp…the mainstream media… prevailed and disheartened so many."

Nina lit another cigarette. "So, Bryce… everything is all arranged?"

Hamilton exhaled slowly. "Monday morning… Omaha Crowne Plaza Hotel. We have verifications that all the regular broadcast networks will be there, and Fox, CNN, NewsNet, MSNBC and C-SPAN will be covering it all live."

"Are you nervous?"

"I have been nervous two times in my life. The first was when I married Cynthia, and the second was the first time I was shot at in Korea. Oddly enough, I'm not nervous about this movement, or the corresponding interviews and press conferences that will come along. I feel more weary and disheartened that this has become necessary, than I am frightened of being in front of the cameras."

"So, are you going to read me your speech?"

Hamilton reached slowly inside his down – filled jacket and pulled out an envelope. He took the envelope from the inside pocket and pulled out several sheets of paper and unfolded them. "I wish this morning to address the citizens of the United States of America. I ask you to listen to my words carefully, for only by listening to what I actually say, either now on live television, or on an unedited video replay or text of this address, will you be able to make your own evaluations of what I have to say.

"It is important that you understand that it will not be possible for you to find any objective analysis of this address, for what I have to say is controversial, and anathema to most of those who report the news in this nation. I ask only that you listen to my actual words, agree with me if it is your belief, or condemn me or suggest me to be a fool. But if you judge me a fool, see to it that it is your own conclusion, not one provided to you.

"Two weeks ago, representatives from fourteen states assembled in Wichita, Kansas to draft a resolution proposing the nonviolent, political withdrawal of those states from the United States of America.

"That conference was a culmination of more than two years of work at the state level to identify the goals to be achieved by such withdrawal. Another point of order was to establish a detailed framework for how this new federation of sovereign states would form and govern. I wish to emphasize that this task was not as overwhelming as you may think: that work had already been accomplished by our Founding Fathers many generations ago. In the recent decades, we simply abandoned those wise and precious principles, portraying them to be the outdated rants of quaint and very morally flawed men.

"I also want to emphasize this next point very clearly: much of our discussion at the Wichita conference centered on the prospects of reconciling our differences with the President of the United States and the leaders of the two houses of Congress from both of the currently dominant political parties. Unfortunately, our request for our executive committee to meet face-to-face with President Malcolm, House Speaker Riley and Senate President Burroughs was rejected out of hand.

"In light of this rebuff, we proceeded to obtain a pledge from one or more members of the state legislatures in each of the fourteen states represented at the conference willing to introduce a resolution in the state legislature to withdraw from the United States of America. It will be the intent of affirming states to form a new union based upon the original Constitution that until recent years, was a governing basis of our federal government.

"It is our goal that such votes will be accomplished within the next forty-five days. There is no minimum number of states that will be required for this process to move forward. If one or two states decide to walk down this path, that shall be their choice, and the new federation will be composed of such states. Nor do participating states need to be contiguous. We believe that technology will provide the same degree of interaction between such states as we now enjoy with Alaska and Hawaii.

"These steps are taken with great reluctance, and in great sorrow. However, as a nation we have forgotten that it was the states that created the federal government, giving sanction and birth to the United States of America. The states are not mere political subdivisions of the federal government. Therefore, each state's first obligation lies with the best interests of the residents of that state.

"Most of all, the states must preserve freedom and economic opportunity for citizens. The ongoing crisis of debt we have been experiencing for far too many years. combined with the policies of the current Administration has made it impossible for citizens of the United States of America to hold any reasonable hope for the preservation of an economy based upon free enterprise. Having a span of renewed economic freedom under President Trump only makes the regression back to overregulation more bitter to accept.

"We feel that in the six months that have passed since the credit rating of the United States of America was again downgraded, our citizens have been shown no reason to believe that there is any real heart among our collective body of elected officials in Washington D.C. to take the steps necessary to restore solvency. Even though we are in an interest rate crisis, the housing market is in chaos and the numbers of homeless are overwhelming resources in many cities, large and small, short-sighted political interests are still taking precedence over finding the remedy to our financial disaster.

"One of the main reasons we have had for decades to revere the United States of America has been our freedom to elect our leaders. Unfortunately, in the most recent national elections, our voting citizenry chose to do nothing but embrace anew the practices that have brought us to the door of despair, and rejected those who offered painful, but necessary alternatives. Therefore, many of us believe deep in our hearts, that this separation is sadly necessary.

"This new union will be comprised of one to fourteen states, and will place the economic security and reasonable provision of public services at the top of its list of priorities. This union will provide an environment in which free enterprise can flourish, engage in fair trade with other nations and abstain from any treaties or international entanglements not in the best interests of its citizens.

"Although the states will have a high level of sovereignty within this new union, it is certain that the states will be as free from interference from the new national government as possible. The degree to which there will be any uniformity of state laws is still to be seen. However, it is evident from the discussions that have been held, that the new national government will not be permitted to legislate rights or restrictions in matters such as the right to bear arms.

"The failed attempt by the Senate to accomplish universal firearms registration that took place four months ago is still fresh in all of our memories, regardless of our individual stances on the matter. I believe it is safe to say, this new union will be a place where the unfettered right to keep and bear arms will never again be challenged.

"Once the roster of participating states has been established, another meeting will be held in Omaha in late December of this year. That meeting will be for the purpose of finalizing guidelines for states proposing to join the new union and send their delegates to a convention to be held hopefully by January. At that January convention, the delegates will vote on an effective date for the withdrawal of the participating states from the United States of America, and the establishment of this new nation.

"Please understand, that my role is one of nothing more than a convening chairman of the Council for a Free America. All that I have shared with you this morning, and all that I will share with you afterwards in response to your questions, is my summary of months of discussions in which I have been involved. I cannot speak for individual states, their legislators or any potential delegates who will be meeting in Omaha as this process unfolds."

Bryce folded the sheets and returned them to the envelope, and once again placed them in his coat pocket. Instead of looking at Nina, he appeared to be staring into space

"You know, Nina. I am a basketball fellow. I don't even care that much for football. Every season I reserve this private box just so that I can be a loyal supporter and have a place to impress guests and speak with them in confidence. So what do you think of the statement?"

"Do you really think those comments about the media deserve so much emphasis, especially so close to the beginning?"

"If we had a fair and objective media, we would never have gotten to this point. Aside from that, what you think about my statement?"

Nina looked at her colleague with a thin smile. "Not too bad. Polish it up a little more, then go out and buy some Vaseline, because Monday morning, the press is going to shaft you, and most of your old friends are going to abandon you."

~~~

John Malcolm had served as President of the United States for less than nine months, and he still greeted Monday mornings with the same attitude as did most Americans. However, this was not a Monday morning like many others. He glanced at his watch to see that only three and one half hours remained before the crackpot former Senator from Nebraska would ruin his day.

Malcolm nervously walked the floor in the Oval Office, waiting impatiently for the arrival of his Attorney General, Julia Stafford. As he wore a path back and forth in front of his desk, the portly Malcolm wondered how he could be anything but trim, taking into account his nervous habit.

He looked down at his desk, to the thick document that rested there neglected. He put on his glasses and nervously ran his fingers through his red hair as he seethed in resentment that his pet legislative initiative to address substandard housing was gathering dust. All the while, the antics of a coalition of laughable secessionists were monopolizing all of the media attention.

Talking heads and pundits who had been counted on to be promoting the housing bill on every available panel discussion were instead concentrating on the motives of the secessionists. It seemed that each was trying to outdo the other in psychoanalyzing anyone attached to the movement.

In his sixty years of life, John Malcolm had never felt as disrespected as when senators and representatives of his own party declined to take the floor of Congress to promote his bill. Rather, they all wanted to be seen on camera denouncing the Council for a Free America, or the Tea Party, or any other groups who fancied themselves to be super – patriots or defenders of capitalism. Further complicating his life was the fact that a smattering of Representatives and a couple of Senators had gone to the floor of Congress and expressed sympathy, if not outright support for those Neanderthals.

Bryce Hamilton and his associates were sucking all the oxygen out of the room. Just a month earlier, requests for comments on the secession movement had been sporadic. Now, the White House was being bombarded by reporters asking about it.

The major networks were beginning to fill their evening broadcasts with anecdotal stories of those in the group of restless states who feared secession. There were interviews with those who felt that they were being forced to leave their homes out of fear of possible repression, and flattering profiles of those involved in efforts to prevent secession from taking place.

Political opponents of the fledgling movement, along with media figures had repeatedly implied that the effort was racist in nature. Now there were reports of incidents in which white supremacist groups in non– secession states were issuing threats against blacks and Hispanics migrating there. In East St. Louis, Illinois threatening signs had been posted, and a Ku Klux Klan group had claimed responsibility.

All around the country, there was a growing number of peaceful rallies and marches being held to oppose secession. Some were held in cities within the boundaries of the states considering breaking away. Many others were held in the other states to express unity with and support for those who wished to remain United States citizens.

The President nearly jumped when his intercom buzzed and his secretary told him that Julia Stafford had arrived. Within a few seconds the door opened and the forty-five-year-old former justice of the California Supreme Court entered the room. As was usual, the attractive blonde woman peered over the top of her glasses at a clipboard as she approached the President.

"Well, Mr. President, the silly hour's almost upon us. I trust that Bryce Hamilton will rapidly dispel any questions as to his level of buffoonery, and that one or two news cycles will relegate him to writing columns on conservative websites."

The President rested on the edge of his desk and motioned for the Attorney General to have a seat in one of the guest chairs. "I wish I could dismiss him so summarily." The President began to lightly tap his knuckles on the desk. "No offense Julia... I thought your advice was right at the time. In hindsight, I wish we would have agreed to that meeting with the leadership of the Council. We may have lost a pivotal opportunity to head this off."

"Mister President, it would never have worked for you to have met with them as if they were a delegation from a sovereign nation. I still maintain it was the right decision."

"I'm sorry Julia... I took your advice and it was my choice. It just rattles my cage to hear Bryce Hamilton out there speaking about the Constitution of the United States of America playing a role in a breakaway nation, as if all they had to do was purchase the copyright."

"Mr. President... for all of his chatter about the Constitution, he has no constitutional basis for what he and his merry band of pranksters are up to. The Constitution does not speak to allowing secession, and I recall from my high school American history class, the issue of secession got settled in a big war. It was in all the papers."

The President shook his head. "I know that. But that Montana character Bridger was on Meet the Press yesterday, spouting all that bullshit about how technology can make all of this work. I hate to say it Julia, but he has a point. Logistically, a nation could form in flyover country, and even if it divided the United States right down the center, the West Coast and the eastern states could function just fine as one nation. As for making it feasible, what these fruitcakes are proposing could be made to work. That's why it's so dangerous."

The Attorney General looked up at the ceiling, and then closed her eyes. "Mr. President... this is going to turn out to be nothing more than a flash in the pan media carnival. Sure, there are going to be rallies all over Texas and in places like Boise and Little Rock. They will start having fantasies of living with low taxes, a bigger and higher wall to keep out immigrants, no gay rights and having their cars washed by black people who know their place. Then when this whole thing fizzles out they will go home all pissed off, renew their NRA memberships, go to Wal-Mart to buy a few cases of beer and a new NASCAR tee shirt."

The President stared at her for a moment. "I guess you think you have them all figured out, don't you?"

"I just don't want you getting so sidetracked with that housing legislation on the line. This is a distraction, and Bryce Hamilton will have his morning in the sun. And the faster his press conference takes place and everyone sees him for the dim bulb that he is, the sooner he begins to fade into the dark where he belongs."

The President stood and folded his arms. "Hamilton spent one six-year term in the Senate. He never really took the initiative on anything. All he really ever did was object to the ideas floated by others. I'm certain that a lot of Americans had never even heard of him before this secession movement plastered his face all over the news.

"His one term in the Senate seems to have been quite forgettable. My father met him before that. Pop was in a different law firm, but one time he and Hamilton ended up as co-counsels in a class action lawsuit. Pop told me that their case would have gone down in flames, if it had not been for Hamilton. It's not that Hamilton is so smart, but he is tough as nails. He may be laughable, but he won't back down. It seems that he was in the Marines during the Korean War. Word is that he doesn't know the meaning of fear. Quite frankly, Julia, I prefer my opponents to be of the type to be more easily intimidated."

Julia sat in silence for a moment to consider his words. "I have staff already exploring every nook and cranny of statutes and past rulings on treason and sedition. Stay tuned."

~~~

Bryce Hamilton and Nina Burton stood out of sight of the assembled media that filled a large room at the Crowne Plaza Hotel in Omaha, Nebraska. Nina watched in amusement as Hamilton nonchalantly reviewed his slightly revised notes. She began to scan the faces in the rows of reporters.

Although the networks were tending to treat the movement as a freak show, the fact that so many members of the White House press corps were in attendance told her that the matter was being given an aura of importance. She knew many of the reporters gathered there, and she knew even better the tall man next to her. She understood why he seemed so relaxed. If the media became combative, at least within that room, it would not be a fair fight.

Hamilton took a casual glance at his watch, and without having anyone introduce him, he strolled to the podium. He adjusted the microphone, and prepared to speak to several million Americans. He glanced up at the crowd to see that some in the room were not paying rapt attention to his presence, so he simply announced, "Thank you... I am Bryce Hamilton, Convening Chairman of the Council for a Free America. I will now begin."

~~~

When he finished the prepared address, Bryce Hamilton looked out over the assembled media representatives. Some were already waving their hands and shouting out questions, while others were snickering and a few were sitting with their faces buried in their hands and trying to bring their laughter under control.

Ignoring the questions that were already being shouted, Hamilton leaned down to the microphone and announced, "I will now take your questions." Offstage, Nina Burton laughed as she saw the vintage Bryce Hamilton in action, exhibiting dignity and enforcing good manners.

He pointed to a young reporter who was standing, but refraining from the shouts engaged in by many of his peers. "Thank you for taking my question, Senator Hamilton. I was wondering if you could address the short timetable that the Council seems to be working on."

Hamilton nodded and thanked the young man for his question. "We know that this process is going to be difficult for the nation, so we don't want to prolong what will likely be a painful transition. In addition, we would like to have as much settled as soon as possible in advance of the next round of congressional and state –

wide elections. We know that as we go forward with this effort, much will need to be sorted out. We feel that it is our obligation to resolve matters as quickly as possible, while trying to avoid making major decisions in haste."

Hamilton pointed to a reporter who was simply raising her hand in silence, but with a hopeful look on her face. He listened attentively to the question, and then nodded. "Thank you for your question. We do have a substantial cadre of attorneys discussing the constitutionality of what you call secession, or as we call it, withdrawal. To ensure that we are on solid ground, we purposely retained attorneys for the task of attempting to prove to us that our plans are not constitutional or legal. After having done so, and being briefed on their findings, we feel confident in moving ahead."

Hamilton called on yet another reporter who was conducting herself in a similarly constrained manner. "Yes, thank you. That's an interesting question. We do not want to pretend that we have easy answers to every logistical issue. The examples that you bring up, such as the military, the banking system and even Postal Service will require negotiations between the new union and the government of the United States of America. However, we feel that in civil matters, technology will ease our way. Plus, for the past two years there have been taskforces and study groups devoted to these matters. Issues of defense provide much thornier issues. I do not wish to minimize the difficulties inherent in that matter. In the case of hostilities against what we now know as America, there would not likely be an issue in terms of joint actions. Preemptive military actions are another matter."

Hamilton purposely called on one of the reporters that found his address to be a source of great amusement: "Mr. Hamilton, it has been readily noted that the states involved in your movement are either overwhelmingly white, or have substantial minority populations that are governed by predominately white power structures and state governments. Several were formerly Confederate states. In addition, many of those involved in the secessionist drive speak of establishing a nation to promote self-sufficiency and offering only very Spartan public welfare benefits. How do you respond to allegations that your movement is, at its heart, a racist movement?"

Hamilton nodded warmly to the reporter, who then sat down with a self-satisfied and expectant smile across his face. "If you wish to tell members of minority groups that they are less capable of achievement than white people, be my guest. However, I don't believe that. If you believe that, I suggest you take a deep look inside your own soul. I don't know how you think you can make assumptions about what is in another man's heart."

Hamilton ignored the subsequent combination of laughter, protests and murmuring, and pointed to another reporter in the front row that had to shout his question to be heard over the boisterous reactions to his previous answer. Hamilton proceeded to give his answer, even though there were reporters attempting to shout follow-up questions. Finally, Hamilton motioned for the frustrated reporter sitting in the front row to come forward.

While others in the crowd continued to demand an opportunity for follow-up questions on the issue of race, Hamilton responded one-on-one to the question about the role of Texas. Although few in the room could hear what he was saying to the reporter, he continued to speak above the chaotic shouting and pleading: "Of course, we expect Texas to play a central role, especially considering its history and circumstances under which it was admitted as a state."

When the media throng realized that Hamilton was going to proceed without them, the din finally settled down. Hamilton returned to the microphone. "So as for Texas, of course such a large state would play a major role in the establishment of this union. Should the Texas legislature vote to withdraw from the United States of America, that is. Once again, this is a matter of state sovereignty, and if Texas decides it does not wish to withdraw, then other states that decide otherwise will proceed. It is important to note that Texas alone ranks in the top fifteen largest economies in the world. Naturally, the economic structure of this new union would be greatly impacted by the inclusion or absence of Texas."

Hamilton pointed to one of the more veteran members of the press corps he had seen frequently on the evening news giving reports while standing in front of the White House. The smiling woman spoke loudly. "Mr. Hamilton, how would you prevent firearms from being trafficked from your new union into the states still belonging to the United States of America?"

Hamilton nodded to her, and then smiled. "Forgive me for this answer… I know your question is meant to be serious and I mean no disrespect… I'm simply going to recommend that you meet with the authorities in Chicago and the District of Columbia, and ask how they have been so successful in keeping weapons out of their jurisdictions."

Hamilton pointed to another reporter in the back row who shouted out, "How can a group of states possibly be able to afford to carry out all the duties performed by the current federal government of the United States of America?"

Hamilton shook his head, looked down, and finally replied: "You really don't get it, do you? Unlike the current government of the United States of America, our proposed new union would only carry out functions that are actually necessary." Hamilton ignored the imploring shouts from some other reporters, leaned toward the microphone and said, "Thank you, and have a good day."

Chapter 2

Television viewers watching NewsNet saw the image switch from the scene in Omaha to the New York studio where a panel was assembled to discuss the press conference. The camera focused in on a close-up of the striking redheaded woman conducting the discussion.

"This is Cynthia Warren, and thank you for joining us at NewsNet for our special coverage of the dramatic press conference just held by Bryce Hamilton, Convening Chairman of the Council for a Free America. So let's begin by my asking Joshua Simmons, managing editor of the Potomac Review, did we just hear a new Declaration of Independence?"

"No, Cynthia… I think we just witnessed an unfortunate man who forgot to take his meds this morning. Bryce Hamilton just went on national television and presented nothing more than a list of right wing and Tea Party fantasies. While he was at it, he removed any doubt as to how unbalanced and rude a person he truly is."

Cynthia turned to Mason Howell, a columnist for the Washington Times. "Mason, do you see it the same way?"

"With all due respect to my friend Joshua, I don't think we were watching the same press conference. In my opinion, Bryce

Hamilton appeared to the American people as the serious leader of a serious movement. I think that those who attempt to laugh him off the stage do so at the peril of their own credibility. I know who some of those attorneys are he was speaking of, those who were specifically retained for the purpose of convincing the movement to give this idea up.

"Further, this is going to be such an intensely studied, closely watched matter, there's no doubt in my mind that the citizenry will not be swayed by media filters. I caution everyone, this can happen."

Cynthia turned to her remaining guest. "Let's turn to Gwendolyn Munro, a freelance columnist who covers national politics and serves as a NewsNet correspondent. Gwen, what's your take on the possibility that the nation really will separate?"

Munro hesitated for a moment. "I think that a major point is being missed here. Beyond the matter of whether the discussed secession or separation or whatever you want to call it is constitutional or unconstitutional, legal or illegal, the real question as I see it lies in whether substantial action would ever be taken to prevent it. What I mean is, the attitude of the left and the Democratic Party in general, and the media is much more of a key than the attitude of those on the right who live within the states in question.

"The President is going to be subjected to tremendous pressure within his party, and even within the more liberal, mainstream media, to simply bid these states good riddance. We would be left with a United States of America consisting of mostly but not all blue states. Nearly every one of the states in the proposed union that wants to break away have traditionally been red states, during the past five Presidential elections.

"My sources tell me that the President has been experiencing a deafening amount of chatter from some of the most liberal members of his party salivating at the prospect of a new Congress free of so many conservatives.

"The gun issue is another key factor. Liberal America has been berating and insulting gun enthusiasts, to say nothing of the botched and aborted gun registration disaster that came out of the Senate. These states wanting to secede are heavily in favor of gun ownership rights. How can the same liberal cadre of politicians, interest groups in the media say on one hand, guns are evil and we should get rid of them, then try to insist that states where gun ownership is a sacred right should not be allowed to leave the United States? At some point, the left has to make a collective admission that they cannot have it both ways. And I think they are falling on the side of saying goodbye, but not necessarily, good luck.

"And deep down inside, the same liberals know that they will have a trading partner next door that can flourish as the bread basket of America as it does now, and provide a place for blue state conservatives to migrate to. A lot of red state liberals will migrate the other way. Then, presto… a liberal paradise in the eastern and far western states. Gone will be most of the members of Congress wanting to restrict abortion, opposing expansion of LGBT rights, wanting to rein in entitlement programs, and promoting gun rights."

Joshua Simmons began to shake his head emphatically: "But it is simply not allowed."

Gwendolyn nodded. "I'm really not arguing that point with you Joshua. I'm telling you that John Malcolm is not going to shed blood to prevent this. This is not 1861. The people of these states see this as a matter of economic survival and freedom. They also know in their hearts that the President is not going to employ force to keep them in the union. And they're certainly not going to back off because John Malcolm and the mainstream press tell them to. And I really don't see any signs of the press doing that, at least not so far.

"And one more thing... I am shocked that there is so little coverage being given to the crisis of crime and disorderly behavior in so many of our towns and cities during the last several months. Some of this is being recognized as nothing more than crimes of opportunity, but there is much whispering going on regarding how this is tied into the rapidly growing homeless population. Many veteran Republicans I have spoken to recently have complained about what they see as a pattern when it comes to media coverage. They tell me that when Ronald Reagan was president, the media could not provide enough airtime to matters of homelessness, but when President Bill Clinton was inaugurated, attention to the homeless seemed to vaporize.

"Now they're complaining that through the Obama years, and in the first few months of the Malcolm administration, homelessness is not being exposed as it was through the Trump years, although statistics show that homelessness in the United States is now at the highest level since the Great Depression. And with housing interest rates so high as a result of the credit downgrade, that's not likely to abate very soon.

"Whether it is talked about or not, there is an undercurrent of fear at hand. People are seeing the rise in homelessness and crime, and anyone with a calculator knows that it's going to only get worse when there is an inevitable crash in funding for social programs. Then, at the same time, people see the government as discouraging them from protecting themselves."

Cynthia Warren turned to the camera. "On that disturbing note, I wish to thank our panel for taking part in this special coverage. This is Cynthia Warren for NewsNet."

~~~

President John Malcolm turned off the television in the small receiving room next to the Oval Office. He gave a loud sigh, and then turned to his only guest at the moment, Howard Litton, Vice President of the United States.

"Howard... I need for you to be as brutally honest with me as you have ever been. I want your take on this... being from South Dakota and all."

"John, I'm scared shitless. Ever since you told me two weeks ago to gather all the information I can from our friends on the ground in those states, I have become less optimistic.

"If you listen to the talking heads and pundits, this whole movement is the Keystone Cops do rebellion. That's been the media theme ever since that first organizing meeting in Omaha over two years ago. But I've been talking to reliable party contacts in every one of the states... our own party, just for security reasons. They have a whole different take.

"State legislators, of both parties for that matter, are very much of a different mind than the politicians here in Washington. This movement is under very serious consideration in many states, and I can tell you these... condescending and demeaning comments from the media and some members of Congress are only steeling their resolve. The people in the states who are involved in this movement have been caricatured by the media as a group of guys sitting around under Confederate flags and cleaning their guns. The reality is, they have been holding seminars conducted by college professors and current and former elected officials... of both parties, I may add. For all practical purposes, they have established some very sophisticated think tanks devoted to a post – secession administration. We know that retired conservative and libertarian professors from Harvard, Yale and other prestigious universities never get much press. But now we know how they're spending their free time.

"The resentment is building over how they are being portrayed by the media. Not just by regular members of the movement, but by those academics who see their work either being ignored or mocked. As an administration, we don't want to go there.

"Texas is in, Arkansas is in, Missouri is likely, and the upper Plains states seem likely to bolt as well. South Carolina seems serious and Mississippi is hard to call because it seems to be headed for some serious fractures. And get this one... the Upper Peninsula of Michigan wants to break away. They want to become a separate state called Superior."

The President leaned down and buried his face in his hands. "Superior?"

The Vice President laughed. "They see themselves being allowed more freedom in mining and forestry. I talked to a friend of mine in Lansing who knows that area well. The mining and logging company executives up there see themselves operating with no EPA or Department of the Interior oversight. Ski resorts are gearing up for a price war against their competition in places like Colorado. They are already estimating how low their unemployment rate can go, and are discussing how much of a population swell they can absorb.

John… some of your major corporate donors are licking their chops at how they can expand in these breakaway states."

"Don't tell me their names. I can't handle hearing that today."

"I got a call from our Commerce Secretary yesterday. When you picked Bill for that job, you picked a good one. He has a knack for getting CEO's to speak to him off the record. He's being told that much of our stagnation in job growth over the past few months is because of this possible secession. Companies are just simply holding off on expanding, hiring or building new facilities. They want to see if this new union becomes reality. If it does, that's where they're heading."

The President shook his head. "They don't see it as too risky?"

"John, the talking heads who tend to favor us keep parroting the prospect of wages going down to four dollars an hour in those states, and the environment being raped left and right. The reality is, auto dealers are looking for new locations there, and developers for housing communities are already scouting for potential land buys in Texas, the Dakotas, Kansas and Nebraska… need I say more?"

President Malcolm looked up toward the ceiling and began to laugh. "And what about Ohio… Indiana… Kentucky?"

"No chance of them bolting. They have not been involved in any major way whatsoever. However, those states will be suffering in chaos if this new union becomes reality. I'm very worried about states like Ohio and Michigan where there are such divides by region. Missouri is another example, whether it leaves or not. To be quite frank, I'm finding it impossible to predict what will happen in some of those places.

"I don't see massive violence breaking out, but I am concerned about the sporadic lone wolf or the small bands of crazies. There is likely going to be waves of migration in both directions. In Ohio, Illinois and Michigan especially, a lot of businesses are planning to move out to what they see as a friendlier environment to run an enterprise. An industrialist friend of mine who owns a plant near Cleveland says that the blame is being placed upon federal regulations, and those state regulations that exist purely as a result of federal requirements. The employment environment that is left behind will be a disaster."

~~~

It was the middle of the afternoon when Bryce Hamilton sat in a booth at the Crowne Plaza bar. Patrick Bridger stepped into the room, peering around as his eyes adjusted to the dimmer light. The former Congressman spotted Hamilton and strolled slowly over and sat down with him.

A waitress arrived to take their orders, and the two casual acquaintances made small talk until the drinks arrived, and they were left to speak in private.

"Congressman, I hope that this morning's opening address met with your approval."

The stocky, distinguished former Representative nodded his head. "Bryce, you did us proud. You gave them a glimpse into what we are heading for, but you did not give away the farm with a bunch of details about things that are still too fluid. Well done." The Congressman chuckled before he took a sip of his Jack Daniels. "You must have done a good job. The talking heads are beside themselves. The funny thing is, they're not talking so much about the substance of what you had to say as they are about your lack of reverence to them as a privileged class."

Hamilton smiled and nodded. "They are so predictable."

The former Senator leaned closer and lowered his voice. "So, in your eyes, where do we stand?"

Bridger took a sip of his drink and began to tap his finger on the table. "The media is totally missing just how far along we are. They're spending their airtime flogging us for extremism and racism. In the meantime, we're close to forty percent support in several state legislatures, not counting Texas, Alaska, Idaho, North Dakota and Arkansas, who are already all in. It's just not official. After the first couple of states vote to withdraw, it's going to open a floodgate. Those states at forty to fifty percent legislative support will quickly fall into line. Let's face it… it's no small thing to vote to secede. It's not something you can ever take back. No matter what you do for the rest of your life, there will be a certain finality to having voted to leave the United States of America.

"We expect that in a few days we can move Montana, South Dakota and South Carolina into the solid category. What everyone is missing is that West Virginia's getting some real movement even though they're not part of the announced group. That is going on under the radar, which is remarkable considering the proximity of a chunk of its population to D.C.. It's in the West Virginia newspapers, but it will still catch a lot of people by surprise. There's a real disconnect between the Washington suburbs in West Virginia and the rest of the state."

Hamilton shook his head. "But what about Alabama, Georgia, and Louisiana?"

"In those particular states, much of the black populations have political allegiance to the Eastern liberal power base. It's not looking as though there will be enough of a lopsided vote in the state legislatures for them to move forward with as much confidence, at least at this time. Of course, I must remember that we are expecting a lot of migration from other states into our union, to take advantage of our pro- business form of government. That can have some effect on the thinking of the state legislators in those more undecided states. People can talk all they want about the Civil War. This will allow those who want to live in economic freedom a place to do so without really leaving their country. Those who want to live in a more socialist United States of America can just stay there if they're already there, and people can move out of our new union if that is their desire. Then we will eventually see who provides the best way of life for Americans to choose from."

Hamilton stared down at his drink. "And what is the latest you've picked up about the intent of the Administration?"

"Remember when Clinton got into trouble with his intern. That's when MoveOn sprung up as a political force to come his defense. Well it looks like we now have a sort of good riddance movement forming within his party, along with a beginning drumbeat in the media to that effect. We cannot forget how important the media is to his administration… how integral a part of the power structure it has become within the Democratic Party over the past couple of decades. They have spent years criticizing what are now the movement states as being opposed to women's rights, opposed to minority rights and being anti-immigrant. I don't believe they're going to clamor for President Malcolm to keep them in the fold."

Hamilton laughed and took a sip of his gin and tonic. "The 24-hour news cycle certainly has had Christmas arrive early. I was flipping channels yesterday, and they were talking about what the new U.S. Congress would be like if there were only thirty-six states. There would only be seventy-two United States Senators. They're even calculating how many electoral votes would elect the next President of the United States."

Bridger shook his head and sighed. "Still, they never seem to discuss why this is happening, do they? Hopefully, Tom Edelstein will prove to be a good follow-up to your press conference on his appearance this evening."

Hamilton arched his eyebrows. "If I recall correctly, he is only thirty-two years old. He's a bright enough fellow, but I just hope that he is seasoned enough and savvy enough for that interview. The media is just holding its breath to pounce on one of us screwing up."

Bridger grinned and picked up his glass to take another sip. "We will certainly know in just a few hours."

~~~

Tom Edelstein took his place in the interview guest seat at the NewsNet studio. He was a minute away from being on national television for the first time in his life. Not much over five feet tall, he knew that he would look diminutive next to the large and muscular program host who always dominated the set, adding to his reputation as tending to conduct tough interviews. As he mentally repeated his favorite verses from the Torah, Edelstein struggled to keep his anxiety under control.

As was his typical demeanor, program host Ben Stirling paid no attention to the young balding man sitting nervously three feet from him. Rather, his full attention was devoted to the last minute discussion with the program producer.

Suddenly, the producer bolted from the scene, then Stirling spun around and began to speak: "Welcome to another edition of America in Real Time. I am your host Ben Stirling, and tonight we're going to swerve from our normal format and devote our entire first half hour to our special guest, Mr. Tom Edelstein from the Council for a Free America. Unless you have been under a rock somewhere, you know that this organization is at the heart of the movement that would allow as many as fourteen states to separate from the United States of America and form a new nation based upon certain principles of economic freedom and individual liberty.

"Mr. Edelstein is a former chairman of the Conservative Caucus in the Kansas House of Representatives, a bipartisan group of legislators. After not seeking reelection to the Kansas House of Representatives, Mr. Edelstein is now serving as a member of the executive committee of the Council for a Free America. Mr. Edelstein, thank you for being on our program this evening."

Edelstein gulped and nearly began to stutter. "Thanks for having me on your program tonight."

"Mr. Edelstein, needless to say, your organization has rattled the cages of everyone within the Washington Beltway. Both

Democrats and Republicans in Congress cannot get to the microphone fast enough to denounce your movement. However, my staff has been doing their own research, and they found that in the states named as being part of this movement, support is building rapidly among the citizenry. To what do you attribute that dichotomy?"

Edelstein nodded and began to speak slowly. "If our movement were to come to fruition, the Washington D.C. power base would see its influence greatly diminished. No Chairman of a House or Senate committee wants to oversee the goings on in thirty-six or forty states, rather than fifty, and no bureaucrat in Washington wants to see his or her regulatory power so diminished as well.

"For that matter, conservatives lose their dreams of trying to force fiscal responsibility onto the rest of the nation, and liberals are no longer going to have an opportunity to try and force more progressive values on populations that they like to deride and label as backward and uninformed.

"However, in contrast to those in the Beltway, the people who live in those states that are considering separating from the United States of America want to see an adherence to the original Constitution of the United States restored. They see no way to do that, other than to use that old revered Constitution as a basis of governing a new union. Many of us are simply of the opinion that the current power structure in Washington simply finds the

Constitution to be too disruptive and restrictive, and have simply abandoned it.

"Conservatives blame liberals for the situation, accusing liberals of viewing the Constitution as an antiquated relic. From our point of view, many who label themselves conservatives have been all too willing accomplices in the constant creep away from the Constitution that has taken place over the past three decades."

Ben Stirling held up his pen to signal that he wanted to ask another question. "Mr. Edelstein, what about all those residents of the breakaway states who are perfectly happy with the current condition of the United States of America, and are in total disagreement with the concept of withdrawing from the federal government?"

"Mr. Stirling, I do not wish to minimize the seriousness of those concerns. As for the desires and feelings of such individuals, I do not take them lightly. However, a social liberal would already be uncomfortable living in certain parts of certain states such as Idaho and Nebraska. A conservative living in Massachusetts would be in the same boat. I believe we have already seen people moving from California for instance, and going to states with lower tax bases and different economic outlooks. A number of the people who operate businesses have relocated to Texas and Indiana, although I add that Indiana is not involved in this movement. There simply will be a migration in both directions. We are not insensitive to the fact that in the process, there will be some significant disruptions for many individuals. Still, we feel the prospects we are holding out to Americans who yearn for an environment in which the principles of our Founding Fathers are adhered to override such considerations."

"Mr. Edelstein, watching Bryce Hamilton's press conference, there was a moment that I think was important, but many seemed to miss. He was asked how such a new union could afford to conduct all the activities that are currently conducted by the government of the United States of America. I thought his answer was a tad flippant, so I would like for you to elaborate."

"Thanks, Mr. Stirling. First of all please remember that Bryce Hamilton takes a very direct approach. I know him quite well. I think he was just reacting to a question from a reporter who is missing the entire point of the movement.

"I think it is safe to say that in our new union, we would only establish regulatory powers as a last resort. We would not establish programs unless there was a clear need for them to exist. In other words, the last thing that we would want to do is replicate the current bureaucratic structure of the United States of America. That is the point of the movement. Of course there would be some regulation of commerce, but only to the extent minimally necessary. There would be some vital environmental regulations, but only as needed to truly protect the health and safety of residents."

Ben Stirling held up the pen once again. "But what about all of the social programs such as welfare benefits, Food Stamps, Medicaid and things such as that? Under any circumstances, a society's going to have a significant number of poor, aged and disabled individuals. Some of your critics maintain that those of you backing this concept of the new union simply want to do away with such programs, and further, claim that this is based upon racial prejudice."

Tom shook his head before replying. "As for such programs, much of that would be left to the discretion of individual states. In addition, most the states that are considering joining this new union have a strong base of church involvement in the lives of their citizens. Such people can be very generous and charitable, I see no reason to expect that to change.

"Such things are yet to be decided, and I am conjecturing right now. But I would be surprised to see such a new union establish some clone of the Department of Health and Human Services, or mimic the food assistance programs operated by the United States Department of Agriculture, or the housing programs operated by the Department of Housing and Urban Development. Once again, I would personally predict that the states would decide the extent to which they want to provide such services and how eligibility for those would be determined. The sticky topic in all this lies in Social Security and Medicare. Something would have to be negotiated in that realm, as everyone who works has paid into that system. That would be one of the more complex issues, but we already have a plan developed by one of our workgroups.

"In fact, for over two years we have been developing plans regarding Social Security and Medicare. We would hope that we could initially contract with the United States for administration of those programs until we phase out into our own systems.

"After the initial transition period, we would probably have a lot of state sovereignty regarding basic welfare programs, but our new union would indeed have replacement programs for Social Security and Medicare. As for Medicare, it would all be operated through the free market system, with individuals selecting their own health insurance providers.

"As for a retirement program to replace Social Security, it will likely be a program in which each individual manages his or her own retirement account according to their own comfort with risk levels in terms of investments. For those who want nothing to do with the stock market in a direct sense, there will always be the option of a fixed income selection.

Stirling leaned in toward his guest. "But won't you have a chaotic situation if each of the states simply found their own way with entitlement programs?"

"You mean, if we went back to having it the way it used to be? I don't think that we would consider the United States of America in the late 1950s and early 1960s to have been a primitive nation by any stretch of the imagination. To digress for a moment, if all regulations and programs enacted after, let's say 1970 were to merely disappear, the lives of the vast majority of Americans would hardly be affected at all.

"Those of us in the movement are often asked about welfare benefits, much more often than we are asked about the job opportunities we hope to provide. But remember, each state already has to put up a large funding share of federally mandated welfare program benefits. That includes a lot of administrative costs to handle all the red tape and intricacies required by the feds.

"We can simply consolidate programs into a basic welfare package. The portion of our state money that was going toward administration of so many federal programs can go into the funds to be distributed to those in actual need. We won't have to have a separate program for a cash benefit, another for food supplements and others for things such as utilities and housing. In addition, I would expect that most states will attach some very strong work and training participation requirements for the able-bodied.

"However, we have established a monstrous benefits system for low income Americans, and we will have to deal with the fallout. I don't have all the answers for that right now. But what everyone has to understand, is that if drastic steps are not taken soon, the entire system is going to collapse anyway."

"Mr. Edelstein, should that happen, and if there were no such secession movement underway, do you actually foresee some kind of economic catastrophe taking place?"

Edelstein slowly nodded. "I don't see how it can be avoided."

Stirling went to a commercial break: "After we return from these messages, we are going to ask our guest to elaborate."

"We are continuing our discussion with Tom Edelstein from the Council for a Free America. Now, Mr. Edelstein, do you actually foresee that entitlement programs can bring the United States of America to an economic collapse, and how does the prospect of the formation of a new union tie into that?"

"Mr. Stirling, we are in danger of collapse, and entitlement spending is just one of those reasons. But let's talk about that for a moment. We have an increasing number of people in this country receiving government benefits, and a declining number of wage earners paying for them. I do happen to be an economist, but one does not have to be an economist to see the train wreck coming. You cannot borrow money to pay increasing levels and varieties of benefits to people who do not contribute to the national treasury. I'm not talking about Social Security, or the very vital assistance given to the disabled. We have a moral obligation to assist them. And people who have been forced to pay into Social Security deserve the benefit they were promised, although we could face adjustments in benefit levels.

"What we cannot afford to do is to issue such an array of benefits upon the able-bodied. I understand the sensitivity of this topic. And by no means do the recipients of most of our social program benefits live in anything resembling a lavish lifestyle. If you are a single parent trying to hold down a job, having a child care subsidy would hardly be considered a luxury. The same with the various medical care and nutrition programs that are available.

"The dilemma is that, the line between the subsidized and unsubsidized hits a point where the difference in disposable income blurs. As much as we may feel good about these programs, and as much as they may be appreciated and needed, you cannot provide them with borrowed money without an eventual collapse. And mathematics will tell you, you cannot tax the high earners enough to cover all those costs. You have to provide an economy in which there is employment for the able-bodied, and an accompanying expectation for them to accept it. People need to be able to provide for themselves, and prepare for a retirement.

"So, the United States of America will see its federal budget melt down soon enough, and the states in the new union we are proposing are going to start from scratch, aside from some reconciliation arrangements for Social Security.

"Over two years ago we hired one of the nation's leading data processing firms to help us plan the method through which we would absorb the data for the Social Security and Medicare transitions. That is in place and waiting to go. I would add that we had to do this without any cooperation from the Social Security Administration."

Stirling held his hands upright. "Whoa… when did that happen?"

Edelstein laughed. "That's a great example of what we have been dealing with. We got coverage in local newspapers about all of this meticulous planning we have been doing. But all the national media ever wanted to ask us about was how things like abortion, guns and gay marriage were going to be addressed in the CSA. So, no one paid attention to the more than two years of work we have done, and now the media narrative is that all of this has happened overnight."

Stirling waved the pen for a moment, seeming to hesitate before his next question. "Mr. Edelstein, I feel obligated to ask this question one more time, as it has been bandied around some in the press. There are those who feel that the Council for a Free America is fixated on cutting back on spending on social programs, and that this has a racial overtone. Would you please address that further?"

Edelstein managed a smile, but also shook his head slowly at the same time. "Mr. Stirling, I will be more than happy to address this straw man. In fact, I would have been disappointed had you not asked that question. First of all, most recipients of welfare and Food Stamps in the United States of America are not members of minority groups. Most are white. And I have to say this as well, that when one makes a direct connection from a comment about welfare to black or Hispanic citizens, I think that is engaging in some very unfair stereotyping and lowering of expectations of people who possess the same levels of capability as everyone else.

"And, I must make this point... I know and you know that the individuals you refer to as discussing this in the media are the members of that very same media. So I have seen this pattern for years... they bring it up over and over when interviewing conservatives, then claim that conservatives want to keep talking about race and how it plays into welfare policy, and subsequently, this movement.

"There is endless speculation as to how members of minority groups will react to the formation of this new union. As for me, I expect many to migrate to the breakaway states to find some real opportunity."

"And let me ask you one specific question about the Council for a Free America. The commentators and pundits on the internet and news programs on the broadcast channels and news websites have been furiously asserting that your organization is being funded by wealthy corporate interests that are trying to buy themselves a tax haven. In particular, the oil industry is being singled out as a suspected prime source of funding for your organization. Would you please address that?"

"Yes, I have heard and seen all of those comments and assumptions. I hope to put that to rest right now. When our organization was formed with the first state chapter in Nebraska, it was decided that it was crucial for any donations to be private, rather than corporate, in nature, and that our records would be made public to maintain total transparency.

"Therefore, from the beginning, this organization requires all state chapters as well as the national umbrella organization to follow strict guidelines. Only credit card donations are accepted, and they must be made directly to a state chapter website or to our national organization website. We accept no checks or cash. Also, over fifty percent of the total in donations we have received consisted of donations of twenty-five dollars or less.

"Anyone making a donation must acknowledge on the online donation form that the donation is being made as an individual, and secondly there is an acknowledgment that all donations will be considered public record. Anyone can go to our state or national websites and view a list of donations by name, city of record for mail delivery and the amount. We anticipated the very accusations that are now being made, and knew as well that the same would be parroted by the mainstream media, who are quick to try and make us appear to be an illegitimate tool of corporate interests."

Stirling began to raise his pen once again, but Edelstein raised his hands, indicating that he wanted to continue. "Mr. Stirling, there's a point that I don't want to be lost in this discussion: if this new union is indeed formed, we expect that many businesses and industries will relocate there. If that comes true, there are going to be some states losing tremendous sums of tax revenue. And for the life of me, I don't see how such states would ever be able to come up with their required portion of the funding for many of the social programs. Remember, states are required by their own constitutions to have a balanced budget. I think that this scenario should give everyone cause to pause and think, regardless of the outcome of our movement."

Stirling simply nodded, then turned once again to the camera. "And we will be back in a few minutes with our special guest, Tom Edelstein from the Council for a Free America."

Chapter 3

"We're back once again with tonight's special guest, Mr. Tom Edelstein from the Council for a Free America. So, Mr. Edelstein, let me ask a question that you say has been a media fixation... how would this new union handle matters of contention such as abortion, gay marriage and so on?"

"You have to understand, that the agenda driving our movement is centered on economic opportunity and individual freedom. We are nearing the end of the formative period right now, and as Bryce Hamilton explained in his press conference this morning, we need to be careful when it comes to speaking for an entire movement composed of so many different people living in so many different states. As he noted, we are often left to conjecture. What I am picking up in conversations and discussions, is that the individual states would have a lot of flexibility and sovereignty. You need to remember that the Tenth Amendment is a key tenet in the formation of this new union. The policy work being done by our study groups takes all that into account.

"I can see different states having different laws regarding things such as abortion and gay marriage. That is somewhat similar to what we currently have in effect among our current fifty states. But once again, and I cannot emphasize this enough, we want to have economic freedom with a major reduction in government regulations and interference in our lives and business.

"As for the matter of gay marriage, for example, some states within this new union may take a very libertarian attitude and allow it, while others may not. The same with abortion… we just don't know, but I will vent some frustration here… I want to once again remind everybody, that economic freedom and a lack of government regulations is at the heart of this movement. Pundits can try to overshadow that all they want with questions about social issues… I say again, that's way down on the list of priorities for most people involved in this movement. We want business owners to drive the economy, and we want employees to see more of the fruits of their labors, and matters of social issues will be addressed in their own good time."

~~~

Bryce Hamilton and Patrick Bridger sat in the latter's room at the Crowne Plaza and exhaled simultaneous sighs of relief as the program ended. Hamilton looked slowly at Bridger and nodded. "You were right about that young man. We could not have asked for more, especially on that program. I don't recall ever seeing that bully Stirling allow a guest to speak so long without interruption."

Bridger laughed. "Something tells me that Stirling knew that the more he allowed Tom to talk, the more everyone would be talking about his program for the next week."

Hamilton took a sip of bourbon. "I think it's safe to say that we are two for two. Tom did quite well, and I don't think I started to drool during my press conference."

"Hardly. I know that the media will still try to caricature us, but both of you came across as presenting our side as a serious cause."

Hamilton looked at Bridger with a sly grin. "As much as I hate what we are doing... I just... I just had always hoped it would never come to this. Still there is this mischievous demon inside me that surfaces from time to time and finds a day like today a little too entertaining. So, what's next on the horizon?"

Bridger leaned back and placed his hands behind his head. "I have been thinking that we need to establish a mechanism to start publicly addressing some of the thornier issues. Most of all, I want to do it out in the open. For example, if we discuss our task force on, say for instance, defense, we may want to be magnanimous, vocal and visual in inviting the press to sit in as observers."

Hamilton nodded. "We don't want to be seen as ducking the tough issues and kicking the can down the road. Plus, maybe people will like that enough to demand that from the current federal government."

Bridger leaned forward and took another sip of his third gin and tonic of the day. "You know, it starts hitting the fan after today. Now that we've announced a loose timetable, that puts a whole new layer of urgency on us. Also, there is nothing like a timeline to whip the media into a froth. I can just see one or two of the news networks putting some countdown clock down in the corner of the screen to measure the time until... Secession."

Hamilton sighed deeply. "Our offices scattered around the states... I think we have to get serious about our security from here on out."

Hamilton could hear a quiet chuckle, and then looked over at Bridger. "What's so funny about that?"

"Nothing really... I just remembered, we don't have to worry about those bomb threats we've been getting. We are supposedly the dangerous extremists."

~~~

Edmund Riley glanced nervously at his watch and saw that it was nearly 10:00 AM. Standing to the side of the podium, where in a few minutes he would resume his routine duties as Speaker of the House of Representatives, he knew that the morning would be anything but routine.

The Speaker had his own preferred agenda for the day, but knew that the previous day's press conference held by Bryce Hamilton, followed by the evening interview by Tom Edelstein, had revised his plans. The Missouri Republican was already looking forward to the moment when the House would recess for the day, likely well into the evening.

He stepped up to the podium and gaveled the body into order. When he heard that the murmuring was louder than usual, and the shuffling of feet and milling around showed no signs of abating, he understood the kind of day he was in for.

After five minutes of housekeeping duties, it was time for the theatrics to begin. He took a deep breath before speaking: "Mr. Hollander of the state of Pennsylvania is recognized." The Speaker sat down in resignation as the tall man from a Pittsburgh suburb approached the microphone.

"Mr. Speaker, I address the House today with a heavy heart, and the hope that what we are experiencing now is nothing but a bad dream. But yesterday, a former member of the United States Senate held a press conference to outline a treasonous plan to break apart our great nation. Generations ago, hundreds of thousands of Americans died in our bloodiest war, but America survived through the guidance of one of our most revered Presidents, Abraham Lincoln.

"All rational citizens of the United States of America have long ago accepted the fact that the bloody Civil War of the 1860's put to rest once and for all, any thought of the right of a state, or a group of states to secede from the union. Now this former Senator is a leader of the radical movement that would tear our nation asunder.

"Further, Mister Speaker, last evening we were treated to the spectacle of yet another spokesperson for the Council for a Free America taking to the airwaves of America to present to the American public, this group's extremist, racist and radical ideology.

"Mister Speaker, it is my hope that the good judgment of the American people will prevent tragedy from happening once again. But should the desires of this dangerous and extreme movement become reality, we need to look at what we would be facing.

"In the very heartland of what is now the United States of America, we would see an illegitimate and illegal, not to mention unconstitutional, confederation form. It would be a place where African Americans would no longer be guaranteed the right to vote, or even to have the guarantee of freedom."

Before Hollander could continue, several shouts interrupted him, and the Speaker nervously tried to gavel the chamber back into order. When the shouting finally subsided, he spoke: "Please continue, Mister Hollander."

Hollander stepped back to the microphone. "It would be a place where anyone who looked Hispanic would be pulled over and asked for identification to prove that they had a right to be there.

"It would be a place where guns would be welcome, but gay citizens would have to cower in fear of their lives.

"It would be a place where workers would be denied the right to be represented by a labor union, while forced to work for subsistence pay while business owners would flourish and be freed from supporting the services they enjoyed.

"It would be a place where the unfortunate would be trapped in poverty by a lack of social services, while the rich are relieved of any responsibility to provide for their fellow man.

"Women would be forced to carry the child of their rapist, and would be forced to remain in abusive households riddled by domestic violence, because there would be nowhere else for them to go.

"Mister Speaker, I ask that each and every member of this body, on this very sad day after yesterday's public pronouncements, go on record condemning all efforts of any states to secede from the United States of America. Further, I call on all members of this body to publicly pronounce today their steadfast pledge, that they will not support this radical and dangerous movement."

Congressman Hollander walked away from the microphone as a mixture of applause, shouts and boos caused Speaker Riley to loudly bang the gavel to once again bring order.

"The gentleman from Wyoming, Mister Crindler is recognized." A short stocky and bald elderly man slowly made his way to the microphone.

"Mister Speaker, I rise today to offer a contrasting point of view to that of my friend and colleague, Congressman Hollander. As a grassroots effort to restore the principles upon which our great nation was founded, common people from every walk of life in fourteen states are considering what just years ago would have been considered the unthinkable.

"My colleague and friend spoke of his emotions of sadness at having to address the proposition of our nation separating into two. In that sadness, I join my friend, many others in this chamber, and millions of citizens of the United States of America. Where our opinions diverge however, lies in the root causes of the constitutional crisis we may very well soon be facing.

"Our nation has unfortunately become divided between those who believe that a bill must be paid upon its receipt, and those who believe that government can provide all things to all people, even if those government activities cannot be paid for.

"This is not a matter of party membership or party loyalty. Sadly, neither of our major parties has been willing to routinely deal with reality. Both parties have been complicit in expanding our debt to the point from which we may never find a way to recover. Oh, certainly, those of us in my Republican Party may have some legitimacy to a claim of being more frugal than our friends across the aisle. However, it is only a matter of degrees.

"We have a society that looks to government to solve problems best left to personal initiative. We have a society that looks to government to orchestrate economic factors best left to private enterprise and the capitalist system that served us so well for so long.

"We have a news media that will unfailingly present a big – government bias to a populace all too willing to tell them just how vulnerable they are without the protective cloak of the state always shielding them from the expected and natural storms of life.

"We have a news media, too often joined by members of a party that includes many of my dear friends, who are quick to brand anyone opposed to a smothering government as being racist, backward or even ignorant, opposed to women's rights or the rights of those who are gay. That is the way differences of opinion are treated in America today, and it is not going to change. If you want to get along, if you want to be liked and adored as an elected official, simply embrace big and intrusive government.

"During the former Administration, we saw an intransigent federal bureaucracy refuse to yield to the reality of an elected President, and work from deeply burrowed in dens of resistance to subvert his efforts.

"Still, there are many Americans who are not ready to submit their ambitions and desire for individual liberty and freedom to those who work within the District of Columbia. Those are the people we are hearing from now. Some become involved by writing letters, some have joined various Tea Party groups, while others are becoming involved in the Council for a Free America."

Now it was Crindler's turn to be interrupted by shouts of protest, catcalls and a smattering of applause. And once again, the Speaker had to resort to energetic use of the gavel before the Congressman could resume.

"There are many individuals in many states who feel that there is no plausible possibility that the United States of America will be able to regain its footing, and return to being the nation founded in the 18th century. They believe that their only chance is to return to our founding principles by establishing a new nation to be governed by those precious, basic tenants of freedom.

"I stand here today to tell you that I am one of those citizens." Once again, the chamber turned raucous, but to a greater extent as those listening understood what was coming next. As the Speaker pounded the gavel, Crindler leaned to the microphone and elevated his voice. "Mister Speaker, today I am submitting my resignation as a member of the House of Representatives, representing the great state of Wyoming. I will be assuming the position of policy coordinator of the Council for a Free America."

As soon as the former Congressman Crindler stepped away from the microphone, the chamber dissolved into chaos as shouts were exchanged and a pair of scuffles broke out on the floor of the House of Representatives. The Speaker called upon the Sergeant at

Arms to help restore order, but as Crindler was struck over the head with a coffee carafe, the Capital Police had to be brought in to escort the bleeding man to safety.

The Speaker continued to bang the gavel, but to no avail. He finally had to resort to shouting that the chamber would be in recess indefinitely.

~~~

Marsha Bentley and Robert Carter were already at the NewsNet Breaking News desk, as word had leaked out that both Hollander and Crindler were planning to offer opposing floor speeches. The studio producer on duty ordered a split – screen shot as the chaos on the House floor was still live on the air, and the correspondents were able to observe and report at the same time.

A stunned Marsha Bentley struggled to begin speaking: "Once again, I am Marsha Bentley for NewsNet, and I am joined by congressional correspondent Robert Carter. Bob... I don't know that we have seen anything like this take place in the US House of Representatives in the last century... or longer. Perhaps our research staff could look that up for us, but at least there's been nothing like this in my lifetime."

Carter shook his head. "No, Marsha... I know that sometimes we laugh at videos from other elected bodies around the world when things have gotten out of hand, but in contemporary America, this is without precedent."

"Wow... Bob, let's start with... I guess we should start with what former... I guess we need to say former Congressman Crindler said. Here we had a member of Congress, not only explaining and justifying a secessionist movement, but then announcing his retirement and his intent to join in its leadership."

Carter shook his head slowly and sadly as the other half of the screen displayed a chamber of Congress that was being emptied by police at the orders of the Speaker and the Sergeant at Arms. "Marsha I am getting word in my ear piece that we have reporters and video staff heading for the outer chambers within the Capitol Building, so hopefully we will be able to have some additional coverage of what may or may not be taking place within that hallowed building. But I must say, Hollander and Crindler probably managed to alliterate every possible stereotype that liberals and conservatives and libertarians can throw at each other.

"Hollander managed to give a rundown of every potential wrongdoing that could occur to people under a purely conservative government, and Crindler was able to paint liberals with all of the usual and horrendous traits they have ever been accused of possessing. At least, if either of these fellows missed any, it got past me."

Suddenly the feed from the House chamber was replaced by live video from another area. Marsha leaned toward the monitor. "It appears that we are seeing live footage from what is usually called the spin room, the area inside the building just outside the chamber where members of Congress go to stand in front of microphones and cameras to give their take on whatever the subject of the day may be. This time... all that we are seeing is an effort by the Capitol Police to encourage everyone to go to their offices, or the bar, whatever works, to restore order in the building.

"Our audio does not seem to be working, but it appears to me that there is still some shouting going on, including some over the shoulder as the members are being escorted away. Thankfully, we are not seeing any more physical altercations. Also, as soon as we can get any kind of report on the severity of the injury to now former Congressman Crindler, we'll pass that along to you. In addition, we will be trying to examine our video while we play back that shocking moment when Mister Crindler took a blow to the head. We're certain that the Capitol Police will be doing the same."

Carter suddenly turned his head to the side, then pressed his earphone firmly against his head as if he were straining to hear. "Marsha... I'm getting word... that Democratic Senator Elaine Ford of Pennsylvania is hastily collecting reporters around her for an impromptu press conference. We... I am being told we are switching to the Hart Senate office building where Senator Ford is going to make a statement about the incredible events taking place just minutes ago in the chamber of the United States House of Representatives. Okay... Senator Ford is now stepping up to a microphone, and we can only hope that our audio and video do well under such circumstances."

Suddenly, viewers watched as the tall blonde woman leaned toward the microphone, in front of a handful of reporters. "I want to thank those of you in the media for so quickly accommodating my request to make a public statement about... the...the unfortunate, extraordinary, but I believe inevitable display of irresponsibility that took place in the honored halls of the United States Congress.

"It is hard for us to believe... I guess that... I just thought that I would never see such a thing. Much will be made of the fact that former Congressman Crindler had to receive medical attention after an altercation that had no place on the floor of the House. However, the incendiary statements made by Mister Crindler unfortunately delineated the thinking of too many members who sit across the aisle, who may not so blatantly express their support for the secessionists who threaten the stability of our nation, but quietly harbor the same sentiments.

"It would be a tragedy for even one state, let alone fourteen, to leave the union of the United States of America. As Congressman Hollander so eloquently emphasized, the soil of our nation has been soaked in the blood of those who gave their lives to establish that our union cannot be dissolved.

"That being said, I will counsel President Malcolm to do everything that he can to prevent a secession by any number of states, short of the use of force. I want my grandchildren to grow up in the same union of fifty states. However, if reality forces us to bid farewell to a portion of the union, then so be it.

"It is apparent to objective observers, that this secession movement, while shouting to all that will listen that it is based upon a desire to regain some supposedly lost concept of economic freedom and a supposed reduction in individual liberty, we all know the truth: this movement is nothing more than a mean – spirited attempt to establish some low-tax Nirvana. Those who lead this treasonous movement seek their own vision of America, one in which all the progress made in rights for minorities and women can be rolled back to resemble 1950 America.

"While the leaders of this movement speak of unsustainable spending and growth in federal government programs, it is the case that many of the states involved in the secession movement are states that receive more in federal spending that is paid by its citizens in federal income tax returns. In addition, many of the same states keep the levels of state taxation low by depriving its citizens in need of many services and benefits taken for granted in more progressive states.

"In my opinion, if such states wish to go their own way, then the remaining United States of America will be able to more easily achieve its full potential for enhancing the lives of its citizens. All too often, progressive legislation is hindered by members of

Congress who feel that they have been sent to Washington to impede progress, and nothing more. Some of us grow weary, because it is like trying to row a boat when others are sitting in the back tossing out anchors. Thank you, and I am sorry that I cannot take any of your questions right now, but I am overdue for a meeting that I assume is still on. Once again, thank you."

The Senator ignored the shouted questions as she turned quickly and disappeared into a meeting room. The camera lingered on the scene long enough to capture the amused and amazed expressions of the media representatives.

Once again, Marsha Bentley and Robert Carter were on the screen. "So Bob, this will be no small matter that a member of the United States Senate has, in effect, stated that she really doesn't care if a lot of what we typically have called red states secede. What do you see as the potential fallout from her comments?"

Carter seemed to be struggling to stifle a laugh. "First of all, Marsha, I would imagine that the first call she will receive will be from President Malcolm. She will be under tremendous pressure to walk back those comments, and try to simply pass them off as simple frustration and embarrassment on behalf of herself and some colleagues.

"In reality, those comments may have been unscheduled, but to me they did not sound unrehearsed. As for the fallout, it may be phenomenal in its impact. While the President will be scrambling to control the damage from those statements, you cannot overlook the element of her adding legitimacy to the desires of the Council for a Free America. It will be harder for other Democrats to denounce that movement, now that one of their most influential and outspoken Senators has taken that plunge."

Marsha folded her hands and seemed to be choosing her words carefully. "But do you think there's any chance that President Malcolm may be among those willing to let these fourteen states go away quietly?"

"I don't think so, Marsha. I cannot imagine any President of the United States wanting to go down in history as being in office when a third of the nation seceded. By the way, Marsha, a little tidbit of some interest just came across the screen… there is a new website by the name of Good Riddance.org. We are being led to believe that it is the official internet site of a newly formed organization by that same name. In a similar vein, there are reports that the White House is being inundated by signatures on an on-line petition to allow these fourteen states to secede with the blessings of the United States of America.

"We received one Twitter message from one of the founders, and if you will excuse the language, it makes a derisive reference to those states, admonishing them that they should exercise caution in, '… not allowing the door to hit you on the ass on your way out'."

Marsha began to laugh and shake her head. "Although this is a very serious subject, I guess we may need to see humor wherever we can find it, because I think that our nation is in for a bumpy ride over the next several months."

~~~

President John Malcolm and Vice President Howard Litton sat in a small receiving room just off the Oval Office. They sat at a small table that held two lunch trays, but neither had a very hearty appetite.

The President looked at his friend of many years. "Howard, everything is spiraling out of control. I doubt that anyone will believe that Elaine said that without my blessing. I just don't feel that way about the situation."

The Vice President rapped his knuckles on the table. "One thing we have to jump on right away was the comment about not using force to prevent secession. Do you want to keep the secessionists guessing, or do you think everyone should know where you stand?"

"I think that everyone has me figured out on that one… I will not see blood spilled to prevent this from happening. My gosh, Howard, we have to keep in mind that each military base located in those states will have a chaotic mixture of divided loyalties."

The Vice President cleared his throat. "Actually, John... I think that there would be almost no chance that the military would follow orders to put down the secession by force."

The President nodded in agreement. "I have the same sense. I think that, when it's all said and done, those state legislatures are going to make the final decisions, regardless of what anyone who works in Washington D. C. thinks is legal or illegal, constitutional or unconstitutional."

The Vice President took a sip of coffee and nodded. "My fear is that the only way we can stop this is to make a case that the logistics are unworkable. Of course, as you know and I know, that is not the case."

The President stood, and then began drumming his fingers on the table. "I don't want this to happen. However, I feel that so many people who have been on my side politically, are not with me in that sentiment."

"I hate to say this, John... I think we have two immovable forces sharing equally unrealistic expectations, but both think that they will be sitting in some ideological Shangri-La a year from now. Everyone should be careful about what they are wishing for."

Chapter 4

Bryce Hamilton was enjoying the light mid–– afternoon
traffic as he made his way in his rented car to the Omaha airport. He
could not get home soon enough. He had not seen his wife of forty-
five years in nearly two weeks, and he missed Cynthia very much.

Just as he turned into the airport complex, his cell phone
vibrated. He pulled over to the side of the street, glanced with
curiosity at the unfamiliar number and answered. He listened for a
minute to a request being made from a producer in the New York
studio of NewsNet. Upon finishing the conversation, he sighed and
drove on to the terminal, but instead of having time to sit and read
and relax before catching his plane home to Lincoln, he parked, then
walked inside and booked a flight to his least favorite city.

~~~

Bryce Hamilton scanned his surroundings with curiosity as
he waited for Ben Stirling to finish checking his notes as a producer
crouched off-camera and counted down the seconds. "Welcome to
another special edition of America in Real Time. I'm your host Ben

Stirling, and I'm very pleased to have with us tonight Mister Bryce Hamilton, a former United States Senator from Nebraska, and the Convening Chairman of the Council for a Free America. If you are a regular viewer of our program, you know that last night we hosted Tom Edelstein from the same organization, and in light of this morning's surreal happenings on the floor of the House of Representatives, we asked Senator Hamilton to come on our program this evening. Senator Hamilton, welcome to our program."

"Thank you, Ben. It's my pleasure to be here."

"All right, Senator Hamilton, what is your take on what happened this morning?"

"The altercation, especially the injury to Congressman Crindler was unfortunate and uncalled for. I hope to never see anything like that again."

Stirling held up his pen as was his habit when asking a question. "But who do you blame for this awful exhibition we saw?"

"I understand that the Capitol Police are still trying to determine just who it was that struck Congressman Crindler. So my only possible answer is, that I don't know."

"But Senator Hamilton, do you feel that perhaps Congressman Crindler, or we should now say, former Congressman Crindler, was too over the top in stating his case for secession? After all, this did take place on the floor of the US House of Representatives."

Hamilton tilted his head and considered the question. "Other former members of Congress have announced their resignations in the chamber. I grant you that the circumstances were different from those who resigned from their seats due to some type of scandal or malfeasance, but he had something to say to his peers, and he said it to their faces. And please remember, his taking the floor followed a rather disgraceful tirade from the lips of Congressman Hollander, one that managed to insult millions of Americans, simply because they disagree with him. Still, I am getting phone calls and text messages telling me that most of the punditry class is concentrating on the Crindler speech, and giving scant attention to what I think were deplorable and prejudiced statements made by Mister Hollander."

"Senator Hamilton, I know that many in your movement have felt that the media has been unfair. Could you comment on that?"

"It is what it is. And it is not going to change. I am not among the conservatives and libertarians who hold out hope that someday balanced coverage will come forth out of a sense of fairness. I suppose that at this stage of my life, if I were to be tasked with covering the news, I would find it somewhat difficult to refrain from being critical of liberals. I learned long ago, that beating one's head against the wall only brings pain upon oneself."

"If you don't mind my saying so, Senator Hamilton, you seem somewhat oddly resigned to what you see is a fact of life regarding media treatment of your movement."

Hamilton laughed. "Please do not misunderstand me. I'm simply a man who tries to recognize and accept reality. I do believe that what we refer to with reverence as the mainstream media has played as large a role in bringing us to this precipice as my friends in the Democratic Party, and liberal America in general.

"For the past decade or longer, any suggestion that we should rein in spending has been met with media derision at first, and sometimes not-so-subtle suggestions of racial prejudice as of late. Suggestions that we should make the federal government back off on regulations concerning business have brought catcalls to the effect that we don't care about the environment or how workers are treated.

"And how dare we suggest that those wishing to come to America do so through proper channels? To suggest that the law be followed makes us prejudiced against Hispanic people or those of other faiths.

"Now our very movement is being accused of being racist at its core. As a member of the Republican Party, at least for now, nothing has incensed me more over the past years than seeing minority people who join the party being derided in the most crass of terms, then have the party criticized because there are not enough minority party members. Your viewers can determine for themselves if there is any possibility of our movement ever being treated fairly by the media."

Stirling seemed to stiffen in his chair: "We must now take a break, and when we come back we are going to continue with Mister Bryce Hamilton, from the Council for a Free America."

Upon returning from the break, Stirling looked into the camera: "For those of you who may be joining us in progress, our guest this evening is Bryce Hamilton, of the Council for a Free America. Senator Hamilton… I would like to ask a question that is perhaps more sensitive than any other I could possibly think of. If the government of the United States of America states its intention to prevent your secession, or withdrawal, or whatever you wish to call it, do you believe that the President will order the use of military force to prevent the nation from coming apart?"

Bryce took a deep breath and hesitated. "I don't know the answer to that. Only the President knows his feelings on that matter. I know that everyone is wishing to avoid addressing that issue. Of course, I cannot speak for everyone in the fourteen states in question. I can say that, in the many meetings I have attended, and the discussions I have held, I have never heard the first expression of desire for any conflict beyond the verbal kind."

Stirling leaned toward his guest. "Are you in any position to assure the American public that should the federal government state its intentions to use all possible means to prevent the withdrawal of states, the movement would yield rather than engage in armed conflict?"

"Ben, let me just say this. It is our intention and hope, that should a state or group of states decide to withdraw from the United States of America, that will be allowed to happen peacefully, without conflict and through diplomatic, but not military, means. I think it is likely that this can be achieved without any armed conflict, and there really is no reason for any. The citizens in those fourteen states simply wish to have their state legislatures vote on withdrawal. Further, should one or more legislatures so vote, if any armed conflict resulted, it would have to be at the initiative of President Malcolm.

"I may be in disagreement with President Malcolm in most areas of domestic policy, especially economic policy and the role of government regulations. At the same time, I have a hard time seeing the good and decent man who is our President ordering violence in such a case. I just do not believe that would be in his heart."

Ben Stirling appeared to be a bit shaken. "Let's move on to the matter of the structure of this proposed new union. You have made it clear as an organization that you would intend to build the union strictly along the lines of our original Constitution. Does that include the amendments?"

Bryce managed to smile at the question. "The consensus seems to be that we would certainly adopt the original Bill of Rights. I suppose that through the course of the next weeks we will be finishing our task of examining the rest of the amendments, although they do not have the same level of urgency as the first ten, especially the First, Second, and Tenth.

"One interesting point of discussion many of us are engaged in regards the Congress. Not a few individuals involved in the movement have expressed a sentiment to have a House of Representatives, but to dispense with the idea of a Senate. Their thinking is that having just a House of Representatives will make our government more efficient, and keep our elected representatives closer to, and more accountable to the citizens.

"As for a Supreme Court, most voices I have heard support a seven-member court. One suggestion is that, should there be just one house of Congress, our President would make nominations to the Court, then have them be affirmed by a majority of the House of Representatives. Once again, media coverage of such matters has been scant, I suppose because it's not as much fun as guessing our intent on matters such as gay marriage, guns and abortion." Bryce finished his comment with a chuckle.

"Senator Hamilton, one more question, and I want to thank you for coming here and with such short notice... I want to ask you a question that was posed to you in your press conference. Your movement seems to be charging ahead at warp speed. Some of your critics are saying that you are proceeding in that manner so that citizens will not have enough time to thoroughly consider what steps they should take. Can you comment on that?"

"As I said at the press conference, while we do not wish to take any actions that have not been thoroughly considered, we want all of this settled before the next set of elections. Also, whatever the outcome of all this, our citizens need to make whatever adjustments are necessary and move on with life.

"At risk of sounding like a broken record, the media has fixated on side issues. The reality is that these discussions began in a number of states nearly three years ago. Some of the states involved had subcommittees of the organizations exploring some of these more delicate side effects of withdrawing from the United States of America. Those subcommittees were dealing three years ago with considering what the governmental and social structures would be should this movement come to fruition.

"Several of the Council organizations at the state level have already prepared plans for the social programs being so widely talked about, how the education systems would be affected and so forth. I am not saying there will not be some critical difficulties. But

Ben, as a nation, the United States of America is already facing critical difficulties, and the fact that they are not always acknowledged does not make them any less real."

"One more question on a related topic: the states proposing secession contain large amounts of land occupied by Native Americans. What about the rights of the first Americans?"

"The CSA will honor all current agreements."

Ben Stirling nodded, and then reached out his hand to shake that of Bryce Hamilton. "Senator Hamilton,… once again, thank you for changing your plans for us, and most of all… I want to thank you for your candor. And when we come back, we will be speaking with a constitutional law professor from Harvard University who claims that the Council for a Free America is simply engaging in blackmail to force changes, and has no real intention of having states secede from the union."

~~~

It was midnight when President John Malcolm finally made his way to his bedroom, and was relieved to see that the First Lady was still awake and reading in bed. Marjorie Malcolm peered over her glasses perched upon the round and lovely face framed by salt and pepper hair.

She watched with a sympathetic gaze as her husband of thirty-two years tossed his clothes onto a chair and crawled into bed, his exhaustion and frustration evident. He reached over and took his wife's hand, gave it a squeeze, then drew it to his mouth and kissed it. "Margie… I don't think I could handle this job if I couldn't look forward to having you with me every night."

The First Lady leaned over and kissed him. "Are you having regrets?"

The President took a deep breath, and then nodded. "Yes… I made a big mistake in running for this office. I seem to have enjoyed campaigning more than governing. I enjoyed the Senate, and I should've stayed there. Margie… I think it's all going to come apart, and that's how I'll be remembered."

Marjorie closed her book and turned on her side to place her head on the pillow next to her husband's. "We're a long way from that."

"I think I have had too tough an act to follow as a Democratic President. There was something about Obama… I can't really put it into words, but there was something about him. I just don't measure up in comparison. Maybe not even to Trump."

Marjorie raised herself on an elbow. "If he did such a damned good job, why do all those states want to bail out of what he left behind? Understand me correctly John,… I think Obama was a fine President. But still, he left a lot of things behind that made a lot of people very unhappy. Actually, I blame them for not appreciating everything he tried to do. In the eyes of the Republicans and the right wing media, he could do nothing right. He was treated by them as a novelty, and he was never taken seriously by those narrow – minded fools. But we got past Trump, and I think that you are doing a sensational job in your own right."

Malcolm ran his fingertips across his tired eyes. "We all know that the media gave Obama cover for everything, almost without question. And I'm okay with that. When I think back to how people on the right talked about that good man, I have no quarrel with anyone who tried to counterbalance all that vitriol that came from the conservatives.

"Of course the media favored him, and for damned good reasons. I get the same benefit to a degree because I have that progressive, liberal label glued to my forehead for all to see. But once this secessionist movement has gained a little more steam, all that good will is going to thin out."

"But John, there's a growing call for you to just take up that good riddance attitude. You can keep favor with your party base, and the press if you just join in."

The President shook his head vigorously. "No… I don't want it to happen. I want to keep us together, no matter how hard it is, I don't want to be the one to give up, the one to abandon all hopes that we can reach some kind of reasonable accommodation in our political divide."

Both grew silent, until Marjorie spoke haltingly. "Did you have a chance to see Ben Stirling's program this evening?"

"Yes… I could've had it recorded, but I was so anxious to see that interview, I canceled two meetings so that I could watch it live. I have to say, if Bryce Hamilton makes an announcement that he intends to run for President of the breakaway states, my ass is had."

"How is that?"

"He's coming across as the fantasy President for all the right wingers and Libertarians in America. He is so blunt, and he breaks everything down into such simple terms. Most of all, he is so… damned… sure of himself. That arrogant bastard…".

The President closed his eyes before continuing. "Those people in those fourteen states who may be wavering, or even opposed, they just may fall in love with that guy."

"What about the things he said about you using force?"

The President began to laugh. "I will divulge to you, my dear, what is officially for now a secret of the highest level. There is no way in hell I am going to use military force to keep them from seceding."

Marjorie leaned over and kissed him. "I can't tell you how relieved I am to hear you say that. It's what I expected, and apparently, Bryce Hamilton suspects the same. But as hard as all of this may become for you... I want you to know, I think you are making the only right decision."

The President began to chuckle. "I wonder if Abraham and Mary Todd had this conversation."

"Whatever... I know that this is not the same. It has a regional quality to it of course. But it's not the same at all. With the instant media... John, can you imagine a reporter from CNN broadcasting live video of a crying Nebraska farm wife whose husband was just killed in a firefight with the U.S. Army?"

The President closed his eyes again and slowly shook his head. "No, and that's why we'll never let that happen. Good night Margie."

~~~

Jim Walters was hidden away in his office on a quiet Wednesday morning. As the Chief of Staff for President John Malcolm, he was being tasked with trying to manage the flow of comments and policies regarding the withdrawal movement. He was being joined in that effort by the President's Chief Advisor for Policy, Francine Lowery.

He was not necessarily looking forward to the meeting with her that morning, as they had never seen eye to eye on many matters. However, he knew that John Malcolm was fiercely loyal to his Policy Advisor. She was also one of the few African-American members of his close staff, and he found her input and advice on minority matters invaluable.

Walters heard a light tap on the door, followed by a petite middle-aged woman walking through. Francine Lowery plopped down in the guest chair, and shook her head as she looked at the ceiling. "Those reporters... I suppose it's because I'm black, but they keep peppering me with questions about whether I think the secession movement is being driven by racism. I keep telling them to bring me specific quotes made by leaders of the movement that speak ill of minorities, and then I will comment." She finally opened her eyes, shook her head and looked pleadingly at the Chief of Staff. She began to laugh: "Please Jim... make them stop."

Walters shook his head sympathetically. "Sorry... I'm not a proctologist. I can't fix assholes." He hesitated for a moment. "I don't think that's going to go away. There's so much fixation on how much this movement is founded on racism."

Francine sighed. "So, the only way I can back that off is to defend a movement wishing to break the country apart?"

"Maybe... I don't know how the boss would feel about that."

"But I don't know how they feel about race... I mean the people running the movement." She closed her eyes and shook her head. "Maybe that's the point... I certainly get the impression from the media that they think they know."

"May as well get used to it." Walters opened a file, revealing several sheets of text copied from the internet. He passed the file to Francine. "I don't know how closely you have been able to watch what some of the columnists and bloggers are saying. You can take these with you and review them at your pleasure. What I want to talk to you about, however, is the overall theme we are starting to see."

Francine took the file, closed it, and placed it in her briefcase. "And what would that common theme be?"

"It can all be summed up in two words: good riddance."

Francine nodded. "I did manage to see that website."

"Well, it's all over the cable news coverage as well as the major networks. I don't know how I feel about that, but too many people on our side are getting giddy."

"Giddy?"

"I'm sure you've heard it. They see a United States free of so many of those right wing members of Congress. They see nothing but progressive Presidents as far out in the future as you can see, getting every Supreme Court and Cabinet appointment approved at the snap of the finger."

"Are they wrong?"

Walters leaned back in his chair and began to nervously drum his fingers on the desk. "No, they're not wrong. In fact, if this secession goes through, that's exactly what will happen."

"So what are the major downsides to all this?"

Walters smiled. "Actually, that's what I would like for you to answer. What do you think?"

The policy advisor shifted in her chair uncomfortably. "Is this strictly between us?"

Walters nodded. "Yes, certainly it is. And I can already tell that you're going to tell me some things you really don't want to say."

"I need for this to stay between us, because I don't want to lose my credentials as a good and progressive liberal. Remember, I'm not telling you what I want to happen, or what I think should happen."

"Good enough. I just want to know what you think the future will bring if the states do indeed bolt."

"Okay. I think that this two – way migration that Bryce Hamilton and Tom Edelstein refer to is going to be major and chaotic. And this is where my being black hits close to my heart. If everybody on the left keeps telling black people that they are going to go back decades in progress if they are living in any of those states that end up seceding, there's going to be a lot of unnecessary fear and anguish."

"Go on."

"Because that's not going to be the case. There is no way that these states are going to be havens for bigotry. Still, fear is going to make a lot of people of color flee, because they are going to be bombarded with warnings that if they stay it will be like living in Little Rock in the 1950s."

"What about the economic side of all this?"

"I think this is where things may get interesting. We all know that businesses have been moving to low – tax states, and those with right to work statutes. I am very afraid that as soon as the secession goes into effect, the remaining United States is going to see an exodus of jobs.

"While our party and the media deny this, and either don't believe it or want to treat it as some dirty little secret, the people involved in this Council for a Free America know damned well how this is likely to play out. If the jobs leave, then the tax base leaves. Not all, of course. Wall Street will still be Wall Street, Manhattan will be Manhattan and Los Angeles and Hollywood will still be doing their thing. And all those farmers in California, Ohio, Indiana and Iowa and Illinois will stay put of course.

"But Jim, this won't be pretty. While we are out there warning that these breakaway states are going to be miserly in terms of social programs and public assistance, the states that remain in the United States of America are going to have their revenues so disrupted and diminished, they will, ironically, be forced to dramatically, and I mean dramatically, pare back to a similar degree.

"We are facing the prospect of increased civil disorder when those more severe cuts have to go into effect. We're already seeing the beginnings of those problems. Remember, the states have to balance their budgets. You take away all that revenue from the states, coupled with the further inability of the remaining federal government to make up the difference, well… On top of that, don't forget that the states planning to secede are some of the most fiscally responsible states. Just imagine what will happen to the credit rating of the federal government. It will take yet another dive.

"Everyone in the world knows that three years ago we reached the mathematical impossibility to repay our debt. When the states in the best fiscal condition are no longer part of the United States, the dollar will crash. We won't go into recession… it will be much worse than that."

Walters sat in silence for a moment. "Are you saying that The United States Treasury may end up going hat in hand to beg to borrow money from the new union?"

Francine Lowery sat for a moment to consider a question that had not before crossed her mind. "I don't want to consider the prospect of having to take out a loan from a republic that was formed partially because its inhabitants got tired of being insulted by those now begging for a favor. Can you imagine the conditions that may be imposed as part of the loan agreement?"

"Is there any way out? What are you going to advise the President to do?"

Francine stood up and began pacing the floor, then turned away and leaned her head on her forearms that were pressed against the wall. "The only honest opinion I can give them… I think he has to let this happen, so it will at least be peaceful.

"I just shudder at the prospect of our having to establish the equivalent of an embassy in Omaha, Nebraska. Heaven help us, Jim. We're going to end up negotiating trade agreements and virtual treaties with what used to be part of our country. We are going to end up in competition with what has been our own heartland. And all I can do… I have to… I have to advise President Malcolm to simply cut the best deal he can with Bryce Hamilton and Patrick Bridger. When he asks me for my opinion that is what I'm going to tell him. Then I'm going to walk out of his office, head to the ladies room and vomit."

Chapter 5

President John Malcolm was just finishing up his 1:00 PM meeting with representatives of the California Chamber of Commerce when Jim Walters quietly entered the room and waited until the last of the delegates had been escorted out. While trying to pay polite attention to his departing guests, the President could see that his Chief of Staff was impatient to have his ear.

Walters literally followed the last of the visitors to the door, then quickly closed it. "Mister President, please come with me. I need to show you what we just recorded."

The two men walked hurriedly out of the Oval Office and to a room twenty feet down the hall where a television set and three chairs were always at the ready for viewing something urgent on the airwaves. Without saying a word, both men sat down and Walters picked up a remote control, turned on the set, and a recorded image appeared.

"This is Carol Rogers, and we are interrupting our regular early afternoon programming here on NewsNet to bring you a special report. We are expecting a video feed at any moment that was recorded by a station in Helena, Montana. Excuse me… I am being told, instead, that the video feed is not working… I am now being told that we're cutting away to Megan Howard from our NewsNet affiliate in Billings, Montana."

Suddenly the scene was of the interior of the chamber of the Montana House of Representatives. There was no sound, so Carol Rogers continued the coverage from the New York studio of NewsNet. "We're still waiting for Megan Howard to begin her report, and right now what you are seeing is the interior of the Montana State Capitol in Helena, and being a native of Montana, I can tell you that the large mural you are looking at in the back of the chamber is a painting by Charles M Russell, entitled Lewis and Clark Meeting the Flathead Indians at Ross' Hole. It was painted in 1912 and… I just got word that… here we go… Megan Howard is now ready to begin her report."

A tall brunette woman suddenly appeared in front of the mural holding a microphone. "This is Megan Howard for NewsNet, and I am standing in the now empty chamber of the Montana House of Representatives. However, before the body adjourned for three hours, just forty-five minutes ago, history was made when Representative Seth Morgan introduced a resolution to the effect that Montana would withdraw from the United States of America. There was little debate, and the resolution passed 74 to 26. I am being told that the measure will go to the Senate as early as late this afternoon, and the Senate President just told me that he expects the vote in that chamber to be taken as early as tomorrow morning. And after the lopsided vote that just took place in the House, it seems to be a foregone conclusion that by tomorrow afternoon, the first domino will have fallen, and Montana will have become the first state to vote for secession since the 1860s. This is Megan Howard, reporting for NewsNet, from the state capitol building in Helena, Montana."

The President and his Chief of Staff sat in silence. Walters wanted to allow his President time to gather his thoughts. However, he finally turned to see John Malcolm looking down while tears streamed down his face.

Walters sat uncomfortably, uncertain as to what to say or do. Finally, it was his boss who broke the silence. "I'm just… I just can't believe this happened so…. how did everyone miss that this was happening so rapidly?"

Walters felt himself trembling. "It was a tremendously smart move on their part. Let's face it, how much media coverage was there in Helena, Montana? The news crews have been hovering in Texas, Nebraska and Kansas. But these guys have thrown down the gauntlet. Mr. President, I think that we need to be ready for at least a couple more this week. Even if they are small population states, they are geographically large. If I was in charge of their strategy, I would try to arrange for two or three more of those big, rectangular states to go rapidly on the heels of Montana.

"Just imagine what that graphic is going to look like… each and every network will have one.… this map showing this large, highlighted chunk of Middle America that plans to leave. Then, in another shade of color they will add the states that are involved in the Council for a Free America. That would be, what, may be a little more than a third of the landmass of the lower forty-eight states? As for just those states that are likely to go by the end of the week, the area highlighted may contain a fraction of the population, but the visual effect will be murderous."

The tearful President considered his staffer's words for a moment. "How long do you think it will be before all fourteen have voted to leave?"

Walters looked down to the floor and shuffled his feet nervously. "I know that Bryce Hamilton refers to votes being taken within the next forty-five days. My guess... I say the die will be cast within thirty." Walters leaned forward and toward the President. "Sir... I know that you inherited everything that has led us to this point."

"Jim... I want to... I need to speak with Francine. Is she still in the building?"

"Yes, sir. She told me she would be around all day."

"Have her meet me in the Oval Office... I want to talk to her right away."

Walters stood, but the President sat motionless and in silence as the Chief of Staff left the room. The President decided to linger for a moment, then reached for the remote control once more and turned the television back on just in time to see the beginning of a special report on NewsNet.

"This is Monica Samuelsson reporting from just outside the headquarters of the United States Capitol Police. The commander has just issued a statement to the effect that after close examination of the video of the assault of former Congressman Crindler on the floor of the House of Representatives, along with interviews of witnesses, an arrest warrant has been issued for Representative Walter Benjamin. Benjamin is a moderate Republican representing a suburban district near St. Louis, Missouri.

"Sources tell us that Benjamin and Crindler had been at odds for several days over some comments Crindler had made in Benjamin's presence, comments that indicated his sympathy and support for the secession movement.

"Supposedly, Benjamin was very unhappy at the mere possibility that Missouri would join the secession movement, and that he would lose his influence as a key member of the House Ways and Means committee. It is no secret that Benjamin has reveled in the power his position has yielded. We are expecting more information on assault charges later in the day. This is Monica Samuelsson, reporting from the U.S. Capitol Building for NewsNet."

~~~

President John Malcolm was sitting on the front edge of the large, storied desk when his chief Policy Advisor walked in, and rested in the chair he pointed to in silence.

"Francine... I suppose I've known you for over twenty years now. Right now, I need for you to be unmerciful in your honesty with me. I think you understand, I am not going to use the military to stop this."

Francine nodded silently, a few gray strands falling to her forehead. "I would find any other answer inconceivable and unrealistic."

"Jim believes this is going to be a cascading event over the next three to four weeks."

"Jim and I are often at loggerheads. However... I think he's right on this. And before you ask me, Mr. President, I don't think there's anything you can do but accept the inevitable with grace, and try to reassure the citizens that will still be residing in the United States of America."

"Francine... I need to... I want you to tell me why we arrived here."

"Mr.... John, the divide is just too wide now to salvage this. I know that every state that tends to be conservative contains a lot of liberals. And I know that every state that tends to be liberal contains a lot of conservatives.

"But the insults, the disparaging comments flying back and forth and snippets of opinion that everyone heard within hours after they were spoken in this day of immediate and instant news… I was talking to a friend from college a few months ago, a girl I hung around with. Now she's a conservative activist. Oh, we laughed about how each of us now spends our time trying to see that the other's causes go down in flames.

"Then we started talking a little more seriously, and we started to try to figure out when and how all the political discourse became so bitter. I told her that it all went back to the things Newt Gingrich said when Bill Clinton was President. She disagreed, and said that it all began when Ronald Reagan was elected, and the left could not accept that a man they regarded as having a simple, narrow view of the world had replaced Jimmy Carter.

"And look where we are now. Pundits and talking heads on our side scream that conservatives are backwards, unsophisticated, greedy and anxious to stomp on the rights of women and minorities. At the same time, the loudest mouths on the right constantly claim that liberals and progressives are unrelenting extremists bent on doing away with all traditional values and weakening the United States economically and militarily.

"When we parted company that day, we were just as close friends, but we were never able to come to an agreement. The only thing we agreed on, was that it has all turned poisonous, and neither of us felt optimistic about it getting better in the foreseeable future.

"John… I really don't know how to say this in any kind way. You have been my friend for so long… I just…"

The President leaned forward and placed his hand on the shoulder of his long-term friend. "It's just us here, Francine. Just say it."

It was then that he noticed that Francine was dabbing at her eyes with a tissue. "John… I just don't know… I just don't know how you won the election."

In spite of the stark statement, and the melancholy that had overtaken him on that day, John Malcolm still managed to smile at his friend's words. "Well, Francine… I avoided ever mentioning the secession movement on my own initiative during the campaign, and when I was asked, I dodged the question. We have been collectively whistling past the graveyard. To my own shock, it worked. However, I detect that there is still more you would like to say."

Francine seemed to be holding her breath. "John… I feel so honored to be working for you in this capacity. But now I feel so torn. You see, I believe in the same things you believe in. During your campaign, you promoted every ideal I have held dear since my college days. But John, my dear friend, even as I was going around the country speaking to groups and state conventions on your behalf, I knew that those principles I hold so dear just are not working. Let's face it. Your campaign never proposed a single idea that would do anything other than make our economic crisis even worse.

"And every time I saw a video of your opponent speaking, I knew deep inside that his proposals would have continued to have provided us the only chance we had to make it through this fiscal debacle as a nation. But I was blinded by my ideology, and swayed by my loyalty to the party... and to you. Maybe I didn't drink the Kool-Aid, but I did even worse... I brought the pitcher and poured glasses of it to hand to everyone else.

"It's all coming to an end, John. And God help me... I worked fifteen hour days during the campaign to help bring it about."

Francine stood up, leaned over and planted an affectionate kiss on the cheek of the President of the United States of America. "I'm going to go back to Arkansas... I'm going to live with my sister and mom for a while to sort all this out. I'm going to try and do what I can with them and my lifelong circle of friends and family. But I think I know what I'm meant for... I will always treasure our friendship, John... I'm going to have Betty box up my things... I'll make sure the letter is on your desk by tomorrow." Francine turned slowly, walked to the door, and did not look back as she left.

~~~

In spite of heavy rain storms on the eastern seaboard that were causing havoc with flight schedules, Bryce Hamilton finally made his way to his stately home in Lincoln, Nebraska. As he walked in the door of the home he had lived in for forty years, he glanced at his watch and realized that twenty-four hours had now passed since his entertaining appearance with Ben Stirling.

He called out Cynthia's name. When he heard the warm and familiar reply, as always, he was glad that that slight touch of a southern twang had never left her voice. He began walking toward the living room and was met by the slender, gray-haired woman with whom he had spent most of his life. After a long kiss and firm embrace, they made their way to the sofa and sat.

Cynthia looked at her husband with an amused expression. "A regular political superstar, aren't we now?"

Hamilton tried to maintain a false, stern expression, but could not prevent himself from breaking out into a laugh. "Are you trying to tell me that I'm taking myself much too seriously?"

"No." She shook her head back and forth. "I'm just trying to keep my own sense of humor alive, because I'm so damn scared, Bryce. I support everything you are doing... I just find that agreeing with you and supporting you doesn't make this any less frightening. You and I have been on this earth long enough to know that the variables are nearly incomprehensible. As my father always said, people plan, then God laughs."

Hamilton leaned his head back against the top of the sofa and heaved a deep sigh. "Quite frankly, at times I already hear that laughter."

Cynthia leaned over and kissed him. "But I understand. There is no choice but to try to salvage what we can."

He seemed to be staring into space. "I just want us to be able to...". His phone began to buzz and he glanced at the tiny screen. "Sorry... I have to take this. It's Pat Bridger. "

He answered the phone and listened for a moment, his eyes growing wide in interest. "I guess I need to start turning on the radio when I drive. Thanks, Congressman. I'll be back in touch with you."

Without any explanation, Hamilton leaned forward to the coffee table, picked up the television remote control, and turned the set on. He punched two buttons, then settled back against the sofa. Bryce and Cynthia watched in silence as a NewsNet correspondent posed in the dimming light in front of the large arched façade of the Texas State Capitol building in Austin. "...... and now reports are surfacing that it may be High Noon deep in the heart of Texas tomorrow. Announcements went out three days ago for supporters to gather on the lawn in front of this Capitol building to show support for Texas legislators to formally vote on a resolution to withdraw.

"As we all know, Texas has seceded one time before, when it joined the Confederacy at the beginning of the Civil War. Texas also has an interesting status among the states, as it is the only one of the fifty states that has ever been an independent nation. The Republic of Texas was established after winning its freedom from Mexico, before being admitted to the United States. Another interesting tidbit is that some proponents of Texas sovereignty contend that Texas has special status based upon certain clauses included in the documents involved in its becoming a state. Of course, that is under scrutiny by many legal scholars who contend that Texas cannot exercise any special clauses, including the legendary right to divide into several states at its discretion.

"Further complicating matters is that some Hispanic activists claim that parts or all of Texas, along with some other states in the American southwest, rightfully belong to Mexico, and were seized under illegitimate conditions. The often repeated adage that we hear is, in regard to undocumented immigrants, 'we did not cross the border – the border crossed us'.

"The pro-withdrawal leaders here in Austin yesterday were granted a permit to hold a rally on the state capitol grounds. However, it is evident from social media traffic and even flyers being posted around the city of Austin, several interest groups, some related to Hispanic interests, others consisting of cadres of students from the University of Texas here in Austin, plan to mount counter – demonstrations.

"To say the least, police leaders are on edge as much as they are on alert. In addition, although it has not been confirmed, we have received reports that Texas Governor Marcus Howell has called up some units of the Texas National Guard to be on standby at some undisclosed staging area outside the city, but close enough to be brought in if things were to get out of hand.

"For those of you who are just tuning in, all of this excitement that began to percolate late in the afternoon and continues now into early evening, came about when a local television station interrupted programming at around 4:00 PM this afternoon, to announce that sources connected to the Republican leadership in the Texas House of Representatives had indicated the possibility that the legislature planned to suspend all other activities tomorrow, to devote its attention to a yet unseen resolution in favor of secession.

"Details are sketchy, but one of our sources who spoke to a staff member of the Texas House Speaker's office, speculated that the resolution would be jointly introduced by two very conservative Republican members of the Texas legislature. The names we have been given are state Representative Henry Banks, and State Senator Walter Rodrigues. It should be noted that Banks has been prominently involved in the criticism of federal interference in the matters of state governments. Banks has been the most dogged Texas critic of the federal government for what he refers to as a failure of people in Washington to be sensitive to the problems of ranchers and other landowners who live along the border with Mexico. He has traveled to Washington to testify to House committees about the damage to property committed by those crossing into the U.S. illegally, not to mention the violence that has made some border landowners fear for their lives within the borders of their own properties, and even within the confines of their homes.

"He accuses the federal government of sacrificing the safety and security of Americans, for the sake of being politically correct in order to gain favor with Hispanic voters. He has also railed against elected officials who minimized enhanced border security during the Trump Presidency.

"He has also spoken in public many times about the 10th Amendment to the United States Constitution, one that is intended to limit federal involvement in its authority over matters of state sovereignty.

"As for Rodrigues, he has been notable as a target of criticism from some Hispanic interest groups for his very blunt criticism of those who have advocated increased Mexican influence over the Southwest states. In one notable town hall setting, Rodrigues became quite animated in asking why any Hispanics would wish to come under the influence of the government of Mexico, considering the drug activity and violent chaos being suffered there.

"Now we have reports that both Rodrigues and Banks are being given special security protection by the Texas Rangers. Allegedly, both have received death threats over the past twenty-four hours, and that is in addition to three bomb threats that have been called into the Texas State Capitol switchboard.

"As we all know, Texas has a long-standing tradition of freedom to own and carry firearms. Now, late this afternoon, troubling reports have been coming into local media outlets that gun shops and firearms sections of department stores and sporting good stores, are experiencing runs on inventory rivaling the ones that took place in early 2019 when the United States Senate began floating numerous ideas regarding gun control in light of the various school shootings in America. It is also being compared to the memorable situation with similar results that took place several months ago when the Senate tried to enact legislation requiring mandatory gun registration.

"One local police authority who asked to not be identified, stated to me that he at first found it inconceivable that there were very many Texas residents who were not already armed, then he found out that many of the purchases were being made by students and residents of some of the neighborhoods of Austin that are home to the more liberal denizens, such as university staff and members of the local cultural community.

"Tomorrow morning, all eyes will be on Austin, and not only will we be watching to see if any tempers overflow, but most of all we will be watching to see what, if any, action the Texas legislature takes. There is rampant speculation as to whether the Montana resolution was enacted independent of any strategy, or if it were part of a planned tip – off of the secession movement. Still others, of a more conspiratorial inclination, think that Montana took the action when it did to send a message to Austin, to make a point that the large and powerful state of Texas will not be calling all the shots."

The scene on the television suddenly was one of another hastily arranged panel discussion in the NewsNet studio in New York. Hamilton shook his head, muted the sound of the television, and reached for his phone to call Patrick Bridger.

~~~

It was 9:00 PM when Vice President Howard Litton led Chief of Staff Jim Walters and Attorney General Julia Stafford into the Oval Office where President Malcolm awaited them. Each of the visitors had already been apprised of the sudden departure of the President's primary policy advisor.

The President looked them over for a moment, and then spoke: "I'm afraid to ask this question, but have any of you heard any news within the last hour that I may have possibly missed while I was meeting with the Governor?"

Howard Litton was the first to speak up. "Mister President, I just got a phone call from Senator Carlyle."

The President shook his head in obvious irritation. "And just what does our wise and noble Majority Leader want now?"

The Vice President cleared his throat. "Senator Carlyle wanted me to make it perfectly clear to you that he hopes that more states in this group will expedite their secession, because we all know that he has nothing but derision for most of the members of the House and Senate from these states. At the same time, he wants you to appear to be doing everything you can to prevent this from happening so he is… he is, uhm, he is suggesting that you declare martial law and a state of emergency in each state that passes a secession resolution."

The President slammed his hand angrily on his desk. "What did you tell him?"

The Vice President allowed himself a chuckle. "I told him that he needed to give more forethought to making such a suggestion, and that you would have no part of it."

Jim Walters spoke up: "The problem with that loose cannon… I mean we all know that he is more than capable of going off on his own and making a statement like that, then trying to make you own it."

Julia Stafford scooted forward in her chair and raised her palms upward. "Do you really want to dismiss that idea out of hand?"

The President leaned forward and nearly came out of his chair. "Hell yes, Julia… I do indeed want to immediately dismiss that suggestion."

The Attorney General held her ground. "But, sir... I see some merit in that idea. I really don't think these characters living out there in sagebrush country really have the stomach for all this. I still think they're bluffing. Take Senator Carlyle's suggestion under advisement. At least think about it, please. It may be a chance to draw them out regarding what they really want from us. I still just think they're looking for some concessions, and to score some points with the right wing talking heads. Plus, it is a low-level threat, but it may be enough to make the secessionists began to back off."

The President strained to regain a calm demeanor. "Do any of the rest of you agree with that?"

The Vice President turned slowly toward the Attorney General. "Julia... I don't know how I'm going to convince you about this... I'm certain that this is no bluff. And declaring martial law is not a low-level threat. This secession talk is no negotiating ploy. The states are going to take a hike, and we owe it to President Malcolm to help him find a way to minimize the damage to the nation... I mean all the current fifty states."

Julia stood and began pacing the floor. "Mister President... I need to come to an understanding with you. Do you, or do you not wish for me to seek a Supreme Court ruling that the states are prohibited from seceding?"

The President stared at her for a moment. "I have a feeling, that in this matter, considering the progression of events, any such ruling, or granting of a stay or an injunction from the Supreme Court would be seen as irrelevant."

Now the Attorney General was the one staring in silence. "Okay... I need another question answered. Shall I, or shall I not, pursue treason or sedition charges against Bryce Hamilton, Patrick Bridger or any of the other leaders of the Council for a Free America?"

The President shook his head slowly from side to side. "You... shall... not."

The Attorney General picked up her briefcase from beside the chair she had risen from. "In that case, Mister President, I resign effective immediately."

The President nodded. "There seems to be a lot of that going around today. Julia... I want to thank you for your service to your country, and wish you the best in the future."

The only sound in the room was the scruff of the former Attorney General's shoes on the thick carpet as she made her way to the door that she slammed behind her. The Vice President and Chief of Staff exchanged glances that betrayed equal portions of relief and anxiety.

The President took a deep breath, blew it out, and then turned to the Vice President. "Howard, I want you to look over the list of Assistant Attorneys General. Make a recommendation within a couple of days, because we don't have time to go on a conventional search, and we have to have the position filled immediately. In addition, I don't want the media talking about this any longer than necessary."

The President turned to Jim Walters. "Come up with a statement from me. I don't in any way want to demean Julia, so let's try to make this a soft landing all around."

President Malcolm struggled to regain his concentration. "I think we are being played by Hamilton and Bridger. This timetable...".

The Vice President spoke up: "It's taken on a life of its own. My sources tell me that a key group in the Montana House was incensed by an EPA directive that came out on Friday. They were ready to give the green light for the opening rounds of development for a new oilfield. It was going to mean nearly four thousand jobs in just one county.

"The EPA stomped on the project, and it turns out that the main developer is a respected acquaintance of some of the more powerful House members. Two years ago, that same developer gave over $3 million in donations to help some of the state universities up there upgrade their science labs.

"Most movers and shakers in the Montana state government view this guy as a philanthropic hero. Remember, Montana is not New York. Good deeds or bad deeds become quickly known to all.

To the good folks in Montana, that EPA letter was the last straw, because to them it was just gross and heavy-handed overreach.

"It turns out that the consensus for the resolution had been quietly building in hushed conversations over the past few months. This is Montana… those last two botched gun control circuses coming out of the Senate already had them at the edge. It didn't take much to push them over. I understand this was not planned by the Council, and it may very well not have been desired by the movement leadership either. Nonetheless, the dam is breaking."

The President shook his head. "And now that brings us to Austin. That is a very dicey situation down there. Of course, the moment the Texas legislature votes to secede, the floodgate is truly opened. After all, just Texas seceding changes everything."

The Vice President nodded in agreement. "You are right. Texas can set itself up as the low tax, low regulation magnet. They had been trying to do this for some time, but their success was always limited because they always had to draw the line at federal laws and regulations.

"If they can also lure businesses and industries with the additional bait of no EPA, no Department of Labor, no federal corporate taxes, and on and on and on…". Litton hesitated for a moment: "Texas has a lot of very arid and forbidding land, and it goes on forever. But that also means that they have a lot of room. Water is a problem for them. But without any federal oversight, they will do what they damned well please to accommodate anyone wanting to set up shop there. The drain of jobs from other states to Texas alone, can be devastating. Some of the other states may offer the same packages, but Texas also has some climate benefits. My home state, as well as some of the others, is going to have a field day with energy production.

"Those willing to put up with those Dakota and Montana blizzards can earn a lot of money. Look, a lot of my family and friends are still there. They keep pissing on me about how much better they could do if this and that federal law or regulation would disappear. Now, they may very well get their chance to prove it."

The President managed a thin smile. "So tell me, Howard. Are they correct?"

The Vice President leaned back in his chair and placed his fingertips to his chin. "In a purely factual and analytical vein, yes they are. However, I don't think that is what should happen. I believe in our environmental laws and regulations. I am convinced that if they are given the chance to do the things they want to do in those states, the environment will be damaged, we will still be dependent on fossil fuels that will someday run out, while exploration and advancement of things such as solar energy are neglected.

"Of course, their ideas are workable. Let's face it, it's the way things used to be. I don't think it will be good for the people living in those states, and I think it would be bad for all Americans. We need to give our highest priority to clean air and water. Workers need to retain the rights to collective bargaining. But it looks like a wide swath of what used to be the United States of America... I'm sorry... I didn't mean to speak in the past tense like that."

It was President Malcolm that broke the tense silence: "That's all right, Howard... I sometimes find myself doing the same thing, at least I have over the past couple of days." The president stood and walked toward a large framed map of the United States resting on an easel in the corner of the Oval Office.

"This morning when I came into the office, the first thing I did was walk over and gaze at this map for a while. It made me feel... I guess I should say, nostalgic."

The President walked back to his chair and sat down. He remained silent for a minute as he looked back and forth between his Vice President and his Chief of Staff. "Howard... Jim... tomorrow morning, I want the two of you to cancel anything on your calendars. I want you to get together and draft a statement for me in the event of a Texas vote for secession. And although I doubt that this will be necessary, have one ready in the eventuality that such a resolution is defeated. Then, I want you to work on a statement to all of our citizens in all fifty states... I want one ready for conceding the reality of the breakup."

Chapter 6

Jim Walters arrived at his office at 7:30 AM the next morning, and commenced going through the three previous days' still unreviewed mail. Recalling the instructions his boss had given him the previous evening, he placed a call to the Justice Department and asked for files on the various Assistant Attorneys General on staff. Understanding that he needed to move ahead rapidly ahead of his late afternoon meeting with the Vice President, he got on the internet to review what information was available to the public about each of the potential candidates.

He knew that the day was going to be interesting, so after spending ninety minutes on the Attorney General vacancy, he decided it was time to see what else was going on. Glancing at his watch, he was surprised that it was already 10:00 AM. He reached for the remote control that still rested on the desk. With trepidation, he turned on the television set on the small table behind him, and then turned to watch.

The picture that greeted him was not the usual set or cast of characters of the morning program on NewsNet. "This is Cynthia Warren, and on this morning's special coverage of activities by the

Council for a Free America and its associated secession movement, I am joined by Joshua Simmons of the Potomac Review, and correspondents Marsha Bentley and Robert Carter. In a little while, we will be joined by Gwendolyn Munro, who has flown to Austin, Texas to provide live coverage of the expected goings – on both inside the Texas Capitol Building, and among the expected demonstrators on the lawn of the Capitol, and possibly the adjoining area.

"First I want to turn to Joshua Simmons, and I want to ask what your crystal ball is telling you about whether a Texas secession vote is imminent."

Simmons clasped his hands and shook his head. "Texas is not Montana… I still think this is nothing but a means to get the attention of the President and the leaders of both parties in both houses of Congress. The secessionist leaders in Texas know that, by the sheer size and legendary status of the state, anything they say or do will make for grand headlines. I see it as nothing more than great theater."

Cynthia Warren turned to Marsha Bentley. "Marsha… I know that you have been in contact with the Texas chapter of the Council for Free America. What does state chairman Les Browning expect to happen?"

"Les Browning is an interesting case. He told me three days ago that the Texas movement leaders fully expect the legislature to vote for secession, but he was unwilling to give even a hint as to how soon it could happen. I have tried unsuccessfully to speak with him after the Montana resolution was passed. This is pure speculation on my part, but Mister Browning does not come across as a type of man who likes to be upstaged."

Cynthia Warren then asked: "So, it's Robert Carter's turn. Any predictions for what might happen today?"

"Unfortunately, there are a lot of rumblings that those Texas National Guard troops have been moved closer to Austin, and are now using a small municipal airport in one of the Austin suburbs as a staging grounds. I know that we have a camera crew on the way to verify that, but such a movement of the Guard indicates that the mayor of Austin and the Governor both believe that trouble could break out.

"We have picked up a lot of chatter on Twitter and other social media platforms that indicate it is possible that a very large crowd of protesters will find themselves in proximity to a very large crowd of pro--secession demonstrators, and the pro--secession group has a demonstration permit to use the lawn of the Capitol building, from 11:00 AM until 1:00 PM today.

"All of that social media chatter makes reference to being on the scene at 11:00 AM. However, only the pro--secession group has a permit, and that leaves open the possibility of the streets around the Capitol building being filled with protesters without either a parade or demonstration permit. That is problematic in and of itself, but what has authorities at the city and state levels most concerned, is a potential for conflict between what could be two large groups of people."

Cynthia Warren began to speak once again, then suddenly halted and pressed her earphone closer to her head. She began to speak once again, but once again halted as her eyebrows arched and she tilted her head in reaction to the information she was receiving.

She paused for a moment, glanced at someone offstage, returned the nod and spoke: "We are receiving several reports simultaneously, and we're going to take a very brief break to sort them out. When we return, we're going to be providing you with some very interesting developments, so stay right here with NewsNet, and we will be back in a moment."

Less than two minutes later, the same NewsNet panel appeared on-screen. Cynthia Warren held a finger upward as she began her report: "We have several things to bring you, and please, understand that these are not in anyone's order of importance, so here we go... I need to tell you first of all that a bomb threat was called into the Texas State Capitol building about an hour ago, but the legislators refused to leave. Apparently, they are intent on carrying on with business, and we understand that their main topic of business is to consider a vote on secession.

"Obviously related to that bit of news, is a confirmation from the Austin Police Department that not only was a bomb threat called in to the Capitol building, but an individual whose identity is unknown at this time managed to somehow place a letter on the front desk of the Austin Police Department's headquarters without being seen, or at least noticed. We have been asked at this time to not read the letter verbatim, although a copy has been provided to local media, NewsNet, and we assume other networks as well. According to this letter, it comes from a Marxist student group on that sprawling University of Texas campus at Austin. The unsigned letter claims responsibility for the threat and claims that a bomb has been placed in the Capitol building. It makes no reference to any specific time the alleged bomb is to go off.

"In summary, the letter further also states that this group opposes seeing Texas join a renewal of the Confederate States of America, and that Texas rightfully belongs to Mexico. We will continue to follow that story, but at least for now, those Texans in Austin have no intention of standing down.

"We have also received word from the Associated Press, that in... I guess around fifteen minutes now, the Governor of the state of South Dakota will announce that just minutes ago, both houses of that state's legislature voted to secede from the United States of America.

"However, perhaps the surprise news of the morning comes out of Charleston, West Virginia. A member of the West Virginia Senate, and we do not yet have his name or a confirmation from him, but a report is coming through that, once again, a member of the West Virginia State Senate is going to announce this afternoon, his intention to introduce a resolution for that state to secede.

"Marsha, have we had any word before that West Virginia had any involvement in the secession movement, or is this just one senator going out on a limb?"

"Cynthia, during the break when you told us what was happening, I called a friend who has connections there, and he just texted me and tells me that the senator is Alan Westover, and that Senator Westover is claiming to have already lined up seventeen cosponsors in the Senate chamber, and twenty-one members of the house also willing to cosponsor."

Cynthia Warren pursued the matter: "Marsha, you know anything more about what might be driving the movement in that state?"

"Coal, coal and coal. We had gone several years now with Democratic administrations exhibiting what many in the state of West Virginia considered to be outright hostility to the coal industry. Working in a coal mine is dirty, hard work, to say nothing of dangerous. Still, having a job in a coal mine feeds your family and puts a roof over your head.

"The coal industry benefited greatly from the loosening of restrictions during the Trump administration. Then on Pres. Malcolm's first day in office he signed an executive order reinstating the Obama restrictions. Some people do not take kindly to seeing their livelihood purposefully diminished, in order to promote what some would call progressive principles regarding the environment. If you live in West Virginia, Pennsylvania, and parts of Ohio and Kentucky, coal is important. Apparently, there are many in West Virginia who have decided that they are not necessarily turning their back on their country… they feel that their country has abandoned them and their families in favor of pleasing cultural and ideological elites."

"Joshua Simmons… and what do you have to say about this surprising news out of West Virginia?"

"I know the e-mails and Twitter messages are going to come at me now, but I have to say this… I think that for West Virginia, of all states, should they secede, would be the ultimate statement of ingratitude. I understand that the Obama administration, with the follow-up by the Malcolm administration, certainly took actions that resulted in job loss in the coal industry, and that Trump did indeed change at least some of that.

"However, as Americans we have to determine what the common good is for everyone, not just for a regional employment scenario. Coal pollutes, and it needs to be replaced by other, cleaner forms of energy. You know, energy development that does not result in workers being forever entombed in their place of employment when something goes wrong.

"My last point is that, West Virginia has more than its share of poverty and opioid abuse, and that state has benefited from the generosity of the federal government for generations to alleviate the poverty in Appalachia. The Food Stamp Program started in West Virginia. I think that for the state to say thanks, but now goodbye, would be shameful."

Cynthia Warren nodded. "And you finished just in time, Joshua, because we are now switching to Gwendolyn Munro who is standing on the edge of the large lawn in front of the Capitol building in Austin, Texas. Gwen... what do you see going on?"

The image on the screen switched from the NewsNet panel in New York, to a petite blonde woman holding a microphone, but crouching. In the background, people could be seen running, and smoky clouds were churning low to the ground. "Cynthia... I hope... I hope you can hear me. Most of all, I hope that the camera is picking up what is taking place closer to the Capitol building. Just a moment... I'm going to move further away."

The image on the screen began to move up and down and back and forth as the camera operator was apparently retreating. After moving fifty yards, the image was once again of Gwendolyn Munro, now standing. "Cynthia... I apologize, but I was getting waved away by a police officer. If the camera can now zoom in on the lawn once again, you can see that teargas is being used to disperse what suddenly turned into physical confrontations between the opposing groups that arrived here a little while ago.

"I also wanted to get away from the teargas... I got a mild dose of it, and hopefully I was not seen vomiting on live television. But just a little while ago, the pro-- secession people were listening to a speech being given over a loudspeaker. Many were holding American flags, others were holding the now common Don't Tread on Me flags, when all of a sudden a large group of counter – protesters came marching up the street alongside the lawn. They began shouting, not in any organized chant, but shouting in a chaotic manner in an attempt to drown out the speaker.

"Then, it got kind of silly and strange... I saw a large group of them come to the sidewalk and begin, if you believe this, they began throwing paper airplanes into the crowd gathered on the lawn. All I could tell from a distance was that these airplanes seemed to be strangely agitating the crowd, many of whom turned toward the street and began shouting back, some angrily raising their fists as they shouted back. That was when I ran up and grabbed one of the paper airplanes, only to find that the paper airplanes were made from paper Nazi flags. I don't know who threw the first punch, but soon there was a melee, followed by the police use of the teargas."

"We are also waiting for…". Suddenly gunshots were heard, and the reporter dove to the ground, but the camera operator was able to keep the image on her. "Cynthia… I can… I hope you were able to hear that, and now I'm going to turn around and… I can see police moving toward… I think someone was shot, and now the police are waving a standby ambulance out onto the lawn, where it appears a wounded person is on the ground.

"Cynthia… I don't know if you could hear that, but even with all the sirens now… I think I just heard some more shots, and now police are moving everyone away from the area… I will check back in with you when I can."

The picture on the screen was once again the assembled NewsNet panel. All appeared a bit flustered by what they had been watching on monitors. Trying to get the program moving once again, Cynthia Warren turned to Joshua Simmons. "Joshua, I know that we are going to have to wait for a while to get more information on what we just saw happening. Does this surprise you?"

"Actually, Cynthia… I think a lot of us saw this coming. This is the absurdity of this situation. A group is meeting on the front lawn of the Texas capitol in favor of joining in with other very gun – friendly states to form a new nation that may as well be called the Wild West States of America, so no one should be surprised that gunfire broke out under the circumstances."

Robert Carter put his hands up in frustration. "But Josh... I don't know who fired the shots, and neither do you."

Simmons responded: "The point is, one of the driving factors behind this secession movement is a desire for an even more free and easy gun culture than already exists in these states. And now you have at least one person shot in the process. That's the point I'm trying to make."

Carter shook his head. "At least we know that the pro-secession people who were allowed onto the lawn had a permit. Further, it was made clear that no guns would be allowed on the lawn. The lawn was cordoned off, and police made everyone wishing to be inside that perimeter go through a checkpoint where they were checked for weapons. I know that says nothing about anyone else in the vicinity, but at least the people who were part of the organized, permitted demonstration will not likely be found to have shot anyone."

Cynthia began to speak once again: "Perhaps we should examine whether... I am getting... Wow... Texas... Texas has just voted to secede from the United States of America. In all the chaos, apparently there were a few media people on hand inside the chamber... I am being told that the vote was indeed taken in open session... I am also being told that some local media were on hand, as well as a busload full of junior high students on a field trip. I trust that they are all safe inside the Capitol building."

Cynthia took a deep breath and hesitated. "So, Marsha, what say you?"

"I don't think that anyone one week ago would have predicted this cascade of events. That early move by Montana, whether it was intended to do this or not, has incredibly speeded up the process. But Texas... Texas. This is the big guy. A state whose economy is the one of the largest in the world, is rolling the dice that it is going to be better off as part of this new confederation of like – minded states."

Cynthia Warren put her hand up to draw the attention of the other panelists. "Something just came to mind... I'm interested to know if anything in that Texas resolution that was just passed actually made a reference to anything other than seceding from the United States. What I mean is, I am wondering if Texas has actually stated that it is joining with the other states. Robert, would it be possible that Texas would secede, but go it alone?"

The veteran correspondent shook his head slowly. "I don't think that is likely. As was said a moment ago, Texas is the big player in all of this. I cannot imagine a scenario in which Texas would want a fracturing of this movement right out of the gate. It would be a different situation if after some years of this new union functioning well, Texas would feel that the remainder of the states involved were strong and stable enough without them. I think they are all in this together, at least for several years."

Cynthia Warren peered into an off-camera monitor. "Now we are receiving word that one person has died as a result of the gunfire in Austin we heard earlier. Apparently, the victim was the man we saw on the ground, and Austin police are not yet releasing his name. They will confirm however, that an arrest has been made in that shooting. Further, we are now learning that two other people were wounded.

"The person in custody's identity is also not being released, but police will confirm that, based upon identification in possession of the suspect, he is reported to be a student at the University of Texas. Austin police also confirm that when the suspect was arrested, in his car they found a Remington rifle with a scope, with one round of ammunition still in a clip. I am certain that we will be hearing more details on that arrest, as well as the shooting victims, as the day goes on.

"Well, the news channels are busy today, and now we are being told that West Virginia State Senator Alan Westover has spoken to local television and newspaper reporters in Charleston, and has confirmed that next Monday morning, he will be introducing a secession resolution.

"Westover is also confirming early reports about his cosponsors, and says that even more legislators have called him to join in. Westover cites what he and his colleagues perceive as unacceptable federal encroachment into state's rights, and abandonment of the 10th Amendment to the Constitution of the United States of America. The senator also goes on to mention the federal takeover of healthcare, repeated attempts to restrict the rights of citizens granted under the Second Amendment and attempts by the federal government to strangle the coal industry, thereby doing great harm to West Virginia's current and future economic well-being.

"In his final point, Westover emphasized that he and many other members of the West Virginia Legislature shared disappointment that the past several years illustrated how deeply entrenched the Washington establishment is. He went on to state that no doubt has been left that the power base in Washington DC cannot be reformed, and therefore must be left behind.

"So there you have it, West Virginia has blindsided much of the country. We just didn't see that one coming."

Cynthia once again looked to the monitor. "Our staff has put together an electronic map we would now like to show you. So now, I would like to introduce NewsNet contributor and Washington Times reporter Mason Howell who is going to introduce us to our brand-new visual aid. Mason…".

The camera cut away to where the tall young reporter stood next to a large map on the wall, similar to those used to report presidential election results. "Thank you, Cynthia. What this map will do is to show you by color, the status of this secession, or withdrawal movement, whatever you want to call it.

"The states that are now the color green are those that have already voted to secede. As you can see, Montana, now Texas, and of course, as of this morning, South Dakota are in.

"Now, we are going to indicate by the color gray, those states with very active participation in the Council for a Free America movement. As you can see, the potential is for a very wide swath of America's heartland to break away. It may be true that the population density is greater along the coasts and some parts of the Midwest, but it is astounding to look at this map and see that perhaps a third or more of the land mass of the continental United States of America could be forming a separate nation."

The camera went back to the panel, and Cynthia Warren spoke again. "Thank you, Mason... I must say that seeing the map in that fashion is a very sobering matter. We know that no effective dates have been established, but the very concept is something that, as an American, I find frightening... I find it almost surreal."

Marsha Bentley broke what had become an uncomfortable and unacceptably long silence for live television. "I think that what is so absolutely stunning, is that this is happening so easily. We all suspect that there is no stomach in the administration to stop this by force. All that would stand in the way of secession now would be allegiance to the United States. But today, there was a full auditorium in Topeka, Kansas at a public meeting held by the Kansas chapter of the Council for a Free America. The state chairman of the organization addressed that very matter.

"He spoke of how difficult it was for him as an American, a Vietnam veteran and a retired police officer to relinquish that allegiance. He then went on to explain that it was difficult to maintain his dedication when the nation had given up all pretense of fiscal responsibility, and was seen by the common people to be disregarding its own guidelines on everything, even citing the shutting out of the financial obligations to the General Motors bondholders many years ago. He also cited the failure to pass Congressional budgets in a timely manner and trying to evade the restraints of the Constitution through Senate action such as attempting to force gun registration.

"I have made no pretense of the fact that I'm a progressive, although I have tried to maintain a balance in my reporting and analysis for NewsNet. Still, even as a progressive I cannot deny the damage done by the hypocrisy."

Joshua Simmons nearly shouted. "There are hypocrites on both sides. Conservatives claim to abhor government involvement in our private lives, and then opposed gay marriage until the bitter end, and still resist the right of a woman to choose what goes on with her own body."

Marsha Bentley slammed her hand upon the table in frustration, startling the rest of the panelists. "That's right, Joshua. But we're at the point now where neither side is willing to forgive the other for the slightest transgression. Neither side, when in power, is willing to concede those hypocrisies. Every slight, every slip up results in an ongoing tit-for-tat exchange. It has gotten so bad that neither side wants to give in, and compromise is seen as weakness. It has become more important to score points and show just how unreasonable and unworthy the other side is. This 24/7 media coverage that we are part of makes it impossible for anyone to have time to cool down, and every statement brings about microphones being waved in front of everyone's faces. And now, we pay the price."

Cynthia Warren attempted to calm the panel by softening her voice as she broke in. "And now I have to interrupt this lively conversation for a break. When we come back, we hope to have another report from Gwen Munro, on the scene in Austin, Texas, where at least one person was killed and two injured by gunfire as altercations broke out between competing factions as the Texas legislature debated a resolution to secede, a resolution that did pass. And we will be right back."

~~~

Jim Walters shook his head as he stood to answer the knock on his door. He muted the sound on the television, and then opened the door to greet a courier who had brought the requested records from the Justice Department. He sat the thick envelope on his desk, turned the sound back up on the television, then sat down again and opened the parcel. He pulled out the personnel files and sighed. He wondered who could guide the President through the legal quagmire he now faced.

Seeing the NewsNet panel back on the screen, he tried to examine the first file and pay casual attention to the broadcast. However, as soon as Cynthia Warren had once again introduced the panel to viewers, she halted. "We understand that we're going to cut away to Gwen Munro in Austin, Texas once more… Gwen, can you hear me?"

The view was now of Gwen Munro, but this time she was standing on a street corner three blocks from the Capitol building. "Cynthia, as you can see in the background, troop transport trucks are bringing hundreds of National Guardsmen into the area. A portion of the troops are being diverted to an office building one block away from where I'm standing. That is where the Texas chapter of the Council for a Free America is housed in a rather conspicuous and vulnerable suite of offices on the first floor.

"That building has been the site of some minor but constant picketing by a coalition of groups opposed to secession. I have been told by police sources, that nearly an hour ago rocks were thrown through the windows of that office, and protesters were able to enter the facility through those broken windows. If the camera can now pan up, you will see that smoke is rising, because the building has now been set on fire. Of course, firefighters are now on the scene, but I have been told that the damage already done is substantial.

"As for the serious incidents earlier at the Capitol building, Austin police have released the identity of the man who was shot and killed on the lawn. He is Aaron Higgins of Dallas, a member of the executive committee of the Texas chapter of the Council for a Free America. Higgins was scheduled to be the next speaker at the rally that was cut short due to the altercations that broke out and preceded the gunfire.

"No names have yet been released in regard to the two individuals who were wounded. However, Austin police do report that neither suffered life-threatening injuries. While information is still sketchy, an unnamed member of the Council told me that both of the wounded are volunteers with the movement, that one is a retired gentleman from Beaumont, Texas and the other is a young woman from Fort Worth.

"The police have now been able to release the name of the suspect in the shooting death of Mister Higgins. By the way, forensics indicates that Higgins and the two volunteers were all shot by the same weapon.

"That suspect in custody is one Martin Larimore, age twenty-one. We have verified that he is a student at the University of Texas, and is from Waco, Texas. School officials will not speak on the record regarding Larimore, but a reporter for a local newspaper has quoted an acquaintance of Larimore as saying that the suspect is the chairman of an on – campus Marxist group that has been calling for Texas to abandon discussion of secession.

"Furthermore…". Gwendolyn paused to listen to her earpiece. "It's not easy to hear right now, but I just got word that more violence has broken out at the Capitol building. Apparently groups of protesters have accosted and possibly injured several members of the Texas legislature outside the building. We understand that this happened just as the first truck full of National Guardsmen arrived on the scene, and a large group of demonstrators even engaged the armed guardsmen.

"Cynthia, if you can hang on a moment, there is more…".

Chapter 7

"Cynthia…and I am hearing from an observer we have on a rooftop…I am now getting word that the confrontation between the anti-— secession protesters and National Guardsmen has developed into a full – scale riot. And… hang on for a moment. I understand that the troops have donned masks, and have been forced to fire tear gas. I have also been told that there have been several injuries due to the rubber bullets that Austin riot squad members had employed when the situation began to get serious.

"Our crew has just deployed a couple of drones with video capacity over the scene, because, Cynthia, right now it is difficult for any members of the news media to get close to the capitol building, as police fear for the safety of anyone in the vicinity. So, what we're going to try to do is arrange to interview someone opposed to the resolution passed today, and if we are able to secure that with the aid of local reporters, we will bring that to you. If we are able to pick up any good footage from the drones, we will get to that to you as soon as possible. This is Gwendolyn Monroe, reporting from a very noisy, rancorous and somewhat dangerous downtown Austin, Texas."

Cynthia Warren turned to Marsha Bentley. "Marsha, could you speak for a moment about the challenges Texas will face if this secession goes ahead?"

"First of all, Cynthia, Texas has the image of a Western, rugged place where a certain ethic of machismo rules the day. That may be true for wide expanses of Texas and its towns. At the same time, it has very large metropolitan areas such as Dallas, Fort Worth, San Antonio and Houston, even though they do have a definite Western flair. But if you look at Austin, the state capitol of this cowboy land is a somewhat liberal island unto itself. A significant portion of the population of Austin, as well as the large cities I previously named, feel that they have more in common with places like Boston than they do sagebrush country.

"In addition, Texas has a large and growing Hispanic population. In fact, some would speculate that in the course of several more years, the demographic shift would have turned Texas into a blue state in electoral terms. With the occasional comments about illegal immigration within the secession movement, many Hispanic people currently living in Texas may not feel comfortable with what is being proposed. That is not to say that Texas is overflowing with undocumented residents, but it does have its share, and a certain natural form of sympathy for one's ethnic brethren does come into play.

"What is sometimes lost in the discussion is that many politicians and media pundits make assumptions that Hispanic residents, especially recent immigrants, legal and illegal, will tend to be politically liberal. But some of my contacts within the Hispanic community tell me that the longer people reside in America, the more they cherish America as a land of opportunity, rather than as a guarantor of comfort."

Joshua Simmons quickly spoke up. "The Texas many Americans think of at first mention is one in which John Wayne rides around killing Native Americans and ordering his black servant around.

"But Texas is more than just a bunch of white cowboys tipping their hats to the lady – folk. Texas is a diverse place, and Marsha is correct about the implications for Hispanics. In addition, the large cities in Texas have significant black populations. This should not just be a decision to be reached by the good old boys."

Cynthia turned to Robert Carter. "Bob, I know that Oklahoma is not Texas, but when you lived in Tulsa for a few years, did you pick up much about life in the Lone Star State?"

"Well, Cynthia, we did receive a list of how the vote in Austin went today, and it appears that around one third of the state legislators with what would be considered Hispanic surnames voted for the measure. We can only take that for what it's worth, but I have always been reluctant to view any ethnic group as a monolithic body in its thinking or philosophy. I do not find it at all outside the realm of possibility, that many Hispanic residents of Texas, and the rest of the state for that matter, do indeed see secession is the only way to preserve a land of opportunity."

Cynthia Warren held up a hand to signify that another bit of news had arrived. "I am hearing in my ear that the intrepid and magical Gwen Munro has arranged for that interview she promised. "Gwen… I have to hand it to you. Would you tell us who your guest is?"

The screen image was now one of Gwendolyn Munro sitting on a bench next to a slender young man. "Thanks Cynthia… I have with me Thomas Manfred, a student at the University of Texas majoring in political science, and Thomas is a member of one of the many organizations opposing the secession movement.

"Thomas, thank you for speaking with me." The student was obviously nervous at being interviewed on national television, but nodded warmly and managed to mumble, "My pleasure."

"Thomas, please give me your reasons for opposing the secession of Texas from the United States."

"Well, I… I feel that this new nation these extremists want to form, is nothing more than a Twenty-First Century version of the Confederate States of America. They don't want to help the poor… they talk about allowing corporations to do what ever they want to do, even if it means hurting the environment and taking away workers' rights. They're going to stop people on the street to see if they belong here, and we don't even know yet who will be allowed to vote."

"Thomas, earlier, back in the NewsNet studio, a panel was discussing whether the state legislature is actually representing the people of present – day Texas. Could you speak to that?"

"Texas isn't just a bunch of white people riding around on horses and firing six – guns with some humorous Mexicans sitting around. But I think that's what a lot of people think Texas is. But a lot of people who live here have Hispanic heritage. Some even believe that if Texas should go anywhere, it should be reunited with Mexico. And remember, there are a lot of African-Americans who live in Texas. Some of them just don't know where they would stand after secession, or if they would even be safe. Look at how so many of these people talked about President Obama. At least, if they form their own nation I'm sure they'll never have to worry about having a black President again."

"Okay… so Thomas, what do you think is going to happen now?"

"I think we have to keep protesting. We have to be out there on the street, and in the faces of all these powerful, rich people, and let them know that a lot of Texans like me, aren't buying what they're selling."

"Thomas Manfred, a junior at the University of Texas. Thanks for joining us. Cynthia… back to you in New York."

Jim Walters finally forced himself to turn off the television, after which he leaned back in his chair and closed his eyes. Thomas

Manfred reminded him of himself in his college days. In fact, at the same age, the Chief of Staff for the President of the United States would likely have voiced the exact same words had he been in the same situation.

There were times when Walters yearned for the luxury of those days when ideal and principle did not have to be balanced with reality. But reality was certainly staring him in the face now.

He turned on his computer and opened his word processing program. He always liked to tackle the most difficult task first, and he knew that the Vice President's strength was in the spoken word rather than the written.

Walters had always found that his best way of proof reading a document, was to read it aloud to himself. He placed his phone in silent mode, took a deep breath and read back to himself what he had just spent forty minutes typing, although the length of the statement did not truly reflect the many pauses and hesitations he had endured while creating it.

"My fellow citizens,

"I understand that the events of late have been very painful and confusing to us all. Our nation was founded in 1776, and after several years of hard work on behalf of our Founding Fathers, the United States of America took shape and became the nation to which much of the rest of the world often turned to in times of crisis.

"Past generations endured great hardships, and many gave their lives to build the United States of America into a nation that provided wonderful opportunities for many. There were some blemishes on our past, the most shameful of which was the practice of slavery, and to this day that sad stain on our history reverberates as we try to eliminate unfair treatment of the descendents of those slaves, many still hampered by the cloud of unequal opportunity.

"Today we are faced with the most stark crisis since the Civil War. Some may say that what is taking place now, is just another form of the Civil War. However, that is not the case.

"There will be no warfare between states. As the President of the United States of America, I will not order the Armed Forces to prevent the secession of states by the use of force.

"Some have advised me to invoke the rule of law. However, invoking the law requires the willingness to enforce a judicial ruling. Once again, I will not order the use of military force.

"One more time, I ask the elected leaders of the secessionist states, the Council for a Free America and all others involved, to please cease and desist from your disastrous intentions. Should you proceed, American citizens, regardless of where they live, will never again be as secure, as prosperous, or as willing to work side-by-side to achieve our common goals, as we are as a unified nation of fifty states.

"However, should this new federation of states come to be, it will be incumbent upon us all to do whatever possible to minimize the negative effects for all Americans.

"While I would give my own life to see our nation preserved, should this secessionist movement come to pass, we must all accept the reality before us, and ask for God's guidance as we tackle the many difficult issues ahead.

"Regardless of whether you live in the United States of America, or a newly formed federation of states, we must never lose sight of the common values that originally brought us together as the greatest nation mankind has ever seen. We must never lose that sense of the common good, the sense of common decency that binds us. Nor must we ever lose that great optimism we have always shared that promises a better life for all Americans."

Walters sat silent for a moment, reconsidering his first draft. Even though the words had come from within him, he was stunned nonetheless.

~~~

Bryce Hamilton sat at the desk in his den in his home in Lincoln, Nebraska. He was content to stay inside for the rest of the day, able to walk through the house at any time and be with his Cynthia.

He sat in front of his computer, catching up on e-mails and clicking on the ESPN website to see the latest news in college basketball. His relaxation was interrupted by the buzzing of his cell phone. He looked at the small screen and smiled. He had been expecting Patrick Bridger to call him at any time in light of all of the new developments.

"Mister Bridger... It appears that no matter how much we tried to avoid calling this a secession, everyone else is using that term. But regardless... I suppose your imagination has been as active as mine over the past twenty-four hours."

"And I have more to tell you. I will give you a rundown of what to expect over the next couple of days. I have to admit, I don't feel that I have a very firm grip on the reins. So, let me fill you in, so that you can start working on your next public statement...".

~~~

It was 7:00 PM when Jim Walters and Vice President Howard Litton sat down in the Vice President's favorite office at his residence at Blair House. They spent a few minutes speaking of the unsettling events of the day, and then the Chief of Staff presented his draft statement to Litton. "I tried to make this sound as if the boss had written it. Hopefully, he will have ample time to consider it."

"Jim... I want to mention something to you before we get started on the statements and the recommendation for a new

142

Attorney General, although my question does relate to that appointment.

"I know that North Dakota is likely to go. I don't know what we do, when the legal residence of the Vice President is no longer one of the United States."

Walters nodded. "I have been thinking of that. I know that when we have a new Attorney General, we will need a priority interpretation. I know that this could have to go to the Supreme Court for a ruling on an expedited basis. And speaking of the Supreme Court, we have two Justices who had legal residences of record and states that are likely to secede, but are yet to make it official. I am fairly certain that all they will have to do is change their legal addresses. You, sir, present a more problematical matter."

The Vice President began to chuckle. "I'm really not certain what to wish for when it comes to a final answer. We are into a lot of crap I wasn't expecting to deal with. I suppose, if necessary, I will have to resign, and the President will have to pick a new Vice to be approved by what is left of the Congress."

The Chief of Staff hesitated for a moment. "Sir… I got a phone call about an hour ago from a reporter friend from my college days. He's good at investigative reporting… I was told that tomorrow, Idaho, Alaska and Kansas are going to have resolutions introduced in their legislatures. Further, Idaho and Alaska are considered to be nearly automatic. The Kansas vote should hit early next week at the earliest. It's likely to be a narrower vote than some of the others, because some of the Kansas City House members are opposed. Still, odds are it will pass."

The Vice President's expression darkened. "I am so glad tomorrow is Saturday. Perhaps secession will take the weekend off."

"I hope so, sir. But it will be a wide open forty-eight hours for the talking heads to have at it. We both know that every news program will be dedicated to one subject. There is the potential for the movement leaders to begin floundering in being given so much time on the air. But Heaven help us if Bryce Hamilton, Tom Edelstein and their crew do a good job of making their case. Since everyone now either knows or senses that force will not be used to prevent this happening, everything is now at the whim of the secessionists. And I still do not fully grasp that this could happen so easily."

The Vice President leaned back, closed his eyes and looked at the ceiling as he spoke: "When it is universally recognized and accepted that an action will not trigger an act of restraining force, the outcome lies with the party showing initiative. Their initiative is to secede. The only leverage that was left to us, except for laughable legal maneuvers that would be impossible to enforce, is to plunge the nation into bloody chaos. And quite frankly, Jim, I could never know with certainty who would end up fighting for whom.

"The idea of using force was a non-- starter from the beginning. And how this nation stayed together for so long, seeing now how easily states can slide away… I suppose the bloody memory of the Civil War provided much of the cohesion."

"Mister Vice President… I really don't think that when the Civil War was beginning to appear inevitable, there were so many political leaders of his own party and members of the press telling Abraham Lincoln to say good riddance."

"I know, Jim. It's almost like we're handing them the keys to the car. I find it shocking that all these spoiled ideological purists seem to find it more important that no one be left to disagree with them, than to look at what's best for all of America."

"Mister Vice President, please don't ask me who it was, but a couple of days ago a United States Senator actually told me that when these states are no longer part of the United States, the average IQ of the nation will skyrocket."

The Vice President shook his head and looked down. "I know… at some point in time, and on both sides of our political divide, disagreement transformed into belligerence."

The Chief of Staff picked up one of the files on a potential new Attorney General. "Before we begin, let me ruin the rest of your evening. Some of the states' legislatures are holding special Saturday sessions tomorrow. And NewsNet announced an hour ago that they're having a special addition of News in Depth tomorrow afternoon. The only guest… Bryce Hamilton."

~~~

It was noon on Saturday when Marsha Bentley opened up her weekly Saturday news program on the NewsNet network. She began the program by introducing her guest, columnist Mason Howell of the Washington Times.

"Mason, this has certainly been a week we will never forget. States have voted to secede, others appear to be preparing to do so and we even had some bloodshed in Austin, Texas, and ongoing coverage shows us that the situation in that city is still tense. Even this morning, there were scattered reports of altercations between citizens on both sides of the secession issue, even though Austin police and the Texas National Guard have a tight grip on the city, including the curfew ordered last night by the mayor.

"My question to you is, since Texas has voted to secede, is the matter decided no matter how many other states join now?"

Simmons nodded. "The genie is out of the bottle, that's for sure. Texas is the eight hundred pound gorilla, with its large population, the landmass and its general influence and legendary status in the minds of Americans.

"Texas provides a long coastline with lots of harbors and shipping facilities, a matter that would've been problematic if only

146

some of the landlocked states were seceding. Oil will be a major source of revenue and jobs in what I am being told will be called the Constitutional States of America.

"The ports are in place, refineries in the states that were closed down by federal initiative in the past will likely expand, to say nothing of the new ones that will be developed. When Alaska becomes free from federal environmental restrictions, that oil will start to flow way down to the Gulf Coast.

"Much emphasis will be placed on water resources, so that agriculture will be boosted free of federal interference over matters such as obscure endangered species. My prediction is that industry in the states, but especially in Texas due to its climate, will likely flourish.

"There is already some preliminary discussion among Council leaders regarding the possibility of constructing a high – speed rail system running from the upper Plains States down to the Texas Gulf ports, or even to New Orleans should Louisiana end up in the new federation. Of course, such a rail system would be built through private investment, as a for-profit enterprise."

"As you know, Joshua, in a little less than an hour from now, Bryce Hamilton is going to be appearing on our network. Most of the publicity for the Council for a Free America has been achieved through appearances by Senator Hamilton, former Congressman Bridger and Tom Edelstein, who appears to be fulfilling the role as the philosophical guru of the movement. Should we be concerned that, at least on a national news level, we are not seeing more of the other individuals who may be playing a key role in the secession movement?"

"Well, Marsha, it is not that other leaders have not been out there and available. Each of the states involved in the Council have state chair people and executive committees that have been quite vocal and visible. However, Hamilton, Bridger and Edelstein are on the national Executive Committee, and the media has seemed to gravitate to covering them out of convenience, as they are often in Washington D.C.

"Even though I write for a conservative newspaper, and I make no attempts to portray myself as being anything but a conservative on a personal level, I still have many friends and contacts within the media who call themselves liberals and progressives. I must say that I have been astonished at how certain some of these friends were that the Council leaders we just mentioned were going to be laughed off the stage."

Marsha tilted her head and laughed. "And why was that?"

"Simply because they were espousing a cause and a movement that was assumed to be extremist and radical. It was the conventional media wisdom that they could not withstand vigorous questions from interviewers without lapsing into some chatter about new world orders, infiltration of the government by space aliens and accusations that the gold at Fort Knox is fake. This is what many of my acquaintances in the media basically expected, and now some of them are in shock that these men did not collapse in their immediate exposure as fools and clowns.

"Not only that, but many who considered themselves to be tasked with undermining President Trump were still feeling their oats when this movement surfaced. They are finding that undermining a sitting President is one thing, but trying to downplay the seriousness of those attempting to form a separate America is a whole other matter."

"Please clarify... how do you think your progressive media friends view them now?"

Simmons laughed. "They still view them as fools and clowns."

"Will anything change that?"

"Yes... when these states secede and form a new country, and the mainstream media view them as leaders of a quaint and backward neighbor, they will no longer feel a need to try to expose and destroy them. However, I do expect them all to pitch books to publishers, books that will ridicule those men and women, regardless of how successful the new federation of states turns out to be."

Marsha thanked Simmons for appearing, and then turned toward the camera. "When we return from a break, I will be talking with Congresswoman Angela Hostetler, Democratic member of Congress from the state of New York, and we will get her take on the secession movement."

Marsha Bentley came back on the screen, and sitting across a small table from her was the forty-five-year-old Congresswoman, a soft-spoken and sophisticated woman who represented a liberal and traditionally wealthy suburb outside of New York City.

"Welcome back to NewsNet's special ongoing coverage of the attempt by a number of states to secede from the United States of America and form a new federation of states, one that we are told will be called the Constitutional States of America. Now joining me is Congresswoman Angela Hostetler of New York. Congresswoman, thank you for being with me today."

"Thank you Marsha, it's my pleasure."

"Congresswoman, I would like to get your overall impression about this secession movement that seems to be picking up steam in speed almost by the hour."

The Congresswoman displayed a warm smile: "Marsha, I do not necessarily agree with those members of my party who have taken this good riddance attitude. As someone who has taken an oath to defend the best interests of the citizens of the United States of America, I feel that to allow, let alone enable this movement does not serve many who live in those states very well."

"Could you elaborate?"

The Congresswoman spoke almost in a whisper: "I'm especially concerned about the rights and protection of women, children and minority residents in those states. The leaders of this movement have shown an obvious disregard, if not disdain for, the concerns of anyone other than white males. They speak of the right to bear arms, the right to make money free of taxation, but they do not speak of voting rights, a woman's right to choose, the rights of gay people to marry or how they're going to ensure that basic needs such as child care for working mothers will be addressed. We hear virtually nothing about their plans to provide healthcare or to ensure that the nutritional needs of children or at risk adults are seen to. Their priorities, are not the priorities of a caring society."

"The leaders of this movement make the case that their vision for this new CSA will by its nature, provide unbridled economic opportunity. Further it is their contention that this will result in enough taxation through revenue that basic needs can be provided by the state when necessary, and that employment opportunities should alleviate concerns over income, even for such people as single mothers. Do you disagree with that?"

"I will concede that some things will be known only after the passage of time. However, it is a great and serious gamble, a dangerous roll of the dice, to believe that you can break away from the United States of America, the greatest nation the world has ever seen, and do even better for your citizens. I see no reason why women and minorities should trust reassuring statements from a white male power structure, without a great dose of skepticism."

"But let's just play with a hypothetical situation. If five years from now, the CSA unemployment rate turns out to be much lower than that in the United States, would you then concede that you may have been wrong?"

The Congresswoman hesitated for a moment, and then flashed her trademark genteel smile. "Marsha, as a woman, if I had a choice of living in a society with virtually full employment, but full of firearms, and without such rights as a woman's right to choose, or to live in a society where those rights were protected and proudly promoted, guns were restricted, but unemployment was at twelve percent, I would personally choose the latter. And I think most women would agree with me."

"Do you believe that you are being fair to the leaders of the Council for a Free America, as they have not yet issued formal statements of intent regarding such matters?"

"I will say this, Marsha. If I were a black woman, I would feel very reluctant about staying in any of these states. Should it tragically happen that secession is actually enacted, there'll be no Department of Justice as we now know it to enforce minority rights, that is, if the laws in these states will even address the matter of minority rights.

"I challenge anyone to present one shred of evidence that this new CSA even intends to allow minorities, or for that matter, women to vote. Once these states are out from under the protective umbrella of the federal protections we now enjoy, they are in effect a foreign country. Authorities in the Justice Department in Washington D.C., will have no more authority to address matters of discrimination in Montana, than they would in Malaysia.

"For that matter, they can sentence minors to the death penalty, sentence people to life imprisonment for marijuana possession... I see the possibilities as endless."

"Congresswoman, should these states proceed with secession, what do you see as any possible avenue to alleviate such concerns."

"I would like to see the President make some type of a counter offer. Perhaps in exchange for his not resisting secession, this CSA could agree to operate its economy with no oversight from the United States, but agree to follow guidelines on individual rights to be provided by the United States Department of Justice. In that way, the CSA could experiment with economics to their heart's content, while assuring the rest of America that minorities, women and children would be protected."

"Thank you for appearing here today Congresswoman, and I'm certain that we will have much to discuss in the future. Now, please stay tuned to NewsNet, as in the next hour, Bryce Hamilton of

the Council for a Free America will be with us right here on…
NewsNet. And we will be back in a few minutes."

Chapter 8

While Congresswoman Hostetler was being interviewed, Bryce Hamilton sat in the green room of the NewsNet studio taking notes. He was saddened by some of the suppositions being made about him and his colleagues, but felt that only time would resolve them, as people had a chance to see the workings of the Constitutional States of America for themselves. Then Hamilton reminded himself that those living outside the CSA would never actually be provided an objective report. At that thought, he shrugged and picked up a newspaper to read until it was time for him to go on the air.

A few minutes later, an intern opened the door and asked for him to go with her. As he walked, Hamilton stretched his arms upward, an old habit from his college basketball days when mentally preparing himself for the beginning of the game.

"Senator Hamilton…". A short, white haired man Hamilton had seen on television countless times reached out to take his hand and escort him to the set. "Mike Silver… I want to thank you for being with us today. As you may imagine, I have been looking forward to this interview for two days." The host motioned to a chair, and both sat down to pass the last minute before going live.

Silver made small talk, asking if his guest had found the green room comfortable, and if he needed anything before going on the air. Finally, the two men turned to face the camera before Silver spoke. "Welcome to this special edition of News in Depth. My name is Mike Silver, your host. I know that if you are a regular viewer of NewsNet, you know that this program is usually broadcast on Sunday afternoons. However, due to the remarkable events that have taken place this last week, we decided to have this special, additional program. We have with us today Senator Bryce Hamilton, one of the leaders of the Council for a Free America, the organization that is spearheading the efforts of a number of states looking to secede from the United States of America. Senator Hamilton, I understand that the proposed name of this new federation of states being floated is the Constitutional States of America. Is that correct?"

Hamilton nodded. "First of all, Mike, thank you for having me here today. I do wish to clarify that the name Constitutional States of America is one suggestion that has been proposed. However, I see no harm in using that moniker, or even CSA for a matter of convenience. The actual name will be determined at a later date by a full body of delegates at an organizing convention."

"Senator Hamilton, I know that you understand that you and Congressman Bridger are at the center of the most momentous event in the history of the United States since the end of World War II. Was there one specific catalyst to which you owe the existence and formation of the Council for a Free America?"

"As you may know, I am a resident of Lincoln, Nebraska. A couple of years ago I happened to see a notice in the newspaper about a meeting that was being held at a local lodge meeting hall. It simply referred to making an effort to have the voices of average people heard in regard to irresponsible actions being taken by the federal government. The same day that notice appeared in the newspaper, I received a telephone call, asking if, as a former United States Senator, I would be willing to become involved.

"I went to that meeting, found that it was originally organized by a group of like – minded friends who seemed to me to be sincere and well-informed. We talked that night of our ongoing financial crisis, the unwillingness of the federal government to constrain its spending or to make any hard choices, as well as such matters as threats to the Second Amendment.

"Of course, weighing heavily on our minds was the fresh memory of how powerful what many referred to as the 'Deep State' had proven to be during the Trump Presidency. That factor was very disheartening for those of us hoping for true governmental reform. By the time the evening was over, I had agreed to become involved on an ongoing basis.

"It was not until the second meeting that I heard of the Council for a Free America. I was told by my new friends that an organization by that name had formed in Topeka, Kansas, and as such matters happen to be known on the internet, inquiries began to come in from many places.

"Our group in Lincoln decided to become associated with the Topeka organization, and we adopted the name, and the movement began to spread. Although there are currently fifteen states with chapters in direct affiliation, we know that there are chapters in various stages of formation in other states as well. They may not be in states that will withdraw, but we certainly welcome their support, their input and the pressure we expect them to place upon elected officials in those states."

"It would be an understatement to say that your movement is the subject of some rather savage criticism. You are being described as everything from racists to gun – crazy extremists, to naïve ideologues looking toward Eden, or your version of it. You probably heard the comments here on NewsNet earlier in the day made by Congresswoman Hostetler. She had some rather harsh presumptions regarding you and your colleagues. How do you react to such attacks?"

"Well, Mike, I was sitting in the green room and watching her interview. In no way do I doubt her sincerity, for she seems definitely convinced that her assumptions are prescient. I guess that one of the things that bothers me the most about our current level of poisoned discourse in this country, are the assumptions we make about each other's intentions. Both sides in this argument toss around comments that the other is out to destroy this or that. People like me are out to destroy women's rights and the safety net for the poor. We want to take away minority rights and make life miserable for workers.

"On the other hand, people like Congresswoman Hostetler are accused of wanting to bankrupt our nation and demolish what have long been recognized as traditional values. Now Mike, I do not believe for one second that Congresswoman Hostetler intends to do any of those things.

"All I can do is assure your viewers that I do not wish to take away anyone's rights or make life unnecessarily difficult for those facing challenges. I wish that I could say that people believe me when I say that, but I cannot in all honesty do so. I have seen and heard snippets of what progressive politicians and members of the media say about me. I'm a racist, I wish to keep women barefoot and pregnant, and I want everyone to carry a Colt .45 whether they want one or not.

"Nothing I do or say will dispel that. I believe in fiscal responsibility, and I believe that citizens should be self-reliant to the extent possible. I also feel that people have the right, and the responsibility, to protect their own safety and the safety of their families. Therefore, I am guilty of all those charges against me."

"Well, Senator Hamilton… I appreciate your tongue-in-cheek qualities. But let me ask you, just how would you establish the economic structure in the proposed CSA? I understand that you plan for this new federation to be a very business friendly, low tax proposition. What about revenue?"

"Thank you, Mike. That's my favorite subject to address. First of all, we have seen the tragedy that results when government falls short of its responsibilities in terms of fiscal solvency. For several decades now, we have seen spending increase much beyond our means, resulting in unconscionable levels of borrowing. We all know now that this debt cannot be sustained, and that is why we are in trouble with interest payments, interest rates, and the resulting collapse of the dollar and the housing industry.

"It is simply breathtaking to be taking such a high percentage of the earnings of the most economically productive segments of our society, only to see it squandered and used for increased spending rather than payment on the debt principal. It certainly did not take long for the new administration and Congress to do away with some of the tax reform accomplished under President Trump.

"It is our intention to keep government expenditures and activities at the minimum level required to provide for the safety and protection of our citizens. We will have a tax base in most states formed around sales taxes, and income taxes will be minimal or nonexistent, depending upon the wishes of each sovereign state.

"We will also hold corporate taxes to a Spartan level. This means that we will have low unemployment rates, which means that more residents will have jobs, make purchases, and thereby provide sales tax revenues. In addition, by providing such a pro – employment environment, fewer people will need government assistance, so the circle of prosperity will be complete."

Mike Silver leaned forward with a grin. "With all due respect, Senator Hamilton, what if it does not work as planned?"

"Mike, if it did not work as planned, then we could end up with too much unemployment, an unstable currency and too much debt. My goodness, I cannot imagine what that would look like, can you?"

The veteran interviewer smiled and nodded: "Touché, Senator Hamilton. But if you are correct, then why would anyone who owns a business or wants to seek opportunities stay in the United States, since you see it as so burdened with taxes that hamper business?"

Hamilton shrugged. "I don't know."

Mike Silver allowed himself a laugh. "We have to take a break, but we will be right back, and then I'm going to ask Senator Hamilton about what he thinks President Malcolm intends to do to stop this movement, if anything. This is NewsNet, and you are watching a special edition of News in Depth."

"We're back with Mister Bryce Hamilton, Convening Chairman of the Council for a Free America. Senator Hamilton, would you please address the issue of steps the Malcolm administration may take to prevent states from seceding?"

"As I have said in a previous interview, I have no reason to suspect that the President intends to use military force to stop the establishment of the Constitutional States of America. To do so would bring unnecessary chaos and tragedy to the people of America. The confusion that would occur within members of the various branches of our armed services would endanger the collective security of the fifty states.

"Our movement has made no pronouncements of any hostile intent. We simply want to leave the United States of America peacefully, and maintain a close and productive friendship and partnership with our neighbors. The United States of America and the CSA will be the closest of allies. We will still be the collective American people. There is no reason for the use of force, and I expect none."

Silver considered his next question carefully. "In a column yesterday a respected and experienced reporter who has covered national affairs for several decades, indicated that it is quite plausible that in the event of such a showdown, the President would federalize all National Guard units in any seceding states. Do you have any comment on that?"

Hamilton shook his head slowly. "The United States military is not going to attempt to occupy a third of the landmass of the continental states. Regular military units would likely be torn asunder by divided loyalties. I doubt that would be the case with National Guard units. The only way that President Malcolm could manage to bring about an actual shooting conflict, would be to expect members of the U.S. military to point their guns at their friends and relatives.

"I think this is a good point in the conversation for me to remind everyone about how the United States of America came to be. The youngest among us, and the poorly educated may think it only natural for states to be managed and dictated to by the federal government as if they were nothing more than mere political subdivisions, much as a township is to a county, or a borough is to a city.

"The reality is that the states created the federal government, and in the process stated which powers would be granted to the federal government, and which ones would be retained by the states. That is why the often neglected 10th Amendment to the Constitution is so important. It may be too quickly and often ignored by our federal government, but it is supposed to be the guiding principle of the relationship between the states and the federal government. That basic principle has often been lost, but it has never been revoked. Sovereign states created the federal government, but that federal government has taken upon itself powers it really cannot hold without the consent of the states. In other words, the states are

163

supposed to assign duties to the federal government. But for decades, in practice, it has been the other way around."

Mike Silver knew that he had the interview of a lifetime. "After the break, we're going to continue with Bryce Hamilton, of the Council for a Free America. Please stay with us."

Mike Silver watched as a producer counted down until they were live on the air again. "And now we are back with Bryce Hamilton of the Council for a Free America. I would like to ask you about the possible effects of your CSA becoming a business friendly haven for corporations and small businesses. Do you feel any obligation to the states that did not secede?"

"Mike, if businesses and corporations flock to our states after withdrawal, then that means only that the states they are migrating from could have kept them there if only they had adopted similar policies. I would say that business practices in the CSA will need to be fair in competition with those in other states and nations. However, fairness in business does not include engaging in disadvantageous practices simply because competitors, including those in other nations, prefer to engage in social engineering rather than profitable business practices.

"In other words, if businesses and industries move to the CSA, the answer is not for the CSA – based businesses and industries to reduce their profitability. Rather, it is up to other societies to re-examine the taxation and regulatory factors that put them at a profit disadvantage."

"But I have heard some speculation that much of that profitability in the CSA would come through more lax regulations in the realm of environmental protection and worker safety."

"But Mike, one thing that the United States of America is no longer doing, is to review existing regulatory constraints on an ongoing basis. Many were removed during the Trump Administration, but now are added onto, rather than being examined for effectiveness and results, or done away with whenever possible. No one wants pollution, and no one wants workers to be unsafe on the job. That does not mean that regulations should not be routinely reviewed to eliminate costly and ineffective statutes and administrative edicts. Should the United States fail to aid businesses and industries to be more efficient and profitable, that is not the problem of the CSA. It is a failure on the part of the USA."

"But Senator Hamilton, some speculate that the migration of jobs to the CSA will leave many states that remain in the United States without sufficient employment opportunities, and a crisis of revenue. Should that happen, will you feel any sense of responsibility?"

"No. Once again, that is a failure of our federal government to recognize that spending has more than outrun income. We are already way in over our heads in debt, with no real prospect of recovery. If we are looking for matters of unfairness, let me say that it is unfair to criticize those ready to take their own destiny in their hands and find a better way."

"But some economists are stating that, should this secession take place, we will go quickly into recession, then a likely depression as the dollar goes into the tank along with the credit rating of the United States. Does that give you pause?"

"No. Our fiscal situation is already lost, unless the United States would take immediate and drastic action. All that has to happen, is for Congress to convene on Monday morning as usual, and pass legislation greatly curtailing spending, and doing away with several federal agencies, then doing away with some volumes of regulations.

"That could happen within a week. The fiscal solvency of the United States of America could be preserved. There would not be a group of states likely wishing to withdraw if faith were restored in the federal government. There would be no likelihood of the recession deepening, let alone our slipping into depression.

"But what we saw over the past several years is that the stubborn power structure in Washington D.C. will do anything to fight reform. As with cutting the budget, in a matter of days Congress could simplify and shrink the federal government. But in recent years it was attempted, and the forces of intransigence were more powerful than the forces of reform.

"It is literally as simple as that. All that is required is a couple of days of voting on some difficult and hard decisions. The United States of America would be preserved, and our economic future would be restored. But all of us know that will not happen. We all know that Congress and the administration do not possess the foresight to do so, or the will to act.

"Therefore, there will be no votes next week to save our nation. States will withdraw, and the United States will continue down the road to economic disaster. You and I cannot prevent that. Congress and the President can. Unfortunately, Congress and the President will not."

For the first time in his career, Mike Silver spent several on – air seconds in silence while staring at his guest.

"Senator Hamilton… I would like to now discuss some logistical issues. How would the CSA provide for a currency? Would there be a separate currency, or would there be a shared currency with the United States of America?"

"I am speculating here, purely on my own volition. Taking into account the recklessness in spending, coupled with a federal lack of serious concern over the stability of the dollar, I would be reluctant to share a currency. It would be somewhat cumbersome, but I see it being like our currency exchange with Canada. As with many other issues, one of our task forces has compiled a plan dealing with currency. There will be a ratio in valuation, and a process would have to be established to pass currency back and forth. I would imagine that establishment of a currency reserve would be one of the few aspects of federalism we would see in the CSA. I am assuming that I speak for many in the movement, that it would be necessary for all CSA states to operate with a common currency.

"And we must realize that technology has us on the verge of being able to make conventional currency an option rather than a necessity. Perhaps this movement will usher in a new era in economics."

"What about the Postal Service?"

"I am anticipating that the CSA would seek to contract with the U.S. Postal Service. They're already present in post offices everywhere, capitol expenditures have been made, and I think it would be fair for the United States to be compensated for use of the services."

"And now for the big question. What about defense?"

"I owe you and your viewers an honest answer... I don't know. I've stated publicly before that I cannot imagine a situation in which the two entities would not unite for the matter of defense, although it would become murky in the matter of preemptive actions. The United States may want to maintain some existing military bases in CSA locations. And I cannot imagine that Fort Knox would not remain a United States federal installation. The matter of Alaska may also call for some special arrangements to be made, due to its proximity to Russia.

"The role of state National Guard organizations is still to be resolved. I would like to provide you with some more solid answers, but right now, I cannot."

"One more question before we sign off… I would like to ask just how firm a timetable for action exists within the leadership of the Council for a Free America?"

"I will confess to being a bit surprised myself at the pace of activity. Remember, the Council for a Free America does not issue commands to state legislatures, or approve or disapprove legislative actions. Things are unquestionably happening fast, and if I may anticipate a question, I do think that it is possible that more resolutions will come rapidly, and that actual withdrawal could take effect much sooner than I previously thought."

The host reached across to shake hands with his guest, and then turned toward the camera. "Thank you for tuning in for this special edition of NewsNet's News in Depth. I thank my special guest, Bryce Hamilton for being here today… I am Mike Silver for NewsNet. Now stay tuned for Saturday Report with Maria Montes, who will have an update on what is happening in Austin, Texas."

"This is Maria Montes, and welcome to Saturday Report. First up on this Saturday afternoon is an update from Gwendolyn

Munro who is in Austin, Texas where the city is still under a curfew and police and Texas National Guard troops are patrolling the city."

"Gwen, how are things in the state capitol?"

The image on the screen was one of the reporter standing on the lawn in front of the Capitol building. In the background, National Guard troops strolled the grounds and the perimeter of the building. "Hello, Maria. Well things have certainly calmed down considerably here in Austin, where just yesterday a riot broke out when demonstrators in favor of secession were confronted and taunted by counter – demonstrators. Police were forced to use tear gas, but in the aftermath, one person was shot and killed and two wounded. Austin police now have a suspect in custody, reported to be a student at the University of Texas, allegedly involved in a Marxist group opposed to the secession.

"The mayor of Austin and the Governor of Texas met this morning and issued a statement to the effect that should the situation remain calm throughout the weekend, the National Guard troops should be able to leave on Monday, and the curfew would be lifted. However, the mayor reassured the public that for several days after the departure of the troops, there will be extra police officers on duty in the downtown area.

"Of course, the big news coming out of Austin is that the Texas state legislature voted to secede from the United States of America. That vote magnified the impact of the secession movement being coordinated by the Council for a Free America. This is Gwendolyn Munro reporting for NewsNet, on the scene in Austin, Texas."

The scene shifted back to the New York studio. "That was Gwendolyn Munro on the scene in Austin, Texas. We're going to go to a commercial break right now, but I want to inform our viewers that all day tomorrow, we will continue special coverage of the secession movement, and all news related to it. And we will be back in a few minutes."

~~~

President John Malcolm's two closest remaining advisers sat at an oak table in the office at Blair House on the blustery but sunny Saturday afternoon. In front of them rested a stack of personnel folders, and scattered across the table were drafts of statements being readied for use by the President at his discretion, in whichever version he chose.

"Jim… I appreciate your taking the bull by the horns on this work. You crafted the statements well, but I can hardly put into words how much I regret our having to do this. But, I think we have done just what the boss asked. The thought of that dedicated man making a speech acknowledging the country is breaking apart on his watch…".

"I know… I guess I feel okay with recommending Mitchell Pryor for the new AG as well. So, I'll get a memo to the boss yet this

171

afternoon. Fortunately, the media have not really picked up that Laura has walked away."

The Vice President's cell phone that was resting on the table began to buzz and rattle. After he answered, he remained silent as he listened, but his attention was obviously captivated by the news he was receiving, and as he said goodbye and tapped a button, he revealed a slight smile. "Please don't be offended Jim... I'm not going to tell you who that was so that you can preserve plausible deniability. You're going to get questions about this, but I can tell you what it was about.

"There's a group... more than a dozen members of Congress, Senators and Representatives from both parties... Blue Dog Democrats included. They're picking up that challenge that Bryce Hamilton tossed out about how a dramatic and immediate budget action could prevent the country from breaking up.

"They plan to work around the clock this weekend, and have this proposal ready to introduce on the House floor on Monday. It contains some extreme stuff. The Speaker has agreed to clear the agenda for them. But, I also understand he is not yet on board."

The expression on the face of Jim Walters was one of shocked surprise. "This is going to be interesting. The Republicans have that maddening five seat majority. For something like this, a lot of moderate Republicans are going to be hiding under their desks.

He's going to need all of those Blue Dogs, but I don't think he can get them all."

The Vice President rested his chin on his folded hands. "Our former, illustrious Attorney General told me that Bryce Hamilton was a quaint intellectual lightweight. I know one thing for damned sure... I know that Bryce Hamilton knows how to put people in a corner."

Walters shook his head and whistled quietly. "How long before this becomes public?"

"It already is. I was told that an hour ago, they released a one paragraph statement. How many Sunday interview shows are scrambling right now to rearrange their guest lists with less than twenty-four hours to go before airtime?"

Chapter 9

Patricia Barrett sat nervously next to Oklahoma Republican Senator Franklin Chiles. Waiting to go on national television as a political odd couple, they sipped on coffee and reviewed their notes. For Franklin Chiles, it was a critical moment. For Patricia Barrett, the Blue Dog Democrat Congresswoman from Florida, it was a commitment of a career.

They were a study in contrasts. The Oklahoma Senator was a tall, barrel – chested former Sooner linebacker whose hair had long since turned gray from his days on the gridiron. Patricia Barrett was in her late thirties, a petite and famously attractive woman.

Barrett knew that whatever standing she had within the Democratic Party the previous day had now been stripped away. She told her colleagues that she would go to any possible lengths to avoid seeing the breakup of the United States of America. Now she was about to give a status report on the work of the maverick band of Senators and Representatives who had hastily assembled the previous day, and worked through the night.

Much needed to be done before the presentation was made on Monday morning, and the members of the group would still not sleep until Monday evening, if then. But it was critical for them to let the public know the level to which they were fighting to make the changes available to the rest of the Congress that could possibly head off secession, and the irrevocable and radical change to the future of America.

Barrett knew that she had already been granted the status of pariah within her party. She spoke publicly of her support for liberal social stances. She spoke at rallies supporting the advancement of LGTB rights. She was fiercely pro- choice on the matter of abortion. And she was a strong advocate for gun control.

At the same time, Patricia Barrett was a deficit hawk. Both on the floor of the House of Representatives and in party meetings and caucuses, she would plead with her colleagues of both parties to cut spending and be more careful and diligent in the use of money taken from people who had worked hard for it. That was enough of a sin within her party. Now she was about to take the lead in stating just how far she was willing to go.

She nearly spilled her coffee when the door to the green room opened and a program staffer told them it was time to go to the studio and be seated at the interview desk. As they walked, the young Congresswoman felt that she may as well have been walking to her own execution.

The young man who escorted them to the studio seated them and brought them glasses of water. Barrett began to scan the room, looking nervously at the cameras and lights that would be trained on them.

For Chiles, being on national television was nothing new. As a long-term Senator, he had often been called on to appear on news programs to espouse the conservative point of view on numerous subjects. However, the subject had never before been so grave and urgent.

For Barrett, she had often appeared on Florida television stations, and had been covered on the floor of the House at times by C-SPAN. This was altogether different.

Suddenly, the program host Charles Bryant came to the interview desk, nearly running as a large digital clock counted down to zero. "Welcome to NewsNet Sunday. I'm your host Charles Bryant, and this morning we have as our guests two leaders in a group of members of the United States Senate and House of Representatives who may be serving as the last chance to prevent the breakup of the United States.

"I am pleased to have with me this morning Oklahoma Republican Senator Franklin Chiles, a veteran member of the Senate, known for being a staunch conservative. Also with us this morning is Congresswoman Patricia Barrett of Florida. Ms. Barrett is in her second term in Congress, and is one of the fiscally conservative Democrats known as the Blue Dogs. Welcome to both of you.

"Congresswoman... I understand that you have for us this morning, a very preliminary summary of the actions your group is going to propose on the floor of Congress tomorrow, is that correct?"

"Yes it... I have... I have what you correctly call, a preliminary overview of the steps we are proposing to address some of the main issues that have caused this unfortunate and potentially tragic secession of states. Most of these proposals, but not all, relate to fiscal matters."

Barrett hesitated for a moment to try to quell her anxiety, and then proceeded after an encouraging nod from the host. "We wish to put into place an immediate across the board twenty percent reduction in the budgets of all federal agencies, except for the Department of Defense. We propose the elimination and revocation of all remaining facets of the Affordable Care Act, better known as Obamacare. We also propose the immediate elimination of the Department of Education and the Interstate Commerce Commission.

"We propose that all non- emergency activities of the Environmental Protection Agency be suspended, and the only remaining duties for that Department should be to respond to obvious and immediate dangers to the health of the public.

"We propose that the standard retirement age for Social Security and Medicare be raised to age 70, through a phase – in process over the next five years. While the details need to be worked out, it is also the consensus of our group that we should initiate a form of means – testing for Social Security recipients in the higher income levels. We also propose the revocation of the Medicare drug program expansion that was enacted during the Presidency of George W. Bush.

"Another part of our proposal would require that work requirements for public assistance and nutritional programs operated by the Department of Agriculture, commonly known as the Food Stamp Program, be reinstated as enacted during the welfare reform legislation in the late 90's during the administration of President Clinton. Of course, that would only apply if the states would accept federal funds for those programs. We are proposing that acceptance of federal funding for public assistance in any form be discretionary on the part of each state. Further, our proposal includes the provision for funds for Medicaid and public assistance to be given to the states in the form of block grants with a minimum of federal oversight.

"We are proposing that the Department of Defense proceed with the closure of the fifteen military bases their own analysts identified last year as being those most subject to closure for fiscal purposes, with the least impact upon the security of the nation.

"We propose a reduction in foreign aid by a cut of 60% overall, and that priority for that remaining funding be based upon a studied evaluation of our national interests in each nation involved in the program. Also to be taken into consideration, is each nation's cooperation in combating terrorism and despotic regimes, and promoting women's equality.

"To spur economic progress, we will be proposing reductions in income tax rates for individuals and corporations. We also propose the total elimination of remaining provisions of what is popularly known as the death tax.

"Further, we are endorsing the enactment of major revisions to our tax code, and within the next week we expect to endorse proposals known as either the flat tax or the fair tax.

"Now I'm going to defer to my colleague, Senator Chiles."

The large man folded his hands and leaned toward the host. "As the Congresswoman mentioned earlier, most of our proposals are economic in nature. However, our efforts are meant to be comprehensive in regards to preventing the secession of a number of states.

"One of the other issues involved is the matter of gun ownership. Many of us share concerns about federal expansion and interference in what many of us feel is a private matter, and under any circumstances, is governed by the rights granted to us by the Second Amendment. As you know, the Congresswoman and I have different points of interest to be presented on Monday. The same is true of some of the other members of our group. Still, we have agreed to a common goal, that being to prevent this secession from taking place.

"As a result, we are proposing that the federal government relinquish any claims of authority to govern the possession of firearms, or the configuration of those firearms. Such oversight will be determined on a state by state basis, with the caveat being that as long as a state is part of the United States of America, there will always be judicial oversight powers to determine if a law is constitutional. In one proposed clause of note, we have agreed that in spite of our other recommendations regarding gun ownership, federal laws addressing automatic weapons should still be in place. We feel that this is a reasonable compromise in a matter that generates such strong feelings."

Charles Bryant had never before conducted such an interview. "I must say, that is an extensive amount of work, considering your group came together yesterday afternoon. I have to go to the most obvious question: President Malcolm is a Democrat, the Senate has a majority of Democrats, and the Republican majority in the House is just five votes. What you are proposing is a comprehensive effort to address a historic crisis. But what do you think the chances are that this will pass the Congress, with enough votes to override a presidential veto?"

The large man from Oklahoma responded. "We need to be very blunt. We are trying to prevent the political fracturing of the United States. Once secession takes hold, it would be very difficult to ever accomplish a reconciliation or reunification if you will. We are in an emergency situation, and only strong resolve, a willingness to make hard decisions and steady leadership will do the job. We cannot nibble around the edges as we have done for decades, shuffling a little money here, moving it around there.

"We all know that only in Washington is a reduction in a requested increase labeled a cut. If we wish to preserve the United States, we have to take this action. Of course, it is unfortunate and it will be difficult and painful. But it will not be as difficult and painful as seeing the greatest nation ever on this earth torn asunder once again. And even though it seems to be consensus that this breakup of the United States will be nonviolent, it will also be permanent. We owe better than that to the generations before us who sacrificed so much to establish, preserve and then defend this nation. We owe it to our children and grandchildren to pass on to them a unified and strong...". The Senator suddenly paused and looked down and began wiping tears from his face.

That was when Congresswoman Barrett continued for him. "We must pass along to the next generations the same great, free and prosperous nation we were blessed to have. This is our only chance, and while we understand that we are slaughtering a herd of sacred cattle in this proposal, there is no choice. It is simply... that... simple. I don't know what more we can do to make everyone understand that.

"Our economy will collapse at the rate of spending we have engaged in over the past several months under our new President.

Enough Republicans have voted with my party to go on a new spending binge the likes of which we have never seen.

"While I disagree with those proposing secession, I know that they are doing so to seek the economic opportunity, stability and freedom they grew up being told existed in America more than anywhere else in the world. So what we want to do, is to make sure that promise, although weakened and wobbly for the moment, still remains, and we will protect it, strengthen it and fortify it."

The Senator had regained his composure and rejoined the conversation. "The next seventy-two hours may be the most critical since December 7, 1941. I know in advance the comments and accusations that will be thrown in our direction. I can anticipate the comments of denial and disputes of facts. But as for our fiscal crisis at least, math is math. Our economy is heading for a cliff, and it is only a matter of how many pieces it will break into before it is finally done for."

"But Senator… Congresswoman. There are many voices calling for the states in this movement to be allowed to simply go quietly into the night. Do you anticipate that some of your colleagues will claim that secession of those states would be preferable to the austerity moves you are proposing?"

The Congresswoman replied: "Charles… I want everyone to understand. I agree that unless drastic action is taken now, our economy is approaching the point of no return. That would be the case even if there were no secession movement. Of course, this proposal came about through our attempt to prevent secession. And I will say, these proposals are more draconian than I would propose if a breakup of the United States were not staring us in the face. Nonetheless, difficult choices must be made, and major cuts simply have to occur. Secession or no secession, the same action will eventually be necessary, and the longer it is forestalled, the more painful the situation will be."

Charles Bryant glanced to the camera. "If you're just joining in, we have with us today Senator Franklin Chiles of Oklahoma and Congresswoman Patricia Barrett of Florida. They are part of a group of members of Congress formulating a last – ditch effort to keep a large number of states from seceding. Since we have much to cover today, and have other guests to interview, our program today will not be interrupted by any breaks.

"Senator, there have been calls for leaders of the Council for a Free America to face charges of treason or sedition. Would you please comment on that?"

"I question whether such charges would stick. I certainly feel that to file such charges would only accelerate the secession. I hope no one takes such a step."

"Congresswoman… I know that it must be difficult for you, as a Democrat, to be doing and saying what you are doing and saying this weekend. I have heard speculation in the last twelve hours that you may be switching parties. Any truth to that?"

The petite woman's expression grew somber. "I became a Democrat at an early age, based upon what my father taught me about the principles upon which the Democratic Party operated. I have always been a Democrat… I will always be a Democrat. I just don't know if I will still be welcome among other Democrats. But, that is hardly my major concern right now."

The host nodded to his guests. "I wish to thank both of you for being here this morning… I know that you have much more work to do, and we will be looking forward to covering the reaction tomorrow from other members of Congress."

The camera zoomed in on the host while the Senator and Congresswoman were escorted away. Out of sight of the camera, two more guests were brought on to the stage and seated.

"Now I am pleased to welcome our next guests, two Democratic members of Congress who earlier this morning issued statements regarding their plan to defeat the proposals just summarized by Senator Chiles and Congresswoman Barrett. Joining me now are…".

~~~

It was the middle of the afternoon when the last of the expected guests reached the White House and joined the other attendees assembled in waiting outside the Oval Office. Hearing from his secretary on the intercom that everyone had arrived, President John Malcolm told her to bring them all in.

The President stood several feet from his desk and shook hands as they filed in. He greeted Vice President Howard Litton, Senate President Lawton Burroughs and his Chief of Staff Jim Walters. He motioned for them to be seated in the guest chairs, then walked around the desk and took his place in his own high – backed leather chair.

"Gentlemen... I guess the challenge has been issued by this informal committee." He looked directly at the Senate President. "Lawton, your reactions?"

The liberal Democrat from Illinois shook his head dismissively. "Out of the question... totally out of the question. We cannot submit to blackmail. This would decimate the principles our party has stood for over the generations."

The President's eyes darted toward the Vice President. The man whose own state could possibly soon secede spoke up. "Mister President... I have to take issue with my friend Senator Burroughs. I trust that these comments will stay among those of us in this room. Senator... I have no doubt that your knowledge of history is equal to mine. And I know that making a reference to principles our party has held for decades is, if you will forgive my crass description, disingenuous.

"The party today bears no resemblance to the one my father joined in his freshman year at Yale. Please do some reading, and go back over comments and essays from Jack Kennedy and Hubert Humphrey. Then try to tell me that this is the same party as the one they led. Kennedy and Humphrey would never have allowed such a national bankruptcy to occur."

The Senate President rose from his chair and glared as he stared down at the Vice President. "That was totally uncalled for. You never have had the dedication to our base to merit your current position. And I...."

The President rose and slammed his open palm upon the desk. "Dammit, Burroughs... I have no patience right now for demands of party purity. We have to make a decision. We have to decide if we're going to take this deal, and the decision has to be based upon the best interests of the people of the United States, not our party."

Burroughs sat back down angrily. "I don't think it is possible for us to accept such extreme and radical demands at the point of a gun from a bunch of self – appointed Congressional vigilantes. I cannot speak for the Democrats in the House, but I can assure you that the members of the party in my chamber will never entertain such an outlandish set of mean – spirited proposals. And I will encourage each and every one of them to turn this travesty down."

The President held up his hands to signify that he wanted calm. "Lawton... I just want to understand. You would be in favor of allowing the secession to happen, rather than accept these proposals? Or is it that you think the secession is a bluff?"

The Senator took a deep breath. "My apologies to all of you... I don't think this is a bluff. But, Mister President, in answer to your question... I do indeed think it best to simply accept the reality of the secession. This CSA outfit can go back to 1950 if they wish. I just don't want to impose such conditions on everyone else in the process. I apologize again for my temper. But I want you to understand, I meant what I said about encouraging Senate members to walk away from this deal."

Jim Walters had been sitting in silence and watching. "I just have to ask this. Does anyone here believe that, secession or not, the United States in either form will pull out of and survive our debt and budget problems?"

The President and Vice President shook their heads slowly. The Senate President shrugged, and then nodded. "We could if we would pass that tax increase bill I wanted."

The President rose slowly and wearily from his chair. "Lawton... I want to be fair. I cannot stand here and state resolutely that I would not be taking the same stand if I were in your position. I don't think there is much benefit in our continuing this conversation. Let me just say this: tomorrow may decide the future of our nation.

If we break apart, we open up a Pandora's Box of possibilities. I... I am not enough of a prophet to begin to know how it will turn out. Except... I don't think it could turn out well."

~~~

Bryce Hamilton sat in the office of his Lincoln, Nebraska home. He had been on the road for much of the previous month, and regretted that he was now hiding away like a monk in the office. Still, he had convinced Cynthia to bring her books and knitting to the office so that she could sit in the leather chair in the corner and at least be in his company.

He was grateful to Patrick Bridger for his offer to fly to Washington that evening, so at least one member of the executive committee of the Council for a Free America could be present in the U. S. Capitol building when the austerity and gun rights proposals were presented to the House of Representatives, and then hopefully to the Senate.

Hamilton sat quietly in front of his computer, sitting still and thinking for minutes at a time, before once again reaching for the keyboard and typing some thoughts and notes. In the back of his mind, he held out hope for alternatives. Still, none were substantial enough to end up among his notes.

All through the early evening, he had received text messages and calls from Bridger and Tom Edelstein. Edelstein had served as a staffer for Senator Chiles during his college days as a law student at

Georgetown University. The younger man was keeping Bryce Hamilton and Patrick Bridger up-to-date with the information that was being passed along to him by his mentor.

The evening wore on, and the old basketball player found that as more notes filled his screen, and more messages arrived, the likelihood of the proposals being accepted seemed to diminish. It was around 10:00 PM that he nearly broke into tears as the inevitability of the situation overwhelmed him.

Chapter 10

Unlike most Monday mornings, Congresswoman Patricia Barrett did not have a cup of coffee in her hands as she drove her Honda Accord into the parking garage of the Rayburn House Office Building. As was typical, she was accompanied by another Florida Congresswoman with whom she shared an apartment.

Also unlike most mornings, although it was only 8:00 AM, the sidewalks were lined with people holding signs or chanting. As she had driven slowly down the street toward the parking entrance, several protesters were seen running out into the streets and being removed from the roadway by police.

Her roommate, was like her, a single woman and a Democrat. They had not discussed Barrett's role in the pivotal proposals that would be presented that morning. Of course, there had not been much opportunity to do so, as she had just arrived home at 6:00 AM after another long night of work on details, giving her barely enough time to take a shower and make herself presentable. Without doubt, Patricia Barrett would be among the more newsworthy members of Congress on that day.

They pulled into the underground parking facility and drove to her reserved space. When she pulled in, she turned off the car that looked at her roommate. "Go on ahead Barb. I need a few more quiet minutes."

The other Congresswoman reached over and took her hand. "Are you sure you're not just trying to shield me? I'm not going to bail on you."

"Thanks… I really just need a few minutes. I haven't slept the last two nights."

"Okay… I'm wishing you luck." Her driving companion got out of the car and closed the door behind her. Barrett watched as her roommate walked away, perhaps one of the few friendly faces she would encounter.

She strolled slowly to the stairway, and then hesitantly climbed her way to the entrance to the Capitol Building. She went to the door to stop at the security checkpoint, and found the swarm of humanity almost disorienting in its contrast to the typical foot traffic that usually greeted her in the morning. As soon as she emerged, several reporters rushed toward her.

She tried to walk rapidly past them with as much courtesy as she could while trying to elbow her way through the crowd. As she walked, she delivered brief thank you's followed by her apologies for the fact that she could not take their questions at that moment. Still, she could not help but overhear the shouted questions in snippets as she scurried away: "… called you a traitor…", "…challenging you in the next primary…", "…becoming a Republican?"

She finally encountered a cluster of several Democratic members of Congress, and as she neared, they walked away in a group. She knew that the tone for the day had been established.

Just before leaving the apartment, she had received a text from Senator Chiles, telling her that the group was having a clandestine meeting in the office of the Speaker of the House. Although the Speaker had not committed his support to their proposals, he wanted them to meet in a secluded place and hopefully avoid some chaos.

As the tiny woman made her way there, she ignored the many shouts directed at her. In her fatigue, she did not even try to differentiate those that were supportive from those containing angry epithets. Upon her arrival at the designated office, a Capitol Police officer was standing guard, and ushered her in.

She walked in to find the rest of her group had already arrived, and were sitting around the guest seating area outside the Speaker's office. Upon entering, she was greeted with various complementary remarks regarding her presentation the previous day on NewsNet. All that she could manage at the moment was a whispered "Thank you" before she nearly collapsed into a chair in her exhaustion.

When she had gotten dressed, she was so tired that she paid little attention to any symbolism of her garb. However, when one of her colleagues asked if she had dressed for a funeral, she looked down and realized she had put on a rather somber looking black dress. It was the first time she had laughed in three days.

While Barrett had become the de facto spokesperson for the group, the role of leadership has fallen primarily upon the shoulders of Franklin Chiles. He stood and looked over the assembled group of a dozen rather daring members of Congress. "The Speaker plans to call the House to order in just a few minutes. As soon as the prayer is over, he's going to go straight to it… I guess there won't be any housekeeping matters. He still hasn't committed, but he wants to get this underway.

"Congresswoman Barrett… without any prompting or any action on your part, he is going to simply recognize you to present the list we finished a little over two hours ago. By the way, there will be some extra Capitol cops in the chamber. Also, the public that does get into the spectators gallery is being given everything but full body cavity searches this morning.

"Congresswoman Barrett… I don't know how much of it you are aware of, but a lot of protesters' signs out on the street this morning made unkind references to you. The Speaker called me a few minutes ago, and told me that he has taken it upon himself to arrange for you to be driven home by the cops when all this is over today, or this evening.

"Everybody ready? If so, good luck in the House… I'm on my way to the Senate chamber to see how much trouble I can cause over there."

~~~

There were seven House members in the unofficial committee. They walked together to the House chamber, and along the way Barrett found herself in the unusual position of hearing encouraging and complementary comments and shouts from Republicans, and seeing other Democrats shake their heads or simply turn their backs whenever she drew near.

When the group entered the chamber, there was a mixture of cheers and cat calls throughout the chaotic room. Suddenly, the Speaker began to bang the gavel loudly, the first step in trying to bring the unusually rowdy assemblage to order. The group of seven members remained together in a cluster as long as possible, and then drifted individually to their seats.

None of the members of the committee really knew just where the rest of their colleagues stood. They had been too busy and absorbed in their work to really follow any news coverage. However, the media had been busy as well, and by the time the Speaker began pounding the gavel for the second time, networks were showing graphics of the expected outcome based upon interviews with members of Congress, some of which had taken place in the middle of the night.

When the noise level had reached an acceptable level, the Speaker introduced the Chaplain to deliver the invocation. It was the last peaceful moment of the morning.

The Speaker immediately recognized the "… Congresswoman from Florida, Ms. Barrett". Upon that announcement, applause broke out simultaneously with derisive shouts of protest.

The Speaker again pounded the gavel, an act that accompanied the obligatory command that "… The House will be in order".

More shouting followed, as Patricia Barrett made her way to the microphone. "Mister Speaker… I rise today to…". Once again, a cacophony of shouts of protest began to drown out her attempt to speak. Many were coming from the spectator mezzanine, and after yet another attempt to bring order to the chamber was made impossible, the Speaker ordered the Sergeant at arms and the Capitol Police to clear the House chamber of anyone without official business.

Barrett stood in silence as the officers made their way to escort the spectators out. However, a portion of the spectators refused to leave, and when police attempted remove them by force, several confrontations developed.

Barrett watched in horror as those who found her thoughts so offensive physically battled the officers, who were quickly forced to resort to the use of tasers to restore order and remove the unruly demonstrators. As the scene unfolded on national television, more protesters and other demonstrators gathered on the streets that surrounded the Capitol Building and the Mall.

It took nearly thirty minutes for the spectators to be removed. That being accomplished, the Speaker once again banged his gavel and ordered the chamber to be in attention to the recognized member at the microphone. But when the rattled Barrett attempted again to speak, she was interrupted by shouts of "… point of order".

The frustrated Speaker ignored those who were attempting to conjure up roadblocks to her speech through means of parliamentary procedure. Equally frustrated, Barrett pulled the microphone closer, and in an amplified voice began to read the lengthy motion, copies of which had been distributed just minutes before she walked to the microphone.

A minute into Barrett's presentation of the proposed budget legislation, members of the House who opposed the effort began to quietly and slowly filter out of the chamber. Barrett knew that it was likely that there would be no floor debate as a result of this ploy. As she went on, a steady stream of legislators abandoned the chamber. Even as she spoke, she was able to see just who was walking out. She could see that most were Democrats, but some Republicans were walking out as well.

When she was finished, the chamber was absent many members. A perplexed Speaker Edmund Riley announced that there had been no requests for debate on the proposed legislation. Upon the conclusion of his words, one of the members of the group that had composed the bill, stood to move that a vote be held immediately. It was Patricia Barrett's roommate herself who seconded the motion.

Speaker Riley seemed almost too stunned to continue. Finally, he ordered that voting commence and that the results be recorded by electronic vote. As soon as he gave that order, a Democrat member left, as did one Republican. Suddenly, the members who had walked out began to stream back in to take part in the vote.

Although it was a Monday morning, millions of viewers watched in anxiety as the shared C-SPAN graphics began to slowly reveal the count. Correspondents and pundits were beside themselves attempting to explain to viewers and to each other, the scene that was unfolding before them. As the numbers changed, analysts and pundits tried to make sense of what was taking place. They discussed the five seat majority held by the House Republicans, then tried to reconstruct that morning's attendance.

The voting slowed down, and television cameras focused on heated debates taking place among the members. Slowly, one at a time, the voting concluded.

"This is Robert Carter, and if you're just joining us here at NewsNet, we are bringing you live coverage of what may be the most critical vote in the history of the United States House of Representatives.

"We are trying to determine if the vote tally we are seeing is final, but we do not know if the final votes have been cast. We are doing some quick math here... I have Marsha Bentley here with me... Marsha, what do you have?"

"Bob, the Republicans have a five seat advantage in the House, but we know that many Democrats walked out, but so did a number of Republicans, and we are not sure if everyone came back. Apparently, everyone wanted to just get this vote over with instead of spending hours in debate. On the other hand, it is to be assumed that those who remained are a mixture of those voting for and against. However, and we do not want to represent this as any more than very crude conjecture, but a vote in the house usually requires 218 in the affirmative to pass, but it appears that the measure failed to...".

The screen was again showing the chamber, and the camera was zoomed in on Speaker Riley. Suddenly, he banged the gavel as he looked at a piece of paper that had just been handed to him.

He looked up and hesitated, then banged the gavel again. "The vote having been taken... votes in the affirmative were 205 and opposed... 208. The measure has failed. The House stands adjourned." The gavel slammed one more time, to the sound of cheers, shouts of protest and members of Congress trying to shout into their cell phones.

At the NewsNet panel desk, there was confusion. "This is Marsha Bentley along with Robert Carter and Mason Howell, bringing you coverage of a rather spectacular event that just took place in the halls of Congress. The House of Representatives just voted to not accept a proposal that was prepared by a group of twelve members of the House and Senate that would have, hopefully, headed off the pending secession of several states. Work on what is being called the last chance bill began on Saturday, and continued through the night, all day Sunday and into this early morning.

"While this was going on in Washington, we had been receiving bulletins to the effect that several state legislatures had assembled in special session to monitor the outcome of this vote. Keep in mind, that most of the states who have been threatening to secede, but have not already passed resolutions to that affect are in the central or Mountain Time zones. Of course, three states have already passed secession resolutions.

"One development we are watching closely is activity taking place in Nashville, the capital of the State of Tennessee. Like Texas, Tennessee has seceded before and was part of the Confederate States of America during the U. S. Civil War. But this time, there apparently will be no armed conflict to prevent... I'm just getting a message in my ear piece... the Tennessee House of Representatives has just passed a resolution for secession... I have just been told that the Tennessee State Senate has also passed that resolution, although in that chamber it passed by just one vote.

"So now... I want to... I am now getting word that the West Virginia Legislature is taking up a resolution as we speak, and I am hearing... I am being told that it is possible that final votes in both chambers in the capital of Charleston could be finalized as early as this evening. This development is very noteworthy, as West Virginia had not been involved in the Council for a Free America coordination or planning.

"Wow... I know that a lot of people were speculating that if the last chance bill did not make it through Congress, it could result in a cascading effect of... I hear you... I hear you, but please say that again. Okay... I apologize to be speaking to the wizard in my ear, but another report just came in, and North Dakota is voting as we speak, as are state legislatures in Oklahoma and Nebraska.

"Okay... Mason, just how far along do you think we will be before the day is over?"

"I guess I can go out on a limb here... I suppose it's not out of the question that before midnight tonight, as many as ten states will have passed resolutions. Due to the political and demographic makeups of their states, I expect that South Carolina and Louisiana will be slower to progress.

"I don't want to minimize the importance of the other states, but just the fact that Texas voted to succeed means that the nation has broken up. Now, it is just a matter of degree. Once again, not to diminish the importance of these other states, but Texas ranks high in the globe in terms of its stature as an economic power. Combine that with the potential for industrial and agricultural development, the energy production factor and the coastline and all those ports, well… Texas is it.

"You see, such importance built up around what we have been calling this last chance motion, that states considering secession came to see this as, in effect, a vote by Congress to show whether it cared if they seceded. I'm certain that this group of Representatives and Senators who set about authoring an initiative to take up the challenge that Bryce Hamilton put forth on that Saturday interview intended only to save the nation.

"However, their proposal took on a life of its own. And even though Speaker Riley has been lukewarm to the details, he was willing to suspend all normal rules and practices of the House to bring this to a rapid floor vote.

"As for the retreat of so many House members during Congresswoman Barrett's presentation of the motion, I am still confused as to whether it was meant as a helpful measure to allow the Speaker to dispense with the usual hours of debate, or if it were a shameful act of cowardice on the part of so many. I am certain that some members of the House simply did not wish to be seen on television in conjunction with this proposed measure."

Robert Carter spoke up. "One thing that seems to have been lost in the shuffle is the matter of the Upper Peninsula of Michigan. Tomorrow, a delegation of local officials is flying to Lansing to present a petition to the governor that would allow that northern region of the state to become a separate entity, so that it can become a part of the CSA. One driving factor is the mining and..." He hesitated to glance toward Marsha Bentley, who was once again pressing the earpiece against her head and pointing her finger upward to get the attention of the others. "Forgive me Robert... I am getting word that in Baton Rouge, Louisiana, debate is now underway in the House of Representatives over yet another proposed secession resolution. That's all I know for now."

Mason Howell spoke again. "I do understand that Louisiana, along with Georgia and South Carolina are not finding that there is going to be the same ease of passage for secession resolution as in some of the other states.

"As we speak, African-American state representatives and senators in those three states are figuratively fighting to the death to prevent secession. Word is that they're calling on members of their delegations to the United States House and Senate to do all that they can to influence members of the state legislature. We have been very fixated on what has been happening in Washington and Austin, Texas. In our distraction, we have been missing some of the real drama going on in some of these southern states.

"Prominent African-American leaders and politicians in Louisiana, Georgia and South Carolina are rolling the dice by stating this is the greatest civil rights issue since the Civil War. There are speakers at rallies telling crowds of African-Americans that important elements of freedom for minorities could be lost. There are accusations that states in the proposed CSA may even deny the right to vote to African-Americans. On a couple of occasions, there have been warnings of slavery being reinstituted. That is how far some of this has gone."

Robert Carter responded: "And people are taking that seriously? In 2021?"

Marsha Bentley spoke up: "I think those words are being used in a symbolic sense. Some of us remember the campaign in the fall of 2012 when Vice President Joe Biden was speaking to a crowd that contained a lot of African-Americans, and he made that off-the-cuff inference that Republicans wanted to put them back in chains. I don't think that he meant that literally, but if your family album contains old photos of relatives who were either slaves themselves, or the children of slaves, then the reading of the Emancipation Proclamation is not such ancient history."

Robert Carter interrupted: "Marsha, do you think that there are people living in what may turn out to be CSA states that actually fear the clock being turned back to 1860?"

Mason Howell responded instead: "I believe that a few do. Look back over the last several years at how conservatives have been labeled, and let's face it, these seceding states are governed by conservatives… I can't begin to count the number of times Democratic officeholders and members of the mainstream media pounded African-Americans over the head with statements that conservatives, and or Republicans, simply did not like them, or worse, did indeed want to take them back to the 1950s. There have been constant accusations that conservatives want to suppress minority voting. "

Marsha Bentley looked into the camera. Once again she pressed her earpiece closer to her head. "I am being told we need to cut away for a quick break… stay tuned, because when we return, we are going to have some more important information to give you. This is NewsNet."

"Thank you for staying with us. My name is Marsha Bentley, and I'm joined here in the NewsNet headquarters in New York by my colleagues Robert Carter and Mason Howell. Mason… I get the definite impression that many states made arrangements over the weekend for their legislatures to be in session this morning to see what happened with this vote."

Howell nodded. "That is correct. In fact, local and regional news outlets were making that known to the public in those states once those plans were formulated. So for the residents of the states, they probably have a better sense of what would be happening today, than many of us in the bigger media outlets."

Marsha Bentley took a deep breath and looked down at a sheet of paper in front of her. "These actions are all coming together. We now have word that Kansas, North Dakota… I don't have anyone else right now. But Kansas and North Dakota's legislatures have voted to go. So we are at around a dozen states…". The camera panned the set to include the large electronic map behind the panel that now illuminated a wide swath of Middle America in light green. To the east, West Virginia and Tennessee looked the same.

The camera focus returned to the panel. Mason Howell began to speak. "The…uhm… the Constitutional States of…". Howell's face was suddenly expressing a look of anguish and he began to visibly cry. "…of America…". He regained his composure and spoke once again. "… has formed". He looked down and away as he attempted to force his words. "I'm… I'm going… to miss my country as it used to be."

The camera panned back to once again show the three of them. Marsha Bentley was dabbing at her eyes and cheeks with a tissue. Robert Carter sat in stone – faced silence. Her voice breaking,

Marsha Bentley spoke slowly. "We need to... take a break now. We...we will be back in a few minutes."

As the camera panned backward to the scene of the panelists in front of the large electronic map and the haunting green swath through the heartland, it was evident that someone in the production staff had anticipated the events. As the station went to a break, the usual, fast paced music had been replaced by a slow and quiet instrumental version of America The Beautiful.

Chapter 11

A laptop computer with cable hookup had been brought into the Cabinet Room in the West Wing of the White House. That was where President John Malcolm, Vice President Howard Little, and a handful of cabinet members had viewed the vote in the House, as well as some of the media coverage in the aftermath. Also on hand was General Sidney Adams, Chairman of the Joint Chiefs of Staff who had been called from his office in the Pentagon where he had been trying to catch up on some paperwork.

Like most top officials in the government of the United States of America, General Adams was finding it hard to concentrate. He had faced combat in Vietnam, two failed marriages, while the third had produced a solid relationship, but also a disabled child. He had learned long ago not to take anything for granted, but seeing his nation rendered asunder was a development that was difficult for him to wrap his mind around.

Adams was a native of Montana. As he sat in the elegant office in the seat of power, he felt as if he were a man without a country as he watched the coverage of the unraveling of the nation he had shed blood for as a twenty-four-year-old Lieutenant who caught a bullet in the hip. It was his most sincere hope that he had been asked to attend this virtual wake simply to answer questions of logistics in a post – secession America.

The President finally stood, took hold of the laptop's remote control and pressed the mute button. "My secretary will be in Jim Walters' office watching. She will come and get us if we miss something.

"This is the absolutely, very last time this question can be asked. I am ready to call a press conference for this evening to make my statement. So I have to know… is there anyone in this room…". He glanced at General Adams. "Is there anyone here who believes I should use the military to stop this secession?"

The President looked slowly around the room. The only hand that rose was that of Calista Myers, the Secretary of State. She looked around, and then displayed a meek smile. "Mr. President… I will publicly support whatever decision you make." She hesitated before speaking again. "I would like to hear what the General would have to say."

All eyes turned toward the only person in the meeting dressed in camouflage, a row of stars decorating each shoulder. The President gestured to the soldier. "General…?"

The General simply nodded and looked down, a display of body language that seemed at odds with his typical demeanor. "It would simply not be feasible... I can see no way that we could stop this simply by a show of force. During the Civil War, there were members of the military serving in the United States Army who left their units to serve in the Army of the Confederacy. But just imagine the situation at any modern military base. It would be chaos... there would be violence... I think it would set off a chain of reactions that would quickly go out of control. The idea is horrifyingly unpredictable. I have already received reports of scuffles breaking out at nearly all of our bases. It is true that they may have involved a couple of fellows here and there, but just imagine that scenario magnified in terms of thousands. Base commanders... unit commanders... their loyalty could be unpredictable. Conditions on our bases could grow desperate overnight. It's hard for me to see widescale armed conflict breaking out. But the outcome would be too unpredictable, and altogether too dangerous.

"I see no way in which the American people would have a stomach for such a scenario. If conflict would break out because we failed to intimidate the breakaway states... I see riots... bombings... civil disorder such as we have not seen in America since the Civil War. There are already too many scared people, and scared people do desperate and dangerous things.

"I have been thinking of all the possible scenarios I could... I have been trying to think of everything that could go wrong. In my opinion, much more would go wrong than would go right. We live in a nation in which food is delivered to markets daily. The same with medicine to pharmacies and doctors' offices.

"The chaos and disorder would bring immediate and severe hardships to millions of people. It is such a big gamble, because if the seceding states would not back down simply by threat... the game is over anyway. If they would call our bluff... if it is a bluff, just try governing that, Mr. President... with all due respect, Sir. And if you are not bluffing tens of thousands will die... even under our most conscientious efforts of restraint.

"All the comments here today seem to be assuming that it is simply our choice as to whether to quell the secession. The reality is, we cannot guarantee that things would not get ugly to the disadvantage of the United States.

"What if the center of the country actually became hostile territory? The food supply would become a matter of immediate crisis. In addition, think about how much of everything would have to cross the middle of the country. Just a few hundred people involved in actions of sabotage could paralyze a lot of things.

"Think about where the oil refineries are located. And if we start playing hardball, we may have to send in paratroopers to secure Fort Knox to avoid another currency crisis.

"If actual bloodshed develops, there is a great potential for what I could describe as nothing else than guerrilla warfare and insurrections in states that were not part of the secession. Every state in the CSA will already have pockets of resistance. I hope that our esteemed Mr. Hamilton and Mr. Bridger and their fellow dreamy eyed ideologues have thought of that.

"There will be significant segments of the populations in the cities who will not want to be leaving the United States of America. They may not be very prone to want to enhance stability. On the other hand, I am concerned about the states that have large segments of their population sympathetic to the cause and principles of the secessionists. And let's not kid ourselves. There are several."

The Vice President leaned forward in his chair. "I'm not sure what my status is here right now… my state seceded today. But I share the General's concerns. Look at North Carolina… Kentucky. Most of all, think about Ohio as an example, because that's a state with a big population that is philosophically and politically segmented.

"Look at one of those blue – red electoral maps of Ohio. The voting patterns in the northern rim of the state would fit in well with the East Coast or Southern California. Then you have a sort of purple Columbus and Cincinnati, and a blue Dayton. But much of Ohio is extremely conservative. It is full of people who could have written that bill that got shot down on the House floor today. You have an Appalachian section of the state that sees the same federal hostility to their livelihood as do the residents in coal country in

West Virginia and parts of Pennsylvania. Our party used to own that territory.

"With the exception of the Upper Peninsula of Michigan, I don't see states trying to Balkanize and fragment. But I do see unrest... I do see the potential for endless violence."

The President folded his arms and began to pace the floor while looking down. "I want to thank you... I want to thank you for being here with me this afternoon. General... Vice President Litton... I thank you for your thoughts." He turned toward Secretary Myers. "And I thank you for having the courage to raise your hand. There will be a lot of Americans who will feel that I should have used force... or the threat of force."

The Secretary nodded. "As I said, Mr. President, I will publicly support your decision. Still, I am haunted by knowing that once we have recognized the secession, there is no turning back. We will be forever weakened. At risk of being out of line... General... I would like to know something. If you received an order from the President to use force to halt this secession... would you obey?"

The President held up both hands. "General... you are under no obligation to answer the question."

The Secretary of State shrugged her shoulders. "With all due respect, Mr. President... I think the question is germane. If the use of military force is simply hypothetical...".

The General glared at the Secretary. "Secretary Myers... I don't think at this time I want to answer a hypothetical question. The conditions at this moment may not be the same conditions hours from now. I am trained to deal with situations that change minute by minute. I try to avoid absolutes when it comes to scenarios that could take place in the future."

The Secretary threw up her hands. "Let's move on."

The President scanned the group one more time. "Now, I need to make arrangements to address the nation, most likely tomorrow evening. Each of you will be bombarded with questions from any reporter you encounter. Just tell them that you have not seen the text of my statement, and that I am still finalizing my thoughts. Everybody try getting some sleep tonight. Tomorrow will be an even tougher day."

~~~

At 4:00 PM, Bryce Hamilton was still sipping coffee to shake off the effects of his 5:00 AM Tuesday morning departure from his home in Lincoln Nebraska. He chided himself for having developed a habit of sleeping in during his retirement years. At least, at that time of the morning, the traffic on Interstate 80 was moderate for his drive to Omaha. He would not have had to leave that early for the drive that was less than ninety minutes. However, one luxury he had come to allow himself whenever possible was a leisurely breakfast.

When he reached the Southwest suburbs of Omaha, he saw a McDonald's sign. Bryce Hamilton may have been a United States Senator who was now one of the leaders of a movement to form a new nation within the American heartland, but he had his own interpretation of fine dining.

Anticipating the morning, and wishing to have time to relax and mentally plan his day, he had dressed for the cold morning in his old hunting coat and black and red checked insulated hat. He also donned a pair of thick rimmed, black framed reading glasses before getting out of his car and entering the restaurant.

He knew that many residents of that area would have been paying rapt attention to his appearances on television, so he changed the tone of his voice when ordering, and posed as if he had bad posture and was unable to stand straight. He received his order, grabbed a newspaper and walked to the most remote table.

As he enjoyed his coffee and cholesterol laden meal, he turned at a slight angle to the window to further reduce the chances that he would be recognized. He pulled out his cell phone and activated the navigation program. It told him that he was only twenty minutes away from the American Legion Hall where the executive committee of the Council for a Free America would be holding its hastily arranged meeting.

In light of the developments, the networks and major newspapers and wire services had dispatched correspondents and reporters to Omaha, the tentative capital of the Constitutional States of America. They had received the press release from the Council for a Free America, one that had been drafted after the morning meeting at the meeting hall located in a working-class neighborhood on the north side of the city.

A real estate investor sympathetic to the Council had hastily made an empty office building in downtown Omaha available to them to use as a temporary headquarters. The building had been the main offices of an insurance company that had been bought out by one of his larger competitors. As part of his deal to buy the building, the wealthy investor had negotiated that all furnishings would be left behind in case he wanted to sell or lease it to someone looking for a good startup facility. It also included a small auditorium that had been used for training and staff development. It would also serve as a good place to hold press conferences, such as the one that would be held at 4:00 PM.

~~~

That time was nearing, and as he finished reviewing the prepared statement, Bryce Hamilton peeked from behind a curtain on the stage of the auditorium. The room was already overflowing with reporters and cameras.

He had changed into the clothing that had traveled in the trunk of his car, allowing him to look as distinguished and serious as he had during his other appearances. He glanced up just in time to see a police officer restraining a young man attempting to enter the room without press credentials. Suddenly the screams of "fascist... hater... bigot" could be heard over the din of the gathering press. As the scuffling took place in the back of the room, a dozen video cameras recorded the scene.

Patrick Bridger and Nina Burton stood next to Hamilton as the tall former Senator glanced at his watch one more time, then strolled slowly to the podium on the stage, and adjusted the microphone to match his height. He looked out over the quieting auditorium: "Thank you... I am Bryce Hamilton, Convening Chairman of the Council for a Free America.

"My purpose this afternoon is to address the events of the past several days, and to speak to what is to come during the next several weeks. I come here today with no sense of accomplishment. Instead, I greet you today in a shroud of sadness and disappointment.

"The executive committee of the Council for a Free America met this morning here in Omaha, to decide how our organization would proceed in light of the accelerating process of states passing resolutions of withdrawal from the United States of America. That factor is coupled with yesterday's disappointing vote in the United States House of Representatives on an emergency bill that may well have prevented the withdrawal of most, if not all states pursuing such actions.

"After the vote was taken, the executive committees of state chapters of the Council for a Free America were surveyed, and it was the unanimous conclusion that Congress had collectively decided to give de facto consent to withdrawal, rather than take the necessary actions to put the United States of America back on a course of fiscal responsibility. The House also chose to pass on an opportunity to recognize, and reinforce their dedication to, the individual liberties provided for in the Bill of Rights, and to grant us a recognition of the constraints on federal power required by the 10th Amendment.

"Therefore, it was decided at today's executive committee meeting that it would be in the best interest of the citizens in all fifty states for the formalization process of the Constitutional States of America to be expedited. I wish to remind you, that the Council for a Free America is an organization, and does not have the role of elected officials. However, we will be facilitating the process through which the actions of the involved states form this new union.

"We know that eleven states have passed resolutions stating their intention to withdraw from the United States of America, and several others are seriously considering similar actions. That means that their elected representatives in both houses of Congress are in difficult situations. We do not wish to prolong a situation in which the status, authority and votes of those officials are subject to question.

"In order for the government of the United States to facilitate the adjustments and reorganization required, our organization will be facilitating a meeting in two days here in Omaha. As we speak, and throughout the day tomorrow, the state legislatures of the states of the new CSA will be naming delegates who will meet on Thursday to establish the effective date of the withdrawal of those states, a date that will be simultaneous with the formal establishment of the Constitutional States of America.

"Originally, we had planned for these actions to be taken in a more deliberative manner. However, events and reality have altered the course of events. I will add, one element that has so accelerated the arrival of so many members of state legislatures at the point of being willing to vote for withdrawal, has been a perceived lack of concern for their presence or absence as member states of the United States of America."

Hamilton hesitated for a moment, and then looked over the assembled media. "I probably should not stray from my prepared statement, but I just want to say… I suppose it's easier to leave home, when your birth family feels that your presence is an embarrassment. The leaving may make you feel sad, but when you step outside the door, at least you are free and allowed to make it on your own." He remained silent for another moment, and then slowly looked down at his notes to resume his talk.

"I am unable to give you an effective date for the withdrawal and CSA establishment. I do think that it is safe to assume that these occurrences, as have many others recently, will see rapid progress.

"Once again, I am not in the position to state any effective dates, but from my conversations with state Council coordinators and legislative leaders, those actions could be just days away.

"Thank you for your attendance and your attention." Bryce Hamilton walked slowly off the stage while dozens of unanswered questions were shouted at him.

~~~

Throughout the rest of the afternoon and early evening, there was rampant speculation regarding the President's address to the nation scheduled for 8:00 PM. However, the lead story on every opening news segment was coverage of Bryce Hamilton's address. Still, the first line shown from his speech on each of those news recaps was the spontaneous and unplanned comment: "… I suppose it's easier to leave home when your birth family feels that your presence is an embarrassment. The leaving may make you feel sad, but when you step outside the door, at least you are free and allowed to make it on your own".

More highlights would be shown, and then the coverage would switch to speculation regarding the Presidential address. Analysts and pundits attempted to predict the text, some even wondering if it would contain an announcement of the President's resignation. Much time was spent conjecturing as to what the tone and mood of the address would be.

Pundits attempted to prognosticate as to whether there would be one final plea for reconciliation. Others attempted to move on and to speculate as to who may end up as the head of state of the Constitutional States of America. Suddenly images of potential CSA presidential candidates were being displayed, accompanied by discussion of the merits and disadvantages of each.

NewsNet coverage began to include reports from the network business program hosts, who began to discuss which industries and corporations were likely to be the first to take advantage of the pledges being made for the new union to be the business friendly environment at the core of its founding.

There was extensive conversation as well regarding the reaction of the stock market. Proponents of secession had expected a sudden rise in stock values, while opponents had predicted a market crash. However, analysts were left to try to explain why there had been little movement at all in the stock indexes.

Time needed to be filled before 8:00 PM arrived. Several networks even reviewed the events that led up to the secession of the southern states as a prelude to the outbreak of the Civil War.

~~~

President John Malcolm sat at the desk in the Oval Office as the networks finished readying the cameras, and aides put the last touches on his appearance and the general ambience of the scene. What was missing was the usual Teleprompter.

The President had been very complimentary to Jim Walters and Howard Litton for the draft address they had presented him. However, due to the extraordinary chain of events that seemed to change by the hour, he decided to put his entire staff into a fit of anxiety by announcing that he was going to speak without a Teleprompter, a written text or even notes.

As for himself, he was past the point of anxiety over something as minor as his own image or stature. In the ninth month of his presidency, the United States of America was seeing at least eleven states, and as many as fifteen, leave the union. That would be his legacy in the history books, and in his heart, it would be his failure. All the consoling admonitions to the contrary, John Malcolm felt that he should have thought of something to prevent this, and chastised himself for not rising above all the others in summoning the wisdom of Solomon.

"My fellow citizens, I join you this evening to talk to you about something that I could not have foreseen the day that I announced my candidacy for the Democratic nomination to seek to become the President of the United States.

"As you are all aware, eleven state legislatures have passed resolutions stating their intention to secede. Others have similar actions under consideration as their debates continue regarding their future as part of the United States of America.

"I have attempted to convince the leaders of these states to remain as part of the greatest nation the world has ever known. I did not feel that there are any differences that we could not resolve and be able to continue as a united and strong republic.

"Unfortunately, it appears that the formation of the Constitutional States of America is now inevitable. Further, it appears that the secession of the states, and the establishment of this new republic within our heartland will happen very quickly and soon.

"Only history will judge whether my decision to not use military force to prevent this action was correct. But after all factors were considered, it was decided that to employ force would not have been in the best interests of the American people. I also believe that I have made a decision with which most of you are in agreement.

"After deliberation, it was decided that not only was the use of military force likely to result in an unacceptable number of casualties, but that it was simply not logistically feasible as well. When all was said and done, what held our nation together was, at the bottom line, a common agreement to live in accordance with the Constitution of the United States. When it became the conclusion of so many that our nation was no longer operating under those principles, dissolution became inevitable.

"I do not agree that we had, as a nation, strayed from our Constitution, nor abandoned the principles that bound us together for so many generations. We certainly had disagreements, and some lively, and at times rancorous, discourse. I still do not feel that these differences justify the actions being taken, but we now must accept the reality, and move on in the best interests of all Americans, regardless of which states in which they reside.

"Therefore, I am inviting the executive committee of the Council for a Free America to meet with me tomorrow, here in the Oval Office. We must establish a working relationship, and the sooner we begin that work, the better the outcome for all of us.

"The work ahead of us is tremendous in its scope. We have to establish agreements on defense, movement between our republics, economic issues such as the status of our currency, and how federal assets will be used on an ongoing basis.

"This process is going to be difficult and complex. A successful transition will require the assumption of goodwill between United States of America and the Constitutional States of America. We will have to trust each other, or neither republic can possibly flourish.

"Last of all, as your President, I wish to offer my deepest and most sincere apologies to all Americans, for failing to prevent this tragedy. I pledge to you that I will do my best to work every waking hour to find the best possible outcome for all Americans, in both republics. Thank you."

Mike Silver joined Ben Stirling on yet another special edition of coverage on NewsNet. The scene had just cut away from the Oval Office, and Stirling began the conversation. "I have to say Mike, when that apology came out of his mouth there at the end, I thought it was the beginning of an announced resignation. It certainly would have matched the look on his face."

"I thought the same thing, Ben. But no matter what you think of John Malcolm as a leader, I don't think that any American's heart was not going out to that man tonight. The pain he was feeling was evident, and just on a personal basis, I hope he understands how little of this has been within his control.

"I suppose one can fault him for having turned down that original request by the Council for a Free America for a meeting, but aside from that, I don't see what else he could have done. It is now widely known that he wanted that last chance bill to pass in the House."

Mike Silver nodded in agreement. "Right now, I'm going to predict how an honest examination of his role in history would read. This man was perhaps not fast enough on his feet. He was surrounded by party members and a media that kept telling him what he wanted to hear. Granted, he should have been more skeptical and looked beneath the covers more quickly. But he wanted to save the country, and at the end, he took a stand contrary to many in his party."

Stirling tilted his head and squinted his eyes. "It can also be said that when he was serving as a Senator in his run-up to his presidential candidacy, he was part of the problem. He did not try to curtail spending. He never called out for his Democratic predecessor to take any steps to prevent the very fiscal insolvency that is at the core of the breakup of the country he is now mourning. President Obama got away with it for two terms, and John Malcolm thought he could do the same."

Chapter 12

President John Malcolm, Vice President Howard Litton and Chief of Staff Jim Walters walked solemnly to Walters' office to speak while the cameras and extra personnel were being cleared from the Oval Office.

The shaken trio was awaiting at any moment the arrival of the Attorney General designee, Mitchell Pryor. Of all the Assistant Attorneys General, Pryor was most senior in age at 62, and although he had only been in the Justice Department for four years, he had a long and distinguished career in federal law, and had made appearances in front of the Supreme Court on several occasions.

There was a tap on the door, and a secretary announced that Pryor had arrived. The nervous attorney was ushered in and Walters introduced him to the President and Vice President. The President motioned for all of them to sit down, pointing for Walters to sit in his own chair.

The silence was maintained until the President spoke. "Mister Pryor, I plan to make your appointment public tomorrow, and I will try to accomplish a quick confirmation for you. In the meantime, you will be the acting AG, and I don't need to tell you that, under the circumstances, you will play a pivotal role."

Pryor was seasoned, but this was something altogether new to him. "Mister President... I will do everything I can to help."

"I know you will, and I have task number one ready for you. As soon as possible, I need your take on whether, or how, I can keep our Vice President in office, in spite of the fact that North Dakota yesterday voted to secede."

The attorney nodded. "Yes, sir."

The President folded his hands behind his head and leaned back in the chair and stretched his legs out. "Dear God... I think that was harder than anything I have ever...".

Walters exhaled a loud sigh. "I don't think you had any alternatives. In the minds of anyone with a sense of our history, our soil is still soaked in the blood spilled in the 1860's. I think you said it well, Mister President. There was no feasible way to prevent it by force, and in my opinion, the country never would've survived such a conflict in as good a shape as we will be in once we settle into this new... I don't know what to call it, really."

The Vice President almost murmured: "As the President said... our new reality."

The President leaned forward in his chair. "Now we have to get our heads screwed on straight to be ready to meet with the... I guess we say, delegation."

The new acting AG spoke: "Every state has so many capital assets constructed by or owned by the federal government. Post offices, highways, dams. It's going to be complicated. On one hand, it was federal revenue that paid for the construction of these things. Then there are shared things such as some of the highways. On the other hand, the people living in those states have been paying taxes into the United States Treasury. I hope all of you see where we are heading."

The Vice President spoke next. "Those items would be enough in and of themselves. It's the matter of defense that's making me crazy. Those bases... and I don't know how many National Guard units there must be in those states. Those are a combination of state and federal assets. I don't know if we can pull off a joint military. My guess is that we're going to be entering into some kind of arrangement similar to NATO."

The President grunted loudly. "I agree with you... I also know that means that we will never again be as militarily strong. That brings danger to us. Of all things on the table, that is one that on a mutual basis, we have to get right."

The conversation lasted for nearly two hours, and in spite of the fatigue they were all experiencing at the end of a tumultuous day, they had covered much ground in advance of the upcoming meeting with the Council. As the meeting was breaking up, President Malcolm touched the Vice President on the elbow. "A word, please."

They waited until the others had left, then walked slowly to the Oval Office and closed the door behind them before taking a seat in two of the guest chairs.

The President rubbed his eyes and leaned forward. "Howard… I need some more of that candor of yours. Is this new federation really going to drain jobs away from the states that stay behind?"

The Vice President took a deep breath, closed his eyes and nodded. "I'm almost certain it will. I'm going to give you that candor you asked for… I think that if I owned an industry, I may not move there myself, but I know that if I was going to build a new facility…".

Litton considered his words. "People who would be considering moving jobs overseas will certainly be less reluctant to move them to someplace that is really still part of America. Under those circumstances they would not face the stigma of taking jobs away from Americans. I see this as a devastating threat to the economy of what will be left of the United States.

"Certainly, the states that are staying with us have a lot of industry. The point is, they have a lot of industry now. But if this new… I can hardly stand to say… nation. If this new country takes off and does well out of the gate, then as far as job retention goes, all bets are off."

The President lowered his head before responding in a weak voice. "Not taking that deal that Patty Barrett rattled off...". He leaned back and looked up at the ceiling. "So is Bryce Hamilton right? Three years from now, are we going to be decimating all of our programs anyway? Are we going to be instituting the budget cuts Barrett and her buddies have suggested?"

The Vice President allowed himself a quiet chuckle. "The timing may be in question, but the outcome is not. It's going to be a spiraling downward effect. We won't develop any more jobs on our turf. All the new jobs will develop on theirs, and even if none would move there, our job growth would be stagnant. Of course, some jobs are going to move there.

"Now, we know that if no new jobs are created in our states, then we're going to go backward. It's just part of our system that companies go out of business. Of course, when things are going right they are replaced by new businesses. That won't work for us anymore, because all the new businesses are going to be... somewhere else.

"So, our tax revenue base declines. The next shoe to drop is that our declining revenue base makes it more difficult for us to cope with our debt. Of course, we are already unable to cope with our debt. Our party keeps talking about increasing taxes on people with a lot of money and high incomes."

The President moaned. "And if we increase taxes, those people are going to go where they can keep more of their money."

"Exactly."

"We have no way out, do we?"

"Well, we can make a public statement that our party has been wrong for a lot of years, and that we have to do a 180° turn and embrace the Barrett proposal for the remaining United States of America. Of course, members of Congress of our party will not vote for that as we just saw, and many of the Republican members of Congress will no longer be part of the game."

The President stood and began to pace the floor. "In summary… we're screwed."

The Vice President stood and leaned on the wall to face him. "Mister President, in light of the situation, you'd be forgiven for using a harsher term."

~~~

"This is Mike Silver for NewsNet, and due to breaking news we are dispensing with our normal 8:00 AM morning update. We are receiving word from numerous sources around the Capitol building and the Pentagon, that the hastily arranged meeting between President Malcolm and Vice President Litton with representatives of the Council for a Free America is not going to be held at the White House as was announced late last night.

"The Capitol is abuzz this morning with rumors, none yet substantiated, that this change of venue has been necessitated by a series of bomb threats against the White House and the chambers of Congress, along with several murky, and I emphasize again, unsubstantiated threats of assassination against members of the administration, as well as Bryce Hamilton, Patrick Bridger and other leaders of the Council for a Free America.

"This development has turned into a matter of great embarrassment to the administration, but for the sake of safety in this precarious moment in our nation's history, the White House and the Pentagon decided it was best to err on the side of caution. We are being told by White House staff that a meeting will still take place sometime today between the President and Vice President and secession leaders. However, the location is being kept tightly under wraps, and in this state of confusion that is Washington D.C. this morning, trying to track even the highest level of officials is proving to be problematic.

"These unexpected security issues have overshadowed what is really the most pressing issue of the day, that is the historic meeting itself. This is a very awkward situation for the administration, for as the President said in so many words last night, this meeting is nothing more than a matter of accepting reality. Now the President of the United States of America must sit at a table and, in effect, recognize the organizers of the new nation forming primarily in the nation's heartland.

"Stay tuned to NewsNet as we continue to cover this momentous development. Our analysts and commentators will be providing you with insight throughout the day."

~~~

"This is Marsha Bentley for NewsNet, and as we are now at 2:00 PM Eastern Standard Time, we are just finally getting some information that may allow us to speculate as to where President Malcolm and Vice President Litton are going to be meeting with former Senator Bryce Hamilton and former Congressman Patrick Bridger, two important leaders of the secession movement that appears to have succeeded in a peaceful fashion, at least so far.

"We have been able to confirm that this meeting is not taking place in Washington D.C., and a spokesperson for the Council for a Free America confirms that it is also not taking place in Omaha, Nebraska, the tentative capitol of the new Constitutional States of America.

"While this is hardly an exact science, all of the news outlets have spent the day tracking plane flights, and it has become somewhat reminiscent of the manner in which former Alaska Governor Sarah Palin was introduced by Republican Presidential candidate, Senator John McCain. In the day leading up to the announcement that Palin was going to be the running mate, flight records were examined in regard to all the assumed finalists for that position. When a flight was tracked from Alaska to Middletown,

Ohio, near the site of the announcement event at Dayton, that was the first confirmation that Palin had been selected.

"What we do know right now, is that while Air Force One and Air Force Two are still on the ground, a military flight from Dover Air Force Base has been traced to a landing at an Air National Guard Base at Columbus, Ohio. In addition, a Nebraska National Guard transport plane has also reportedly landed there.

"Now we have been told that the FAA and the Pentagon have restricted flights in regions of central Ohio, and Ohio Air National Guard fighters are now conducting extra patrols in the airspace over that part of the state.

"Of course, Ohio is not a state involved in the secession movement and is likely viewed as a neutral territory. Still there are... please hold for a moment, because I am getting some news in my headphone...".

The reporter leaned slightly to look at the monitor screen that was built into the desk. "Okay... here we are. A reporter from the Columbus Dispatch is on the scene at Urbana University, a small liberal arts college about an hour from Columbus, and he reports two landings of Ohio Air National Guard helicopters on the university grounds. Further, he reports that a large number of Ohio State Highway Patrol troopers have cordoned off a wide area around the university's student union building, and that there are a lot of men appearing to be Secret Service personnel patrolling the immediate outside of the building.

"This same reporter says that a member of the administration who spoke with him under the condition of anonymity, confirmed that the head of President Malcolm's security detail is a graduate of that university, and hastily made arrangements for this meeting to be held at a place outside the typical beat for the national media, and a place easily defended if the worst would happen.

"Okay… my earphone is again… Okay… Assistant White House Press Secretary Helen Browning has just confirmed the meeting is taking place at the small town of Urbana, Ohio, and although she will give no more specific information, she does confirm the meeting is taking place somewhere on the campus of Urbana University. Please stay with us as we take a break, as we continue to provide you with more information on this meeting. This is Marsha Bentley for NewsNet, and we will be back in a moment. Stay tuned."

~~~

Two Secret Service agents guarded the door to the meeting room in the student union building. The senior agent glanced over his shoulder and nodded to his younger companion. "Ever see that photograph from the end of the Civil War… the one of Grant and Lee sitting under that tree at Appomattox Courthouse? That's what this puts me in mind of. But this time the country did break apart. At least we didn't lose several hundred thousand people this time."

The younger agent shook his head. It was a surreal experience to look through the window in the door to see the President, Vice President and acting Attorney General of the United States of America sitting in negotiations with the men who had orchestrated the secession of the center of the country.

President John Malcolm paced the floor continuously throughout the meeting. Howard Litton felt concern over the demeanor of the President, having never before seen him exhibit some of the mannerisms and stuttering on display during this meeting. As he watched the President in action, he reminded himself that no President since Abraham Lincoln had faced the nation's dissolution. But the mannerisms and the speech problems were of concern to him, and he had spent as much time with John Malcolm over the last twenty years as anyone in the President's family. He knew the man's history, and he felt a cold chill.

John Malcolm halted to collect his thoughts. "Gentlemen, while this may appear to be a minor detail, I do want to insist that the pool photograph of this meeting will show us all at this table in a pose of discussion. I do not think it would be in any of our best interests to pose standing together as if we were having some type of summit meeting."

Bryce Hamilton responded: "I agree, Mr. President. I have no desire for you to be subjected to any more criticism or punditry than will already be the case. I think that the simple photo showing us at work to resolve issues, coupled with some reserved statements and press releases will help to get us all past this first, difficult step."

Patrick Bridger spoke next. "President Malcolm, I agree with you that the matter of defense, and defense installations and assets will be our most difficult matter to resolve. What do you think about the Speaker's proposal that we establish a joint commission to work out the details?"

Vice President Litton responded instead. "The President and I are very open to the suggestion. But please keep in mind gentlemen, the establishment of this new republic is going to take place very much in advance of such an agreement.

"People say that we can just be like NATO. That concept may be fine, but just consider, say… Lackland Air Force Base in San Antonio, for example. Personnel at that base come from all over the place. So the base is in a seceding state…". Litton turned to look at Hamilton and Bridger. "Pardon me, gentlemen… a withdrawing state. We are going to have a mess at every installation. Do we say that if you willingly enlisted when you were a resident of Illinois, that you are still held to your enlistment agreement, and do we tell an Airman from Montana that he is not?

"Do we jointly fund the bases, and for that matter do we jointly fund a mutual defense system? I understand that is not going to be immediately acceptable to the CSA. Are we going to just contract for installations on a state-by-state basis, and go on from there?"

Bryce Hamilton answered. "Probably the latter. After all, there are Air Force bases in many different places, as is the case with the Army. It means that the United States would retain most naval and Marine bases, but geographically, I see that as logical. Beyond that, I think that is simply a matter of playing the cards we have been dealt."

Present Malcolm turned angrily and slammed his hand against the wall. "Senator... I don't want to hear about cards having been dealt. Your organization consciously and purposely spearheaded the movement that has brought us to this point. So don't act like these matters are some damned surprises that are blindsiding you."

Bryce Hamilton stood and pointed his finger at the President. "And that movement that you refer to so derisively, was caused largely by the failure of both political parties, but in particular your party to address urgent issues and your resistance to everything President Trump tried to accomplish. And, Mister President, with all due respect, in your first months in office you did nothing to give us any hope and confidence that our actions would not be necessary."

Outside the room, the two Secret Service agents who had heard the hand slam the wall, were peering in with their guns drawn.

Vice President Litton reached out and gently took hold of the President's arm. "Mister President... please sit down. You're going to wear yourself...". Before the Vice President could finish, the President picked up one of the cushioned armchairs and dashed it against the wall, breaking it into pieces. The Vice President signaled to the concerned agents just outside the door that they were not needed.

The room was silent for a moment. Finally, President Malcolm looked down, took a deep breath, and muttered to the group, 'I did not mean to lose... I... I'm sorry." He looked up and scanned the faces of the stunned participants in that meeting. "Perhaps we can agree to assure the public that the Armed Forces of the United States of America will, as always, protect the American people." He looked toward Bryce Hamilton. "Senator... I would propose that we ask the Chairman of the Joint Chiefs of Staff to explore ways in which the apparatus of the various National Guard organizations in... your states... and ours...could coordinate the future of such bases."

Bryce Hamilton nodded and sat down. "Mister President... an excellent suggestion. If you make a public announcement regarding that idea, please be assured I will strongly endorse the wisdom of it. And... Mister President... I know that we have several more topics to cover, but I do wish to say… not for a moment do I want you to think that I don't appreciate the extraordinary situation in which you have been placed. Only Lincoln, and perhaps Franklin Roosevelt on the day of Pearl Harbor, has ever faced such a crisis."

~~~

"Welcome back to NewsNet for our ongoing coverage of the historic meeting held today. I'm Charles Bryant, and right now we are going to one of our NewsNet correspondents, Mitch Collins, who is now at the small central Ohio town of Urbana, where a historic meeting has just ended between President John Malcolm, Vice President Howard Litton, along with acting Attorney General Mitchell Pryor, and two leaders of the secessionist movement, former Nebraska Senator Bryce Hamilton and former Montana Congressman Patrick Bridger. I understand that we now have Mitch Collins live at the scene. Hello, Mitch."

The scene shifted to the brick building at the small college that was now the focus of the nation's attention, and a tall young blond man moved into the scene holding a microphone. "Thank you Charles… as the camera scans the scene, you can see that I'm standing several hundred yards from the student union building at the local college, Urbana University. That is where, during a two-hour meeting, the leadership of the United States of America and organizational representatives in effect representing what will soon be established as the Constitutional States of America identified issues of the most pressing concern to both sides.

"As of this moment we do not have formal statements or anyone ready to come to the microphone, but a White House spokesperson, Michelle Flannery, who was quickly dispatched here to central Ohio, spoke with some of us in the media just a couple of minutes ago. Everyone is flying by the seat of their pants right now, so we are in the position of paraphrasing a lot of unofficial comments, including some from sources who are asking to not be identified. However, due to the nature of some of the information we're receiving, one may suspect that these leaks we are getting are actually planned and purposeful.

"So here's what we have so far: the meeting is being described as businesslike but candid. By the way, some of us are interpreting the word 'candid' to imply that some emotions may have been on display here today.

"Topics covered included a possible effective date for the secession and concurrent establishment of the Constitutional States of America. We do know that as early as tomorrow, there will be an assembly of delegates from the seceding states to determine the date of birth of that new union. And Charles... I would like to take a moment to update our viewers on the list of seceding states, as it has changed even today. By the way, this roster was presented to me less than thirty minutes ago by a Lincoln, Nebraska attorney named Nina

Burton. She is serving as the official documentarian for the Council for a Free America, and is reportedly a member of the same law firm in which Bryce Hamilton still has a limited role. Once again, here is a list just provided to me a little while ago by Nina Burton, and includes states whose legislatures voted today to join the CSA: South Carolina, Texas, Arkansas, Idaho, Nebraska, Kansas, North Dakota, South Dakota, Montana, Wyoming, Texas, Alabama, Alaska, West Virginia and Oklahoma so now we are up to let's see… fifteen states. Ms. Burton informed us that earlier today, resolutions for secession failed to pass in the Mississippi, Georgia, North Carolina, and Utah state legislatures. So we may be at the final roster now, with this one interesting possibility hanging out there: officials from several counties in Michigan's Upper Peninsula arrived in the Michigan capital of Lansing this afternoon to deliver petitions to the governor's office, asking for a special election to be held exclusively for residents of that portion of the state to determine the public sentiment for forming a separate state to be named Superior, and that the state of Superior join the Constitutional States of America.

"So now, Charles, it appears that the Malcolm Administration today granted what is, in effect, recognition of the CSA as a newly established, sovereign nation within the American heartland. And today, topics included discussion on what basic functions can be shared between what will now be two nations, such as defense, postal services, trade and the passage of citizens across the borders.

"Consider this, Charles. To fly from, say Boston to Los Angeles, one will likely be flying through what will now be the airspace of another nation. It is not expected for there to be any restrictions at all, and all speculation indicates that Americans collectively will be able to drive anywhere they want free of any types of checkpoints. Just imagine the first time you drive across the border from Texas to New Mexico and see a sign proclaiming a welcome to the United States of America.

"It is being strongly hinted at that secessionist leaders forced Administration officials to accept that there will not be a common currency. Of course, one of the core issues that led to where we are today is what secessionist leaders have repeatedly referred to as a failure of financial stewardship on behalf of the United States that has provided us with a Dollar of wavering value. Secessionist movement leaders have made it well-known in public comments that they want no part of the currency valuation of the United States of America, and that point was reportedly driven home once again today here in Urbana. And Charles, for millions of Americans in both the USA and the CSA, that is going to prove to be a real inconvenience.

"Americans and Canadians have long dealt with a currency exchange situation, but when you soon have all of these states with a separate currency that will be flowing back and forth across borders in staggering amounts on a daily basis, this is going to be a real challenge for the banking systems in both nations. I would expect that the currency will be in the same denominations, as is the case with Canadian currency. But this volume is going to be a challenge.

"Of course, the most vexing problem that had to be addressed today was that of defense. The ownership and operation of existing military bases is a complex matter under such circumstances. Preliminary reports tell us that a major breakthrough was accomplished when President Malcolm directed that National Guard officials in the Pentagon encourage state National Guard administrations to work together, under the general supervision of the Pentagon officials. There will have to be some kind of financial sharing agreement worked out for matters of common defense. It is likely there will be some kind of mutual defense pact to be activated in the case of threats to any portion of the fifty states. One point emphasized over all others today in matters of defense, was that, in the interim, the military of the United States of America will be assumed to be the point of the spear, if you will, in the event of any threats. There is also speculation that residents of the CSA states will be eligible to serve voluntarily in the Armed Forces of the United States of America. As for the CSA, I think we are heading for a temporary military force composed of what are now National Guard units, some naval units in CSA states along the Gulf Coast, with some issues regarding Army and Air Force bases that will have to be dealt with expeditiously."

Charles Bryant's voice was heard next. "Mitch, have you heard any more today about a rumored exodus of officials from the

Malcolm Administration in light of all the developments over the past several days?"

The reporter shook his head and sighed. "Well, Charles, most of the media has staff trying to chase that story down. We do know that Julia Stafford resigned suddenly as Attorney General, so the acting AG, Mitchell Pryor, was in attendance at today's meeting. But there are issues developing rapidly, most urgently being the status of Vice President Howard Litton. He was elected from a state that will soon no longer be part of the United States. We understand that acting AG Pryor is researching the matter, but it is likely to end up in front of the Supreme Court in some expedited fashion. Of course, there are two members of the Court from what will soon be the CSA, but they are now legal residents of Virginia, and it is not expected that there will be any problem with them.

"However, there are some rumored situations that are providing for some palace intrigue, for we are receiving little side comments and vague hints that there are several Cabinet members considering resigning as a group over dissatisfaction with the President's overall handling of this secession crisis. There are three cabinet members from seceding states who are said to be embarrassed, and others who feel that President Malcolm should have been more forceful in trying to make the Council for a Free America back down, although they are publicly backing the President.

"Of course, all these cabinet members are members of the President's own party, while other members of the Democratic Party have been vocal in wanting to let those states go, buying into what is being referred to now as the 'good riddance' point of view. And even within a mainstream media acknowledged by nearly everyone now to be as favorable to President Malcolm and to his Democratic predecessor Barack Obama, as they were hostile to Donald Trump, there is a divide between those who look forward to a more liberal and progressive United States, and those who wanted President Malcolm to give the secession movement a public thrashing, if not pursue charges of treason and sedition.

"But we all know now that resisting secession is now water under the bridge. It was the consensus of the President, Vice President, and the Chairman of the Joint Chiefs of Staff that use of military force to prevent the secession was unworkable, and that without the threat of force, bombast and the beating of chests would have been an exercise in futility resulting in a show of weakness. So now we... I see now that two limousines have pulled up in front of the student union building, and a contingent of men and women who appear to be Secret Service personnel are providing a protective corridor to those waiting limousines. And as I speak, there are now helicopters hovering above the campus here at Urbana University in central Ohio... two fighters are protectively circling low...I can now see that people are being ushered from the student union building to the limousines, and while I cannot see who they are, I'm assuming they are the people who made history here today.

"Now the limousines are driving away, and it now appears that two helicopters are landing on what from a distance appears to be the football field. So, Charles, it appears that the die has been cast. We may all find out by midnight tomorrow night, when we will be referring to the thirty-four states of the United States of America."

The camera went out of focus and viewers were once again looking at Charles Bryant in the New York studios of NewsNet. "Thank you, Mitch, and now we're going to take a quick break, and when we come back we will be speaking to three NewsNet analysts who will try to read the tea leaves for the rest of us. Stay tuned to NewsNet for the latest information on the formation of the Constitutional States of America. And we will be right back."

~~~

Neither Bryce Hamilton nor Patrick Bridger were able to sleep on their flight back to Lincoln, Nebraska. They had flown from their meeting at the university back to the Air Force Base at Columbus by helicopter, then got back into the Nebraska Air National Guard plane to take them back to their original point of departure from the Guard installation located at the Lincoln Municipal Airport.

They were the only passengers in the troop transport plane, but Patrick Bridger looked around for any crew members before speaking. "Bryce… I know we are going to land in a few minutes, but there's something I want to mention to you. When you and I were being led to the limousine after the meeting, did you notice the man in the dark gray suit who was taken into the room?"

Bryce nodded. "I think I remember… tall guy with black hair… about fifty?"

"Yes, he is the one I'm referring to. Well, when we arrived at the student union, I nearly bumped into him in the hallway, and I could not help but notice his lapel pin. He's a doctor. I think he must be the President's physician. He would have been along for the ride today."

Hamilton hesitated before speaking. "You know… I've been thinking about it ever since we lifted off from the football field. He's breaking." He began to drum his fingers on the arm of his seat. "He's an okay fellow. I hate to see him like he was today. I did have a couple of unhappy exchanges with him when we were in the Senate together. He's known for having a hot temper with his adversaries. At the same time, the word is that he's a teddy bear with his own people, with a few exceptions. Still, what I wouldn't give to have photos of the expressions on everyone's faces today when he smashed the chair against the wall. If one of us had done that, one of those Secret Service agents would've dropped us."

Bridger began to rub his tired eyes. "As much as I disagree with that man, we all need for him to hold himself together."

Hamilton argued with himself for a minute. "It's alcohol."

"How bad?"

"He binges for a while, and then he goes off the wagon. He and I were never close when we were in the Senate, and in fact, people tell me that when my name comes up in his company, he never mentions we served together. We certainly were not friends, and when we did come into contact, we always ended up arguing. But if you ask him about me... he doesn't remember me except as a face passing by in the Senate chamber.

"But that may not at all be an act. I swear, there were a couple of times when he and I could not avoid speaking to each other over committee business, and then he was unable to recall conversations we had had two weeks earlier."

Bridger shook his head and whistled. "Blackouts?"

"That was always my suspicion. And then, when he got the nomination and pulled away in the polls, it became my worst fear. John always had a knack for being a closet drunk. Everybody covered for him... the party... his staff... hell, even his wife helped him with his cover story, claiming he had digestive problems. That was why we were always told he missed early-morning meetings now and then... digestive problems. But then, he could turn it off for a long time. In fact, I heard that through his whole campaign, the only time he drank was at functions, and then he would nurse one drink along for the whole evening."

"So when does he fall off?"

"When he's under a lot of stress."

Bridger leaned back and shook his head. "God help us. So is that what we were seeing today? He was needing a drink?"

This time it was Hamilton who looked around before continuing. "That's not all. That would be bad enough but it's not all. Right after he won that narrow re-election to his Senate seat, he was all unglued because he was afraid that his win was going to appear so unconvincing, it was going to hurt his chance to win the early primaries and get the Presidential nomination.

"But he was so adept at parroting the liberal party line, the media got behind him in such lockstep fashion, that there was no way he was going to lose the nomination to a moderate. He kissed every union ass that wasn't sitting on something, and any Democrat who dared speak of fiscal restraint was gone by the third primary."

Hamilton turned to face his companion. "Pat… I remember the day I realized no one was going to stop John Malcolm from becoming President. That was when I knew it was all over."

Chapter 13

As the plane began to descend for its landing, Bridger looked at his watch and moaned. Just as the wheels touched down, he glanced down at his briefcase. "I just remembered, right before we took off from Columbus, I got a text from my brother in Sioux Falls. He was going to forward to me a segment from America Alive from early this afternoon. I never had a chance to get my phone or laptop out and see if it got here."

Hamilton began to laugh as the plane completed its bumpy slowdown on the landing strip usually reserved for use by the local refueling unit of the Air National Guard. "I thought you and your brother only watched NewsNet."

The men began to unbuckle their seatbelts and gather their belongings. "Larry likes to see what the other side is saying. They get pretty honest when they think no one is listening who doesn't agree with them."

Hamilton stopped their progression to the exit. "You know, Pat, the same is true of our side." The two men walked on to the narrow door where a mobile set of steps was being rolled up to meet them. They thanked the crew and shook their hands as they departed, then went down the steps in the chilly darkness.

Bridger laughed as he walked toward where Hamilton's car was parked nearby. "What you say is true Bryce, but it's so much fun to watch them when they're preaching to their own choir. I think that while you're driving, I'm going to see if I have that program so we can play it on the way back to my hotel."

Hamilton opened the trunk of his car, and they put their luggage inside. "Once again Pat, you're more than welcome to stay with me and Cynthia tonight."

"Thanks, but I left some stuff at the hotel. Sorry for all the extra driving."

They got inside the car, and Hamilton shook his head. "I don't mind at all. At least I hope I can listen to that mysterious interview you want to play."

Bridger laughed. "I don't think that it's so mysterious. It just may be entertaining. Tom Edelstein versus Victor Hightower."

Hamilton began to laugh as he began to slowly drive the large car toward the exit road that led to the state highway, then onto Interstate 80. Bridger opened his briefcase and pulled out the thin computer. Hamilton looked over and laughed. "You must be rather savvy with that stuff."

"Actually, I may have to call my brother if I can't figure this download out. Wait... there it is."

It was difficult for Hamilton to fight the urge to watch as the sound of the news program recorded earlier that day came to life. "And now I am joined by California Congressman Victor Hightower, and Tom Edelstein, a member of the executive committee of the Council for a Free America. Gentlemen, welcome to both of you."

The host was Timothy Powell, a former staff member for one of the more liberal and influential members of Congress from the state of New York. Tom Edelstein was the first member of the Council for a Free America he was able to secure as a guest for his program.

"Congressman Hightower, I want to start with you in light of some of the comments you made late yesterday afternoon on the floor of the House of Representatives. You suggested that while President Malcolm did the correct and humane thing by ruling out the use of force to prevent states from seceding, the seceding states should not be so easily left off the hook. Would you like to explain?"

"Thank you, Tim. You are right, I do support the President's choice to not send the military might of the United States to crush a handful of National Guard units and clusters of militia members who fancy themselves ready to engage in some warped visions of re-creating Lexington and Concorde. All they would need would be some Tea Party member riding a horse through the streets of Boise, Idaho screaming, 'The liberals are coming'.

"But in all seriousness, Tim, we have to remember that these states are going to inherit a lot of infrastructure that was paid for by the United States of America. This action is going be very detrimental to the United States, and since their leaders are claiming that their brilliant, low tax and business friendly policies are going to make all of them rich, I think that this CSA should pay damages to the United States Treasury, and if they refuse to do so, the United States government should impose a trade embargo."

The host turned to his other guest. "Mister Edelstein, how do you respond?"

"Thank you, Tim. First of all, let me say that I do share the Congressman's sentiment that the President did the right thing in forgoing the use of force. As for his interesting point of view regarding the outcome of such a hypothetical conflict, that fortunately will never now take place, I would just point out that what would have been unleashed was a chaotic and dangerous situation with an unknown outcome. I would certainly not feel comfortable making any assumptions as to in which direction any military units or commanders would have pointed their weapons. But fortunately, once again, that has been avoided.

"As for the concept of the Constitutional States of America paying damages for leaving the union, I will remind the Congressman that discussions are already underway regarding such matters of what I will call inherited infrastructure. I think that when all is said and done, fairness will be the theme of the day."

The host turned back to the California Congressman. "Congressman, do you share the fears of some that this new union will drain jobs away from the United States?"

"I am certain that corporations will want to go there so that they can operate without any Labor Department oversight. I think they are also seeing dancing visions of low wages and an absence of safety regulations in their dreams. And by the time a generation has gone by with unrestrained oil and natural gas pillaging with all their fracking and shale shenanigans, the Plains States are going to look like some post-apocalyptic wasteland from a science fiction movie."

The host turned once again back to Tom Edelstein. "Any reply?"

"Our new union is going to offer all Americans the prospect of living in greater economic and individual freedom. People who want to live somewhere where they can keep more of the money they earn during a hard day of work, or harbor dreams of starting their own business without government interfering with their ambitions at every step, are going to find a home there.

"What is going to happen is that job opportunities will be seen in unprecedented abundance. I think we are going to see businesses and corporations competing for employees who have a history of a solid work ethic. I don't think that low wages will be an issue, and I think that employers who do not give a high priority to the safety and best interest of their employees will lose those employees to employers who do."

The host motioned for him to continue. "And what about the Congressman's concerns about environmental issues?"

"Any student of American history knows that in our past there were many instances of egregious disregard for the environment, and that health issues related to such things as pollution were not correctly addressed. Those things should never have happened. I don't think any of us would disagree about that."

The Congressman replied angrily. "And you and your people want to go back to the days when industries polluted the rivers and filled the air with toxins. After all, you're bragging about how you're going to be free of all this governmental oversight. What's to stop you from doing the same thing?"

Tom Edelstein shook his head. "This is a new day. Can you imagine what would happen in this day of picture phones and camcorders if an industry started pouring pollutants into the river, or too much black smoke rose from a factory? And one more thing if I may... I think that we learn from experience. I think that we are past those bad practices from generations ago."

The Congressman shot back. "You talk about learning from the past. Then you talk about these problems having taken place a long time ago. The corporations who will be operating in this new...

whatever… they have only been in operation since reasonable federal controls have been in place. They don't relate to those old times. In other words, they'll have a minimal history to learn from."

This time it was Tom Edelstein who did not wait for the moderator to interject. "Congressman, with all due respect, I don't know how anyone with your individual voting record, or the policy history of your party over the last forty years, can say that you have learned from history, unless you are attempting to purposefully bring down our economy. It is either that, or you suffer from an abominable lack of understanding of basic economics."

The host began to wave his hands. "I'm afraid we have to stop it right there, but gentlemen, I thank you for a lively debate. In a little while we will be…".

Bridger turned the computer off, and Hamilton drove in silence for a moment before commenting. "That young man has proven himself. I think we have someone to oversee the economy."

Bridger began to chuckle. "I think we should aim higher with that young fellow." He turned to Hamilton with a wide grin. "Of course, we are nothing but a movement of old white fundamentalist Christian guys." Both began to laugh. "But Bryce… I think he would make a hell of a vice president."

Bridger's phone began to buzz, indicating that he was receiving a text message. He read the short message on the screen, and then turned to Hamilton with a satisfied smile.

"We got the Scott Conference Center on Pine Street. We are on for tomorrow evening at 8:00 PM. That should be convenient for everybody in the Eastern, Central and Mountain Time zones. Word is going out to all the media right now."

Bryce Hamilton glanced at the man who was helping him to change the world, for better or for worse. "Do you think that most of us are on board for an interim leadership? We're going to need a few months of lead time to get set up for elections."

Bridger nodded. "I think everyone understands… Mister President."

"I never signed on for anything like that."

Bridger laughed. "Now Bryce, I want you to remember John Malcolm's comments about accepting reality. Please… just get us on the right track. You don't have to run when election time comes around. I don't think there will be any shortage of good people waiting in the wings."

Hamilton looked at the former Congressman, shaking his head and laughing. "Pat… I know we haven't known each other for very long, but I feel confident in saying… and with all due respect… you are a horse's ass."

~~~

The next morning at 9:00 AM, Marsha Bentley stood in the cool drizzling rain outside the Scott Conference Center in Omaha.

"This evening, the building behind me will be the site of the focus of America. Tonight, delegates from all of the states planning to secede from the United States of America will be gathering here in this building on the campus of the University of Nebraska, Omaha.

"It is expected that these delegates will pass a resolution establishing the effective date of their withdrawal from the United States. That same date will then serve as the establishment of the Constitutional States of America.

"Our NewsNet staff is working to secure interviews with some of the delegates, but in the midst of reports of death threats against them, most of the delegates are being kept in seclusion for their own safety. For security reasons, we will not ask the camera crews to scan the tops of the surrounding buildings, but there are police snipers on rooftops, and we're being told that they are local and state police. We are trying to confirm reports that federal authorities have taken a hands-off approach to this entire event.

"There are reports that demonstrators opposed to the breakup of the United States are gathering in three nearby municipal parks here in Omaha. In any case, due to threats that have already been received, and the gravity of the business to be held here at the Center this evening, it is expected that police will only be allowing into the building those who are verified to be delegates, and a limited number of media representatives.

"Omaha police are watching those gatherings closely, as there have been Twitter messages hinting at the possible use of Molotov cocktails by the demonstrators, and police are tracking down a rumor that a member of an underground leftist organization based in Chicago is intending to attempt to assassinate Bryce Hamilton. The last word we received was that Chicago police have been unable to locate that individual.

"Some people claiming to represent the demonstrators appeared at the City Hall here in Omaha as soon as the doors opened just one hour ago to apply for a parade permit. That was denied, but still the city has not ordered police to take any actions against the assembling crowds, as the parks are public property. However, one police Captain I spoke to on the condition of anonymity, says that once the demonstrators begin to impede traffic, they will be cleared away."

"Marsha… this is Mike Silver back in New York. I was wondering if you are getting much information on the delegates themselves."

The reporter nodded toward the camera. "Mike, all through the night names of delegates had been filtering in to us here at our temporary media headquarters at the Crowne Plaza. They are indeed, an interesting mix. For example, one of the delegates from Tennessee is the former owner of a business that sold healthcare devices. He claims, ironically, that his company went under as a result of provisions in what is commonly called Obamacare. His name is Harlan Mallory, and Mister Mallory says that not only was his business disadvantaged by new taxes on medical devices, but he could not afford the health care mandates for his employees.

"By the way, I know there has been a lot of talk about the issue of race in this secession movement, but Mister Mallory is a black man, one of two black delegates to be here this evening. The other is a Mister Walter Smathers, one of the two West Virginia delegates. Mister Smathers was a union steward in one of the coal mines shut down six months ago due to pressure by the federal government, and Mister Smathers is one of many contending that the federal government did away with many mining jobs in that state to appease environmentalists.

"Of course, many of the delegates have backgrounds that you would expect. There are lieutenant governors and other state officeholders, as well as businessmen and women and everyday citizens who became prominent within their state committees examining the issue of secession."

"Marsha... this is Mike Silver again, and I'm afraid we're going to cut away to Gwen Munro, who is in Austin, Texas with some breaking news. Gwen... Gwen... this is Mike Silver in New York... can you hear me?"

Suddenly the scene was one of the reporter crouched down behind a hedge, while in the background was the Texas Capitol building. Also in the background, viewers could see a haze of smoke and people running around. "Mike… this is Gwen. I have taken cover because a few minutes ago I heard what I thought was gunfire… about twenty minutes ago I was near the front steps of the building interviewing a Texas State Senator to get his thoughts on the upcoming meeting this evening in Omaha, when all of a sudden I heard a loudspeaker telling us to take cover.

"As you can see in the distance, there is smoke hanging low to the ground, and that may mainly be teargas, but I have also heard some explosions, and a couple seem to have been very close.

"For the last fifteen minutes, I have seen several police helicopters overhead, and in the distance I can hear more loudspeakers, though I have been unable to make out what they are saying. In fact I have been unable to find out… Mike… can you hear that?"

"Gwen… were those gunshots?"

"Mike… I'm sure those were gunshots, and now more sirens are getting closer and…". Suddenly, the correspondent was interrupted by the sounds of two loud blasts. "Mike… if the camera can… pan up a little… I can see smoke… and now flames at the front of the Capitol building. I would imagine that the Austin police are wishing those National Guard troops were still here.

"Mike… there are some vans going past me right now, and they appear to be from the Texas Rangers. Mike… now I hear some chanting and shouting in the distance. Now, about half a block away... I can see three streets filling up with demonstrators, heading this way.

"Mike... it looks like those Texas Rangers are going to be putting up barricades and yellow tape around the Capitol building, I suppose as more of a symbolic line to be drawn against the demonstrators, but some damage has already been done, and now fire trucks are pulling up in front of the building, and there are still some flames visible and smoke pouring into the air from the building's entrance.

"Mike... I have just been handed a note... I now understand that someone was able to get close enough to throw some type of explosive at the front of the building... two Texas Rangers who were standing guard in front of the building, were gunned down. Apparently those were the shots we heard just a while ago. And Mike... I hope you're getting a good view of this... three busloads of police in riot gear went past me a moment ago and they seem to be heading to the Capitol building to join the other officers who are already on duty, and the contingent of Texas Rangers."

"Gwen... this is Mike once again... I am being told in my earpiece that a reporter for one of the Austin television stations witnessed a bus full of Austin police officers coming under fire from someone in a crowd of demonstrators."

The scene was once again of the reporter two hundred yards from the front of the Capitol building, now standing, but clad in a protective vest. "Mike... all that I can see is that the police departing those buses seem to be in a hurry to deploy themselves around the grounds here. Ralph... if you can catch the scene behind us now... there are now demonstrators approaching the Capitol grounds from three different directions... now they are breaking into a run as they approach... Mike, the ones in front... they are carrying... something. We are going to take cover."

The scene was once again of Mike Silver in the NewsNet headquarters in New York. "We will try to get back to Gwen Monroe in Austin, just as soon as we know that she and our crew there are safe. Okay... I am now joined by NewsNet contributor Mason Howell of the Washington Times. Mason... there is trouble in Austin and reports of large groups of demonstrators gathering in Omaha, and of course, Omaha is where delegates of more than a dozen states are meeting this evening. First of all, is this evening's vote a foregone conclusion?"

"Unfortunately... I believe it is. They are not going there to debate any longer. My sense is that, possibly within days, the United States of America we have known for decades, will be drastically altered in its composition."

"And what about the immediate situation with the demonstrators. Can they be a factor at all in the outcome of this vote?"

"All that this behavior is going to do is harden the resolve of the delegates. I can only assume that, to most of the delegates, the demonstrators are symbolic of many the reasons they want to secede in the first place. Things have been happening so quickly this morning, that I didn't have a chance to share this with you yet. But right before I came on the air, a press release was issued by a group called the Coalition To Preserve American Rights. They are taking responsibility for the protest this morning in Austin and the one that appears to be building in Omaha.

"This apparently newly – formed organization claims to represent those who do not wish to leave the United States of America. They further claim to speak for various minority rights groups, women's groups, environmental organizations, the pro-choice movement and organized labor. It is impossible to determine at this point just how many different groups and organizations have granted this Coalition the authority to speak for them, but reports are that they are managing to assemble massive, and I emphasize the word massive, crowds to protest today and try to shut down this secession movement. It appears that they have selected Omaha, naturally, as a target because of the location of tonight's meeting, but also Austin, Texas as a symbol of all the state capitals.

"Also, before I came on the air to join you, a report came in from an anonymous police source in Austin, to the effect that police there had received a tip regarding a virtual bomb – making lab near the campus of the University of Texas. Earlier this morning, police raided that house, and they found the lab in the basement. The troubling part of the report is that it appeared that the basement had indeed been used to make bombs and Molotov cocktails.

"All that the police found however, were the leftovers from such activities, and now there is concern that there are more bombs and Molotov cocktails in the hands of the demonstrators in addition to those that went off at the front of the Texas Capitol building this morning.

"We are still awaiting information on just who lived at that residence, but our source also reports that in the same basement were several empty rifle cases, and empty boxes of handgun ammunition. Further…".

"Mason… this is Mike… I have to interrupt you to go back to Gwen Munro at the Texas Capitol building … Gwen… go ahead."

Viewers were suddenly greeted with a long – distance view of large crowds of demonstrators rushing through the perimeters around the Capitol building. "Mike… this is Gwen… I'm going to ask the crew to train the drone-mounted camera on this unbelievable scene outside the Capitol building here in Austin. About five minutes ago, this crowd of… I don't know, perhaps a few thousand demonstrators altogether, converged on the Capitol grounds, and when police used loudspeakers to tell them to halt, they simply rushed the police. I am staying down, because some of the demonstrators have actually taken up positions as snipers around the area.

"Two of the buses that brought police to the scene earlier this morning have been destroyed by what we believe were Molotov cocktails, and just a few minutes ago we received an unverified report that two bombs went off outside the central police headquarters.

"The National Guard is expected to arrive back in town later in the morning… I don't know if you could hear that… I am hearing more shots being fired. We do know that two police officers were wounded a little while ago by what was believed to be sniper fire… I now see more low hanging smoke up near the capital building… Austin police are now firing tear gas everywhere into this massive crowd.

"I see… Mike, this is getting serious… I just saw part of the mob break through the rear of the police perimeter and they are charging through the firemen still on duty at the front of the building… Mike there is gunfire breaking out now in both directions. I don't know if the camera is picking all of this up but there is now a pitched battle going on, I see police wearing masks and using batons… there goes more teargas canisters into the mob…

Mike I just heard even more gunfire, and now the crowd is scattering. Mike... I can't verify this from this distance, but police appear to be opening fire at the demonstrators attempting to storm the capital building... okay... I just saw several demonstrators fall to the ground. This has descended into combat. And we're going to pull back further, because a bullet just ricocheted off a police van just about twenty feet from where I am crouched on the ground."

The scene immediately switched back to Mike Silver and Mason Howell. "Mason, I understand that while we were on the scene with Gwen, some more news arrived here at the studio."

"That's correct Mike. The mayor of Austin has declared martial law. Schools are being shut down and students being sent home, and businesses are being asked to close for the rest of the day. People are being asked to stay in their homes if at all possible, and now we have a report of disturbances in a couple of neighborhoods between residents on opposing sides of this issue.

"The mayor is announcing that all off-duty Austin police have been activated, and other local law enforcement agencies are assisting the city, as are departments from other cities. In addition, Texas Rangers are being brought in from other parts of the state. It is expected that National Guard troops will be back on the streets of Austin within the next ninety minutes.

"I also want to comment on what Gwen told us about the possibility of snipers in the area. The Austin Police Department has

268

issued a warning for all residents and individuals working in the vicinity of the Capitol building to stay inside and lock their doors because of that very threat from snipers. We understand that Texas Air National Guard helicopters are in the air over the city assisting police to spot... and this is a word they are using... eliminate... the threats."

"And Mason... I am now being told that three Austin police officers and one member of the Texas Rangers have been killed in the violence so far. In addition, ten demonstrators have been reportedly killed, and there are reports of eight fatalities as a result of neighborhood disturbances. We are also being told that there are an unknown number of individuals who have been wounded.

"We are now getting word that anti-succession riots have broken out in Dallas, and Houston, Texas, as well as in Tulsa, Oklahoma. In San Antonio, the city hall is surrounded by protestors demanding that Texas be reunified with Mexico. Also, in St. Louis, there is rioting and the Missouri National Guard has been called up. That comes on the heels of reports we have received that during the past two months, there has been a slow but constant migration of city residents to East St. Louis, across the river in Illinois.

"Now, our producer is telling me in my ear... I think that... I am being told that Gwen Munro is calling in information, but the situation in Austin near the state Capitol building is too chaotic and dangerous for a live report. But Gwen is reporting by text that the demonstrators did manage to get at least two Molotov cocktails into the Capitol building, and that a fire is reportedly spreading throughout the front portion of the structure. And now we are going to break away to Omaha, where Marsha Bentley is on the scene with some breaking news there. Marsha…?".

"Mike, I'm still here at the Scott Conference Center, where the delegates from the seceding states are to meet tonight to make their withdrawal official and to establish an effective date for the birth of the Constitutional States of America. As you can see, security is being beefed up here in light of the events this morning in Austin, Texas.

"Extra officers are being brought in from Lincoln, as well as other towns and sheriffs' departments in this part of the state. A number of National Guard units are being assembled and will be arriving later. The deadly turn of events in Austin has caused local authorities to prepare for the worst, and we are observing that riot gear is becoming the uniform of the day for the police on hand. Special attention is being given to the security of the delegates, and again, in light of the Austin news, police have already taken up positions on the rooftops in this part of Omaha.

"The sky is simply swarming with helicopters, and while some are carrying news crews, most are police helicopters interspersed with several National Guard craft. They are keeping a very close eye on the demonstrators at the three locations, and the

Omaha Police Department has made it a point to bring in bomb –
sniffing dogs, and are making them very visible to the
demonstrators.

"Mike, one local businessman I spoke to earlier this morning
expressed his concern that the atmosphere was already growing into
something resembling anarchy. He says that when he woke up this
morning he had a feeling of not knowing in what nation he was
living. He says that Nebraska and all the other states that will send
delegates here today are in a state of limbo, and will remain that way
until the effective date of the withdrawal, and the residents of the
states can go on with life in whatever form it will take."

"Marsha… Mason Howell here. In talking to Nebraska
residents, what are you picking up regarding their confidence in their
future as part of this new breakaway union?"

"Thank you, Mason. Last evening, I happened to speak with
a member of the Omaha City Council. She expressed tremendous
sadness over what was happening, and even broke down into tears
while we talked. Still, she felt that what was happening was as
necessary as it is unfortunate. Then she made this interesting point –
she told me that if this had happened in say, the year 2000 or 1980,
her sorrow would have been much more pronounced. But she said
that it's much easier to leave the country, when it is no longer the
country you grew up in. She went on to say that, when she thinks of

the United States of America, she thinks of it in the past tense, and has for some time."

The scene went back to Mike Silver and Mason Howell in New York. "So, Mason… I think we are starting to see… I'm getting word that we are now going to go to the floor of the United States House of Representatives, where Democratic Representative Michelle Culbertson of California is speaking to address the vote to be taken this evening. She is now coming to the microphone….".

The C-SPAN feed from the House floor showed a tall, silver haired woman approach the microphone. "Mister Speaker… I rise today to express the horror I feel at the prospect of tens of millions of Americans losing their citizenship in the greatest nation the world has ever seen.

"In spite of the sad legacy of slavery, occasional situations of exploitation of vulnerable societies around the world and the engagement in some unjust wars, America is still the nation that others flock to.

"Now we face the specter of millions of innocent citizens being stripped of the privileges and protections afforded to citizens of the United States of America. And why is this happening Mister Speaker? It is happening because corporations want a tax haven. It is happening because oil and gas companies want a vast swath of North America at their mercy to rape the environment for profit. It is happening because those who wish to fill their own pockets, can do so at the expense of workers who will be subject to accepting the crumbs they offer.

"Mister Speaker, this new so-called nation will be nothing more than a return to workers living in company towns, living in company houses and spending their meager wages at company stores. There will be no workers' rights, either in terms of collective bargaining or safety.

"This will be a nation where no one who looks different will be safe from discrimination, or even violence. Not a single official involved in the secession movement, has promised that black citizens will be permitted to vote. More astoundingly, there has not been a single pledge put forth that slavery will not be permitted.

"There will be no rights guaranteed for women, either in the workplace, the home or the womb. Mister Speaker, this is a day when crucial rights diminish for many, but progress more rapidly for the remainder."

Chapter 14

Viewers were once again seeing Mike Silver and Joshua Simmons in the NewsNet studio. "Joshua, as a conservative columnist, how do you react to a statement such as that?"

"Mike, as much as I don't want to see the nation fracture like this, what we just saw on the House floor was a liberal member of Congress parroting the attitudes of some in her party and the mainstream media that played no small role in bringing about this crisis. I will acknowledge that there have been conservative politicians and commentators who have been brutally biased against liberals and Democrats. However, Americans who simply opposed reckless spending and the growth of government found themselves over the past several years, subjected to a constant drumbeat of commentary telling them they were racist at worst and uneducated at best.

"We reached a point where there were a growing number of states with concentrations of citizens who came to feel that they no longer belonged in the United States of America, and for that matter, were no longer wanted. Again, I don't want to see this happen, but I am haunted by what Bryce Hamilton said about leaving home when you're no longer wanted by your own family.

"We finally hit a point in this country where two philosophically opposed forces felt that the argument of the other was illegitimate. And that divide grew so wide, it brought us to where we are today."

"And Mason… wait a second… we are now going to return live to Gwen Munro in Austin, Texas who is going to give us an update… Gwen?".

The scene now showed the reporter standing on the lawn in front of the Texas Capitol building. "Thank you Mike… behind me you can now see that the police and Texas Rangers have control over the grounds of the Capitol building. In the back you can see some smoke still coming out of the building, and the two police buses are still smoldering.

"In the distance, in three different directions I can see smoke, and sirens seem to be everywhere. The large crowd of protesters has been disbursed after the use of a lot of tear gas, and the latest report I have received is that fifteen demonstrators have died here on the grounds, but it does not end there. There are believed to be four law enforcement officers who lost their lives today.

"There are also reports that officers in helicopters killed three protesters who were firing rifles at police from the tops of buildings nearby. There are now four civilian casualties from related disturbances around the city, and the central police department suffered moderate damage from two bombs that went off outside, but did not result in any injuries or deaths.

"I have notes everywhere here… the building that housed the offices of the Texas chapter of the Council for a Free America was firebombed, and is currently in flames.

"Once again, the city is now under martial law and there is an 8:00 PM curfew this evening. Only individuals with urgent business are going to be permitted on the streets.

"There is said to be tremendous anger on the part of the groups and organizations who are hoping to stop Texas from seceding, and they're voicing their sentiment that Texas is going to go backward in social progress and minority rights. There is word of great anxiety on the part of the Hispanic community, most of all, those who have not entered the country legally. Rumors and nightmare scenarios are running rampant through many minority neighborhoods, not just in Austin, but in other Texas cities as well.

"Social media, including Twitter, are ablaze with quotes from some politicians and pundits suggesting that members of minority groups may find their lives drastically changed after secession. Groups opposed to secession were expecting much more lead time to organize protests and marches, but as was the case with the rest of America, events took place at a more rapid pace than anyone could've expected.

"We are also hearing anecdotal bits and pieces regarding the plight of undocumented immigrants attempting to leave Texas and other seceding states for those remaining in the union. New Mexico officials have been reluctant to comment on reports that in the past week there has been a major increase in the flow of such individuals into their state."

"Gwen… Joshua Simmons here. How are African-Americans reacting? It seems that they have been the emotional targets of some rather interesting rhetoric over the past few days."

"Josh… a couple of days ago, I spoke to the pastor of a large, predominantly African-American church here in Austin. I asked him for his reaction to the types of comments and predictions you refer to. He told me that he was not at all happy with the secession, but he also said that he has five adult children, and he has seen very little happening over the past two decades that point to a bright future for them. He says that he's going to take a wait-and-see attitude, and reserve his judgment for later. He added that he is simply not buying the forecasts being offered by what he referred to as alarmist talking heads and politicians trying to scare people in a time of crisis."

Once again, the faces of Mike Silver and Joshua Simmons filled the screen. "Joshua, I want to ask you about what may happen tomorrow. Assuming the delegates vote to secede at this evening's meeting, does that totally erase any possibility of the use of force to preserve the union?"

"Mike, I found it quite interesting when Tom Edelstein appeared on another network with Congressman Hightower. When that topic came up, the Congressman implied that should force be used, the surrender of the seceding states would be almost instantaneous.

"I make this point with the greatest reluctance… I don't want to see any violence break out, more than has already taken place today. What the Congressman seems to forget is that almost all the states involved in the secession are states in which gun ownership is an important part of life for so many of its residents. That has been one key element in the divide that has brought this problem about. It's hard to put into words, but many of the states remaining in the United States are those that have more restrictions on gun ownership and possession. I may be oversimplifying this, but just who is it exactly that is going to go into Texas, North Dakota and Wyoming and overpower them if the military is in a state of chaos and division?"

Mike Silver shook his head for a moment, and then turned to the camera. "And now we are going to go back to Marsha Bentley in Omaha, Nebraska, the epicenter of everyone's attention. Marsha… now, what's going on in Omaha?"

Marsha Bentley was once again on the screen, but this time inside the Scott Conference Center. "Mike… all of us in the media who were broadcasting from outside have just been brought into the

278

building. We are not able to get a good camera feed right now, but just before we were quickly ushered inside, the police were beginning to put on their masks, telling us that they were anticipating the use of tear gas.

"One of our observers called us a few minutes ago to tell us that the demonstrators were in the process of filling the sidewalks on Woolworth and Pine Streets that lead to the Center, and that some of them had left their points of assembly at staggered times so that they can converge here in mass. We are being told that many demonstrators have come in from other parts of the country, and that they may number over fifteen thousand strong.

"I asked an Omaha Police Lieutenant about the march. He told me that the demonstrators had assembled in public areas, and were free to march on public sidewalks. However, he went on to explain that if they poured into the street, they would be in violation of city statute, and could be arrested. Unlike in Austin, there has not been as much as a hint of any weapons or explosives in the hands of the demonstrators. But I would like to add, dogs that can detect explosives have been brought in from other towns to bolster the several owned by the Omaha police. Those dogs had been deployed at the gates through which nearly all of the demonstrators have been filtering to leave the public parks where they assembled. Still, with so many demonstrators, the dogs cannot screen everyone.

"I believe it is safe to say that the Omaha demonstrators are being greeted with a much more muscular security arrangement than had initially been on hand in Austin. And as National Guard units are expected to arrive within the hour, that show of force will only become more impressive."

"Marsha… Mike, here. Have you heard any more about when or how the delegates will be arriving later today?"

"Mike, all details about security around the delegates is being held close to the vest by Omaha police. In fact, there have been so many threats that are being taken seriously by authorities, we have been told that there will be one camera feed that will be shared by all networks and stations during the actual meeting of the delegates. As they want to keep the number of people in the building at an absolute minimum to reduce the chance of any danger to the delegates, correspondents on hand who had been hoping to be in the room this evening, are going to draw cards to see which one, I repeat, one correspondent will be reporting live from within that room."

"Thank you, Marsha. We will be checking back in with you soon. Right now, we would like to update our viewers on other matters related to tonight's historic secession vote. We have reports that downtown Austin, Texas is a virtual armed camp. Local and area police, sheriff's deputies, Texas Rangers and the National Guard have quelled most of the disturbances we witnessed this morning, unfortunately resulting in several deaths and many injuries.

"Throughout the city of Austin, there are still scattered disturbances, some of which have resulted in exchanges of gunfire, and we understand that there are more casualties as a result. In addition, several government buildings have been damaged by fires and explosives. That includes the Texas Capitol building, and the office building that contained the offices of the Texas chapter of the Council for a Free America. It is reported that the office building has been gutted by the explosion and resulting fires.

"Austin police are still investigating the bomb lab that was raided this morning. A preliminary analysis of the materials and residue in the basement of that house do indicate that crude bombs were likely assembled there. In addition, three empty rifle cases were found, along with containers that had held handgun ammunition.

"The police are so far not releasing the names of any suspects, but we are being told that the owner of the house has been located, and he has verified that the occupants of the rented home identified themselves as students.

"In addition… I'm getting a message that… Omaha, Nebraska police have just reported that they have intercepted a van containing numerous, primitive explosive devices such as firebombs and Molotov cocktails. We understand that the van was in a line of vehicles being inspected as they drove toward the section of the city where tonight's meeting of delegates is being held.

"We are being told that the driver of the van is not providing any information, but police are assuming that the materials were somehow going to be distributed to some of the demonstrators.

"We are also being told that Omaha authorities have decided to move their perimeter even farther away from the Scott Conference Center. According to a text from Marsha Bentley, that action is now becoming apparent as the barricades and yellow tape are being moved farther away, and Marsha reports that she has once again stepped outside and can see the demonstrators beginning to arrive at the scene. We hope to soon have live images, but the ever-changing circumstances there are making that difficult.

"Now that the police know that at least some of the demonstrators intended to do some real damage, I would expect that security will tighten up even more, and that does not bode well for our coverage.

"We are also being informed that the riots that broke out in several other Texas cities and in Tulsa, Oklahoma and St. Louis are being successfully quelled by law enforcement and National Guard units."

~~~

Bryce Hamilton looked around at his companions in the police van as the vehicle was ushered through the police barricade and pulled up in front of the brick – columned front of the Scott Conference Center. It was the culmination of a tedious several hours, individual delegates having called the police Captain coordinating their transportation so that each could be picked up individually and taken to the headquarters.

If the situation had not been so serious, Hamilton and the delegates in the van, dressed in police riot gear, would have found great humor in their disguise. Several more similar vans with similar passenger cargoes followed. As each van pulled up in front of the Scott Center, the delegates disembarked, followed by several actual officers carrying trunks containing the clothing the delegates would be wearing at the meeting that evening.

Although everyone inside the building was involved with the meeting, or were media covering the event, the group shuffled through the lobby before anyone noticed something was amiss. Real officers were mingled with the group, and the ill-fitting uniforms seemed to camouflage body shapes, gender and age.

The costumed delegates and officials were escorted to two large rooms adjacent to the meeting room so that they could change clothes, and have some time to rest and collect their thoughts in the remaining hours before they would convene. Bryce Hamilton emerged from the changing room, accompanied by two real officers in riot gear, and gazed toward the lobby where the media milled around, still unaware that the state delegates and most of the fifteen member executive committee of the Council for a Free America were in the same building.

Before leaving the police headquarters, Hamilton and Patrick Bridger, along with other members of the executive committee, had mapped out their plans for the remainder of the day, barring any more unforeseen circumstances. They knew that their plans could be changed at any moment by violence or requests by the police to yield to matters of security.

While they were still in the changing room, Hamilton had taken a few minutes to watch the television and see who was on the scene from NewsNet. He turned to one of the escorting officers and asked, "Would you recognize Marsha Bentley?"

The officer flipped up his mask to reveal a grin. "Whenever she's on television, I stop whatever else I'm doing. You want me to fetch her?"

Hamilton smiled and nodded. "Please… and bring her on back to the meeting room."

Hamilton strolled into the larger room being prepared for the meeting. A minute later, the officer returned with the correspondent. He thanked the officer, who then reluctantly walked away, and then Hamilton put out his hand to the correspondent.

"Ms. Bentley… Bryce Hamilton… I suppose you already knew that."

The reporter nodded. "I should be fired if I had not known who you were."

284

Hamilton gestured toward a nearby table. "Please, sit down."

The reporter retrieved a digital recorder from her briefcase. "May I use this? It helps me avoid misquotes."

Hamilton smiled and nodded. "That is fine. In fact, Marsha… I wanted NewsNet to speak with me today, even if no one else has a chance to."

The correspondent laughed. "When that officer came and got me, I think that everyone else in the media in that room understood that something was up. But even when you came out in the hallway, I think I was the only one who spotted you."

Hamilton laughed. "That's just as well for now. And feel free to quote me on this if you wish… I confess to giving NewsNet preferential treatment, because your coverage of our movement has been quite evenhanded. So if you would like to ask a few questions, please go ahead."

"Senator… are you going to be placed in nomination to be the first President of the Constitutional States of America?"

Hamilton took a deep breath, and then sighed slowly. "It is possible. Someone has to serve as a chief executive on an interim basis. As you are probably aware, we plan to hold elections in advance of those to be held in the United States. We will then elect a President and Vice President, and members of our national legislature. I will not run for President in that election. I have no plans to ever run for office again. Instead, I am going to dedicate my remaining years to the great and many tasks ahead.

"For example, we don't know if our legislature is going to consist of one or two bodies. For that matter, will the Democratic and Republican parties even be relevant in the Constitutional States of America?

"A driving force in this movement has been a peaceful rise of resistance against encroachment of the federal government in our lives and businesses. Starting now, we have to determine just how much authority and power our union will grant our national government. We have no illusions, Marsha… this is going to be difficult and painful."

"I would like to ask you about President Malcolm's decision to not attempt to prevent all of this from happening by use of force."

"Politically… President Malcolm and I are polar opposites. But I do want to say this… I think that history will uphold his wisdom in that decision. It was not only logical and feasible… it was the only humane choice, to avoid unnecessary conflict. Regardless of our differences… I will be the first to say that John Malcolm is a good and decent man, and he has been steady at the helm through this crisis."

"But do you hold him responsible for his role over the past several years… I mean, is he partly responsible for the conditions that brought about this crisis?"

"No more than any other member of Congress or government official… and I stress, of either party… who have simply failed to accept the reality of basic mathematics and matters of income versus expenditures, and allowed dedication to the Constitution to slip.

"Now you take that kind of fiscal recklessness, and then combine it with a situation in which a nation has reached such a divide in its values… and by values I'm not talking about things such as LGBT rights, or even abortion for that matter. What I refer to is a basic respect and tolerance for differences of opinion… respect for those who achieve… people of faith…an emphasis on self-reliance and character.

"Add to that the growing scorn being expressed for the Constitution and derision directed toward our Founding Fathers, suggesting they were nothing more than a bunch of greedy bigots whose words and deeds must be disregarded because some were slave owners.

"The nation simply became too fragmented. And there were several states in which the sentiment was overwhelming to get off a sinking ship. It's one thing to hang in there and tackle problems when you feel that you share a common cause. It's more difficult to continue when you have no choice but to accept that you are no longer in agreement on the common premise that capitalism and respect for an earned dollar are at the core of our nation's economic strength."

"But doesn't the challenge seem overwhelming? Everything from a currency, establishing a treasury, arrangements to be made for Social Security, the list seems to go on and on. Do you ever wonder if you have taken on an unworkable effort?"

"It is going to be tremendously problematic. In some ways, it may be similar to what a nation experiences after a war. Still, while it may have been more comfortable to have maintained the status quo, in the long run, I think we would have suffered more greatly."

"So, Senator… are you predicting dark days ahead for the United States?"

"Marsha… what is going on is unsustainable. I see economic tragedy just over the horizon. Sadly, I question the ability of the citizens of the United States of America to be able to handle what is coming. When I say that, I am speaking in terms of a collective lack of strength to cope with the coming adversity. I could say much more, but now I find myself in a very strange position of having to shut up, short of meddling in the affairs of the nation of which I will no longer be a citizen shortly."

The reporter glanced up and saw that Patrick Bridger was waiting nearby, so she decided to wrap up her interview.

"And Senator… that brings me to the question of the day. Do you know when that will be… your last day as a citizen of the United States of America?"

"Actually no. That could be decided this evening."

The reporter got up, then thanked Hamilton for the interview and rushed away to transmit the recording to New York. She told herself that it may not have been as good as video, but it was much more than any of her competitors had. As she trotted through the lobby, she was greeted with a hail of questions from other reporters. Smiling as she sped by them, she headed into the restroom, went into a stall and closed the door, then connected a small cable from her recorder to her notebook computer.

~~~

Jim Walters sat at his desk, somberly re – reading the letter. He glanced up to look at the equally morose Vice President. "So when do you plan to give this to the boss?"

"The moment the secession is official. That could be as early as tomorrow."

The Chief of Staff took a deep breath and closed his eyes. "I suspect the same. After all, it's not like two weeks from now everything will be nailed down tight. Tomorrow… six months from now… it's going to be absolute chaos and confusion." He put the letter back on the desk and stabbed a finger at it. "The Justice Department couldn't come up with any wiggle room?"

"None at all. Once my state secedes, it's over. He has to have a replacement ready for Congress to ratify."

Walters began to laugh and shake his head slowly. "Of course, we really don't know how many votes are needed to even do that. All the House and Senate rules have to be modified. Can you imagine just how pretty that is going to be?"

Litton shrugged. "But just imagine what the Democratic Party's majority is going to be."

"I know." Walters leaned back and stared at the ceiling for a moment. "He's not doing very well today... not that anyone can blame him. Last time I saw him was around 8:30. He was rather short with me... really on edge. I think he canceled all his appointments this afternoon. I'm just leaving him alone."

"Have you talked to the First Lady today?"

"I've fought the urge. I've never involved Marjorie in any business."

"I think she watches him pretty closely. What do you think?"

"She has a very subtle move when it comes to sniffing a drinking glass. Sometimes she acts as if she picked up the wrong glass, then sets it down and picks up her own."

The Vice President closed his eyes and shook his head. "He's already fallen off the wagon."

"Are you sure?"

"That outburst at Urbana… I used the restroom in the hallway right after he did. He must have had a flask on him. I could smell it. I looked down in the trashcan. There was one of those little travel sized bottles of mouthwash."

Both remained silent until the Vice President spoke again. "He's really not strong and stable enough for this job… you know that don't you?"

"Even under the best of circumstances… and these are hardly the best of circumstances."

~~~

"This is Cynthia Warren with more ongoing coverage here in the NewsNet studio in New York, and I am joined now by Ben Stirling, who most of you know from his evening program America in Real Time. Ben, we are now just four hours away from the scheduled start of the meeting of the CSA delegates. We understand that NewsNet's own Marsha Bentley has just been selected to provide the media pool coverage of that event. What do you think the atmosphere will be like in that room this evening?"

"Well, Cynthia, I think it's going to be an evening of mixed emotions for the delegates. There will of course be a sense of relief once the decision is official. At the same time, it will have to be a very somber setting. I understand all the criticism leveled at the secession movement leaders, and some of it I consider to be quite fair. But at the bottom line, these are Americans who never wanted to see this day arrive."

"Are you shocked at how easily these states have seceded… or will have seceded?"

Stirling sat quiet for a moment. "On one hand, the whole chain of events seems remarkable. Yet, what could the federal government have really done to prevent it? President Malcolm was right about use of the military. That was a non—starter.

"He could've threatened to freeze the flow of federal dollars into the states, but that would've simply played into the hands of the secessionists. There was hardly a chance for an economic embargo against those states, considering so much of our food supply originates there, and the map of the CSA screams two words – energy production.

"All those factors were coupled with the sentiment within his own party and the media to simply say farewell to those states and… the game was over."

"But what will happen with the economies of the United States and the CSA?"

"It will be very rocky for the CSA in the short term. I expect that business will initially be conducted in United States dollars, but I am certain there will be rapid movement toward a separate currency. It looks like some progress is being made behind the scenes to address stability for retirement benefits for people who are already at age 55. Aside from that, the matter of Social Security is murky. The same goes for Medicare.

"I think that when all is said and done, three to four years from now, the mechanical aspects of the economic relationship will be ironed out. But I cannot help but think there's going to be this tremendous rivalry. Many of the states remaining in the United States are going to be dominated by Democrats. Certainly, there will be exceptions, such as Indiana and Kentucky, but in terms of the vernacular we usually use to describe our politics now, the United States will be predominantly blue, but the CSA will be as red as a sunset.

"So, the United States will have an overall theme of attempting to prove that big government leads to prosperity and equity for all citizens. In contrast, the CSA will try to show how limited government and lower taxes will help all to prosper."

"And let me ask you this, Ben… Ben, I'm sorry, but I'm getting word that we are going immediately to Marsha Bentley in Omaha with some new developments."

The scene went to the lobby of the Scott Conference Center, where the correspondent spoke into the microphone, while a dozen riot police stood guard just inside the door. "Cynthia… things have taken a sudden and nasty turn here. About ten minutes ago, protesters began pelting police and National Guard troops with rocks and fragments of bricks.

"I had been outside speaking to some police officials when that happened, and we were all quickly ushered back inside the building. Just before the crowd began to launch the rocks, a chant began of 'Stop the Nation of Hate', over and over again.

"Just as I was coming in the door, I turned to see that police were beginning to fire tear gas, rubber bullets and beanbag guns into the crowd. Then I… I am being told now that we have to be moved farther back in the building."

Chapter 15

Suddenly, viewers were once again seeing Cynthia Warren and Ben Stirling. Cynthia glanced up at the camera. "Okay... I just got word that Tom Whitley from our Lincoln, Nebraska affiliate has managed to become, as we say, embedded with the Nebraska National Guard, and is now in a helicopter overhead in Omaha. Tom... this is Cynthia Warren. If you can hear me, let us know what you are seeing right now."

Viewers were suddenly seeing an aerial view of the scene in Omaha, and the thrumming sound of a helicopter forced the reporter to nearly yell. "I don't know how well this is going to work, because I'm also operating the video... we are now directly over the Scott Center... by the way Cynthia, the helicopter I am in is part of the effort to keep order, so hang on.

"The scene below is... well, I'm not good at judging crowd size, but it is safe to say there are thousands of demonstrators converging on the Scott Center. Oh... whoa... the demonstrators have just broken through the perimeter and are now on the grassy area in front of... Cynthia, we just heard live gunfire. I don't know if you could hear that over the noise of the helicopter.

"Demonstrators have just overpowered the police and Guardsmen, knocking them down and are beginning to beat several of them. The area is now full of altercations, but there was a line of troops in front of the building, and they fired into the charging demonstrators. We are swinging around now to get a different view, but I see several people on the ground.

"Wait a minute… I can't believe this… I just saw a group of demonstrators break through the lines at the side of the building, there was a cascade of rocks and bricks thrown through a couple of windows, and those were followed by what must've been gasoline bombs or some kind of Molotov cocktails or something of that nature. There is now smoke pouring out of the Scott Center.

"Cynthia… I hope you're able to see the video I hope I am sending your way. There are three fire trucks converging on the scene. I think they were being kept on standby about a block away. They are trying to get through, but now demonstrators are not only blocking their way, they are trying to get up on the trucks… I don't know if you can see this… some of the demonstrators are actually trying to pull the firefighters out of the fire trucks.

"Oh… my… the police are now firing at… they are shooting the demonstrators who are attempting to commandeer and stop the fire trucks. Demonstrators are falling to the ground. It is nothing but madness right now… lots of demonstrators are running away, but now a large group is surging toward the Scott Center, still pelting the

National Guard troops with debris… they are being fired upon… I repeat, they are being fired upon, but still, many are now engaged in physical combat with the troops and riot police.

"The fire trucks have made their way through, and are now beginning to send streams of water through the broken windows. I cannot say for sure at this time, but it appears that the fire is in just one small section of the building.

"Cynthia… the whole area is now being subjected to a heavy teargas bombardment. But even through the smoke, I can see that paramedics are on the scene and attending to the casualties as best they can under the circumstances. And I must say, it looks like there may be many people hurt, and I suspect, killed.

"Okay… many more teargas canisters were just launched into the crowd. Now the riot police and National Guard troops are advancing on the retreating protesters. I can't say for sure, but it looks like there's a steady assault of rubber bullets and beanbags taking place. Now the crowd is beginning to break up and scatter.

"Cynthia… I can't be completely accurate because of the fog from the teargas… I'm going to estimate that I see around twenty bodies on the ground in front of the Scott Center, and nearly a dozen in the area where the fire trucks were attacked. Okay… I'm being told now that we are going be leaving the scene for a while. This is Tom Whitley, for NewsNet, Lincoln."

~~~

Franklin Margolis peered out over the restless room full of members of the White House press corps. He stepped to the microphone and unfolded a piece of paper. "President Malcolm wishes to express his deepest sorrow over the loss of life today in Austin, Texas and Omaha, Nebraska. He asks that all Americans, regardless of where they live, to express their differences in a peaceful manner. Further, the President wants to emphasize that in a time of crisis such as this, the best instincts of all Americans must prevail."

Margolis felt his pulse racing and beads of perspiration trickling down the blonde hair on the back of his neck. "I can take a few questions now." He looked up and saw a reporter from NBC standing and holding up his hand. "Go ahead, Larry."

"Why haven't we seen the President today, considering that this evening more than a dozen states are likely to secede from the union?"

The Press Secretary felt his blood turning cold. "President Malcolm is monitoring the situation carefully, and feels that it is best to stay in constant touch with his advisers."

A CNN correspondent shouted out a question without being called upon. "Is the President in communication with Bryce Hamilton or any of the other secessionist leaders?"

"Like I say, the President continues to monitor the situation carefully, especially the outbreaks of violence in two American cities today. I am not free to discuss any individual conversations the President may be having with any particular people at this time." The Press Secretary looked at his seating chart. "Roger Hughes from CBS?"

"There are rumors that Vice President Litton is going to resign as soon as the vote is taken tonight. Does the President have any statement to make about that?"

The Press Secretary took a deep breath. "Howard Litton remains the Vice President of the United States of America until the nation is notified otherwise. President Malcolm has no plans to ask Vice President Litton to step down, and if I may anticipate your next question, nor are there any hypothetical discussions underway regarding any replacement."

Margolis pointed to a correspondent from MSNBC. "Are there any plans to send federal troops to Austin or Omaha to help preserve order?"

"The President believes that local authorities and National Guard units are more than sufficient to take care of the situation. The President also wishes to exercise caution in that regard, lest anyone misinterpret the sending of federal troops into a city in one of the secessionist states."

Margolis took a deep sigh and pointed toward the back of the room in the direction of Leonard Jackson. The elderly man had represented a conservative website for many years, and had provided

White House press secretaries with several uncomfortable moments. "Yeah, Leonard."

The correspondent stretched his frame to attempt to stand straight. "I ask this question with the utmost respect…". Mutterings went through the group, including a couple of impatient expressions of, 'Here we go again'.

"We all know that not many in this room will acknowledge this issue… but is the President unable at this time to carry out his duties because of alcohol abuse?" The room was immediately filled with derisive expressions and many boo's.

Margolis closed his eyes and shook his head. "President Malcolm is fully in charge of his administration and his duties, and I think that I can speak for all administration officials in saying that such a question is totally uncalled for and without merit."

The press secretary nearly shouted a curt "Thank you", then turned sharply and exited the room. The aged reporter in the back gathered his coat and briefcase while ignoring the many harsh comments being hurled his way. But as he left the room, he did catch a couple of clandestine and knowing nods as he departed.

~~~

Vice President Litton was removing the last of his personal items from the desk in his little corner of the White House. He heard a knock, and then saw Jim Walters poke his head through the door. "We have a problem. Crazy Lenny asked the question."

The Vice President placed his briefcase on the desk and began to rub his eyes. "Okay."

The pair walked slowly and reluctantly down the long hallway until they came to the office of the President's secretary. Walters approached her first. "Meg… we have to see him."

The slender black woman shook her head, while trying to convey an unspoken message with her expression. "He's not feeling very well."

The Vice President nodded. "Is he on the phone?"

The secretary shook her head.

"Is there anyone with him?"

The secretary nodded. "Marjorie."

The two men exchanged glances, and then walked slowly to the door of the office of the President of the United States of America. Pulling rank, Howard Litton led the way in.

The President was sitting slumped on a leather sofa, his wife next to him and running her hand across his forehead. A coffee carafe rested on the table in front of them, and a half-full cup was next to it. The First Lady greeted them at first with a scowl, then an understanding nod and a wave of the hand for them to approach.

The Vice President sat down slowly next to President Malcolm. "Mister... John... the questions are coming at us."

The President partially raised his head. "How blunt are they?"

The Chief of Staff spoke up. "It was Lenny...".

The President managed to laugh. "Say no more. How did Margolis handle it?"

The Vice President leaned closer. "With all the righteous indignation he could muster."

The President nodded and looked up. "What's the latest from Austin and Omaha?"

The words slipped out before Jim Walters could catch himself: "How long have you been...?"

The President laughed once again. "How long have I been out of it, you mean? It's okay Jimmy... it was a logical question for you to ask. After all, you've never seen me like this before, although I am sure you've heard the rumors. But these other two...". He gestured to the Vice President and his wife. "They've been through this with me too many times before."

The Chief of Staff hesitated before speaking. "In Austin, three police officers and two National Guardsmen were killed. Also, eighteen demonstrators died. In Omaha, things are still little more sketchy, but what we are hearing is that two police officers and two National Guardsmen died, along with one firefighter who was dragged out of his truck and beaten to death. So far, we have thirty-two demonstrators confirmed dead."

The President stood on wobbly legs, stretched, and began to pace the floor slowly. "And what about the delegates?"

Walters responded. "They managed to get inside to safety somehow. The protesters managed to hurl a couple of crude firebombs into the building, but nobody was hurt by them, and the fire got put out quickly enough.

"By the way, a NewsNet correspondent was able to record an interview with Bryce Hamilton before any of the others knew he was even there. If it means anything, sir, he had kind things to say about you."

The President stood in silence for a moment. "Anybody have a clue as to how this is going to go down tonight?"

The Vice President spoke. "They seem to be holding everything pretty close to the vest. My guess though, is that tonight they may set the effective date. And I think it's going to happen fast."

The President turned slowly. "How quickly? It's already Friday."

Howard Litton considered his words carefully. "Perhaps... even tomorrow. And if that is the case... I guess I go back to private life."

The President shook his head and looked down. "This is totally unfair to you, Howard. You've been a good and loyal friend... and public servant."

"Thank you... Mister President. But you have to be thinking now about a replacement for me. Every hour that Ed Riley is next in...". The Vice President began to laugh quietly. "Sorry... forgot he was from Oklahoma."

Jim Walters interjected: "And our Senate President is from South Dakota."

The President began to pace the floor again. "So, the line of succession goes right to the Cabinet... Secretary of State."

Marjorie Malcolm spoke for the first time. "I am finding this particular line of conversation very unsettling."

Her husband walked over and placed his hand on her shoulder. "Just dealing with reality."

The First Lady took her husband's hand. "I know... I'll just never get used to it."

The President glanced toward his Chief of Staff. "Get in contact with the Secret Service right away. I want them to take

304

Calista Myers to Camp David… yet this afternoon, if at all possible. And have them increase the security. And the Cabinet members next in line… I want them scattered around the country and secured at military bases. We don't want to be totally decapitated by some kind of terrorist attack… from any source… domestic or foreign."

The President walked toward Jim Walters and placed his hand on his shoulder. "And call General Adams…Def Con 3… only for bases not located in secession states. I don't want any hostile powers trying to take advantage of us because they think we're so distracted."

The President turned to Howard Litton. "Get word to Bryce Hamilton. Explain this to him, so there is no misunderstanding."

The President paced some more. "Now we have to just watch and wait."

~~~

"Good afternoon, and welcome to NewsNet for ongoing coverage of the secession crisis. My name is Robert Carter, and I'm joined right now by NewsNet contributors Mason Howell of the Washington Times and Joshua Simmons of the Potomac Review.

"Joshua, we are now just two hours away from the scheduled meeting of the delegates from the secession states. It appears that there is no turning back, so give me your take on what happens the first day this new union exists."

"Actually Robert, I expect there to be legal challenges filed in every one of the states, simply because there is no right of secession."

The moderator turned to his other guest: "Mason... do you agree with that?"

"To what court would dissenting groups or individuals file motions? These states would be saying that they are no longer part of the United States of America, so they would not be expected to recognize the authority of any United States federal courts, including the Supreme Court."

Joshua Simmons responded: "The Constitution has no provisions for allowing secession. And the Civil War settled that."

Mason Howell shook his head. "I agree that the Constitution makes no allowance for secession. But through the generations we have come to establish all kinds of institutions and rights that are not mentioned in the Constitution. And as for the Civil War, I think it is a bit of a stretch to maintain that a military victory can establish a rule of law."

Robert Carter interrupted the exchange: "I would like to get your thoughts on another issue that has gained increasing attention over the past twenty-four hours... and that is the issue of immigration. This morning, our legal correspondent Mark Hansen spoke by phone with Nina Burton, a law partner of Bryce Hamilton. Mrs. Burton has been asked by the Council for a Free America to draft a proposed policy to be adopted collectively by the states in the CSA.

"She told Mark that she had discussed the matter with many of the delegates, in order to find out what consensus of opinion was. From what she told Mark, the sentiment of the CSA will be to grant citizenship to all residents who were citizens of the United States of America prior to the secession. However, the CSA appears to be heading for granting a lenient process for citizenship applications for those who were brought here as minors, but those who came to America illegally as adults cannot become citizens. However, if they have lived in America for more than twenty-four months, they will be granted work permits and the right to reside in those states absent criminal backgrounds. That does appear to leave the door open for deportations of the more recently arrived. In addition, she hinted that border security between Texas and Mexico will be significantly beefed up. Mason… any comments?"

"None of that surprises me. Most of the states that will comprise the CSA have a tougher overall slant on matters of law and order. They are simply less likely to establish laws through a lens of political correctness. The way in which they approach stopping the future flow of illegal immigrants will be a key factor, especially since travel from states like New Mexico and Arizona will likely remain effortless and unrestricted.

"I have nothing to base this on except gut instinct, but when it comes to matters of things such as public assistance, medical care and school enrollment, the CSA states will not likely be magnets for illegal immigrants."

The moderator turned to his other guest: "Joshua, what do you see happening within the CSA regarding immigration?"

Simmons shook his head and threw his hands up. "I think that what we are going to see will only bear out the concerns of those who believe that the secession is about nothing more than establishing a white people's paradise. I'll bet that the undocumented workers who will never be granted the right to become citizens and vote will, however, be granted the right to pay taxes to make up for the low or nonexistent tax rates for the wealthy and corporations. Serfdom will have returned to the North American continent."

Mason Howell closed his eyes and shook his head. "Josh... look at what providing services to nonresidents has done to the economies of the border states. Look at the effects on the schools and hospitals in Arizona and Southern California."

Robert Carter held up his hands and laughed: "Time to move on to another subject. Once the CSA states are no longer subject to oversight and regulations of the United States government, what is going to happen in terms of jobs? Joshua...?"

"Well, I suppose this is one area in which Mason and I will find some agreement. I fully expect that employment will boom in the CSA states, through energy production, agriculture, mining and forestry. But I expect that to be accomplished at a terrible cost to the environment. Also, I hold no illusions regarding the future of workers' rights in the CSA. I am concerned that the remaining United States will suffer economic difficulties in trying to hold on to industry while ensuring that workers are treated fairly."

"Mason... just how much in agreement are you with Joshua?"

"Well, I do agree that it is likely that the CSA will have no problem in providing jobs to its residents. Where I disagree... I see no reason to think that those industries Joshua just cited cannot flourish while still maintaining responsible protection for the environment. As for those remaining in the United States, they will have to make some hard decisions regarding their attitudes toward industry and the relationship between labor and management."

Robert Carter turned to face the camera. "I want to thank my special guests, Joshua Carter and Mason Howell for their insights. When we return in a moment, Cynthia Warren will be giving us an update on the events today in Austin, Texas and Omaha, Nebraska. This is NewsNet."

~~~

Bryce Hamilton and Patrick Bridger glanced at each other and laughed as Tom Edelstein reached for the remote control and turned off the television tucked away in the corner of their meeting room. They turned to scan the room as two technicians readied the camera that would provide the shared video feed to the nation.

The room was being purposely kept plain and unremarkable. There was no bunting, nor were there any banners. The austere atmosphere was to be in keeping with the solemnity of the coming evening.

The stench of smoke and wet embers permeated the building. A building maintenance crew had boarded up the broken windows so that no more incendiary devices could be tossed through. Aside from that, no cleanup or repairs would take place until the following day, when the delegates would have to be moved to a nearby National Guard facility to conduct further immediate business.

Preparations were also under way for setting up a temporary CSA capital building in a large hotel along Highway 680 on the south side of Omaha. Guest reservations were being canceled, visitors were being moved to other facilities, and Nebraska state police and the National Guard were already beginning to secure the premises. Their move into the downtown office building would have to wait until better security could be arranged.

Tom Edelstein stuck his hands in his pockets and gazed upward as if he was trying to remember something. "All the state treasurers are on standby to cut off the fund exchanges whenever they get the word."

Patrick Bridger nodded. "Everything set up with the bank here?"

Edelstein laughed. "Yeah... but it's going to be chaotic for a while. Every employer in every one of our states will have to get the routing numbers to send in the income taxes, while still forwarding Social Security and Medicare payments to Washington. This is all going to be hell to sort out."

Bryce Hamilton took a deep breath. "The transfer of military personnel... that is going to be no small chore. And the ones overseas...".

Bridger sighed loudly. "Bryce... ever since you told me about the Def Con status, I've been meaning to ask something. Did the Vice President mention anything specific?"

Hamilton nodded. "He told me that the President gave the order just as a precaution. But he confided in me... he's worried about North Korea. Our commander there has been told that our troops there are going to have to maintain the status quo. He said they can't afford to lose all the troops from the CSA states. We have no idea how many will decide to terminate their enlistments. But those that do will have to be replaced."

Hamilton muttered something to himself. "When we have our own forces established, we'll have to decide whether to supplement the United States forces there."

Tom Edelstein groaned. "That could go nuclear way too quickly. I wonder how we will be looked upon if our withdrawal is blamed for a nuclear exchange?"

Bryce Hamilton placed his hand on the younger man's shoulder. "I can show you my list of the things that could potentially be blamed upon our actions tonight. Let me know when you have an hour free to read it."

~~~

Marsha Bentley sat nervously at a small table in the back of the assembly hall. She watched as delegates came into the room, some alone, and others in groups of two or three chatting in a subdued tone as they made their way to their seats.

She glanced at her watch, and saw that it was 6:50 PM. A cameraman nodded to her as a producer counted down the seconds. "Good evening. My name is Marsha Bentley, reporting from Omaha, Nebraska. We are at the Scott Conference Center at the University of Nebraska, Omaha.

"I am a correspondent for NewsNet. But this evening I am reporting on behalf of all the broadcast and news networks, to bring you coverage of the historic meeting of state delegates who will vote in a little while on secession from the United States of America.

"As of late this afternoon, a total of fifteen states have enacted votes in their state legislatures to secede, and all are expected to join in the formation of the Constitutional States of America. Along with the state delegates here tonight are several members of the executive committee of the Council for a Free America, the organizing body for the secession movement. Also in attendance this evening will be two observers on behalf of the individuals who live in Michigan's Upper Peninsula, and are considering becoming a separate state.

"In a few minutes, the convening chairman of that organization, former Nebraska Senator Bryce Hamilton will gavel the meeting to order. We have not been provided with any agenda, but I have been told that this may be a very brief meeting due to the security disruptions today.

"The atmosphere here this evening is anything but festive. Earlier today, the immediate area around the Scott Center was the scene of a deadly confrontation between demonstrators protesting the establishment of this new union and Omaha and area police and National Guard troops. Many protesters died in what became a pitched battle, as did several police and National Guard troops, and even one firefighter. In the course of that melee, a portion of the Scott Center was set on fire by what were believed to be Molotov cocktails or some similar types of devices.

"There was much concern earlier today for the safety of the delegates, and I am still not at liberty to tell you how they were brought into the building unharmed. Due to the threats and the violence experienced today, it is expected that the delegates will be kept under heavy guard for some time.

"I believe that you can now see on your screens the room as the last of the delegates file in and take their chairs. As you can see, aside from the tables at which the delegates are being seated, there is nothing else in the room really but for a podium and the American flag standing to my right of that podium.

"Now, Bryce Hamilton is approaching the podium...".

The tall, silver haired man in a dark blue suit and red tie approached the microphone. "Good evening, ladies and gentlemen. My name is Bryce Hamilton, and it is my duty to serve as the Convening Chairman of the Council for a Free America. I would like to call this meeting to order.

"Is there any business to come before this body? If so, please stand and be recognized."

An attractive thirty-ish woman in a pantsuit rose. "My name is Allison Webster, and I am a delegate from Oklahoma. I would like to move that all fifteen states represented here withdraw from the United States of America, effective at midnight tonight, and that the vote be taken by voice vote."

An elderly, bald man at another table rose slowly with the use of a cane. "My name is William Masterson, delegate from Tennessee... I second the motion."

314

Hamilton looked out over the group. "Is there any further discussion?"

A woman in a Western style dress rose: "Call for the question."

Hamilton took a deep breath. "All in favor, say aye." A chorus of affirmative shouts echoed in the room. "All opposed, say nay." The statement was greeted by silence. "It is the ruling of the Chair that the motion passes. Is there any further business?"

A young, red-haired man in a Western hat stood. "My name is Walter Young, delegate from Idaho. I move that we decree by voice vote that effective midnight tonight, the states represented here shall have entered into a union to be called the Constitutional States of America."

A rotund man stood. "I am Franklin Massey from South Dakota, and I second that motion."

Hamilton gestured the gavel toward the crowd. "Any further discussion?" He remained silent for a moment. "Hearing none, all in favor say aye." Once again, there was a chorus of affirmative votes.

A tall, elderly woman rose. "I am Helen Worthington from Oklahoma. I move that Bryce Hamilton be named interim President of the Constitutional States of America by acclamation."

There was a spontaneous outburst of shouted "ayes", and as Hamilton stood there with a look of helplessness on his face, there

315

was laughter in that room for the first time. He looked out at the crowd and simply smiled and nodded.

There was then silence in the room, as Hamilton began to speak, but faltered at first. "I… I would….". He cleared his throat and seemed to strain to stand up straight. "I would like to invite the color guard from the local National Guard installation to come forward and strike the colors."

Suddenly, a group of three men in Army dress uniforms seemed to come from out of nowhere from the back of the room and marched to where the flag of the United States of America hung on a pole topped by a golden eagle. Those in the room watched in stunned emotion as the soldiers stood at attention while lowering the flag, removing it from the pole, then solemnly but meticulously folding it.

The flag having been secured, the young lieutenant in command barked more orders, and the men marched at attention from the room, the flag held by the Lieutenant. Suddenly, throughout the room, the sounds of quiet sobbing could be heard.

Bryce Hamilton once again approached the microphone, visibly shaken by the business he himself was conducting. "I wish to thank the delegates. We will reconvene tomorrow morning, at a time and place that will be disclosed only to the delegates for security reasons. We will also make arrangements once again for a shared media feed."

Hamilton picked up the gavel again, and then pounded it on the podium. He sighed deeply. "This meeting is adjourned."

The camera stayed on Bryce Hamilton for a moment, and then panned the room as the delegates rose and entered into clusters of conversation. Finally, the image on television screens across the country was once more that of Marsha Bentley.

"All right... we have just seen... I am so... sorry... I was born in Kansas. Just the thought that it's no longer...". The reporter's face was red and her mascara had run down her cheeks. "This has just been so... well we are now... less than four hours from the breakup of the United States of America... the establishment of the Constitutional States of America".

The rattled reporter shook her head a few times, took a deep breath, and continued. "When the clock strikes midnight tonight, people in fifteen American states will be living in a new nation, and it is expected and assumed that the capital of that new nation will be here in Omaha, Nebraska.

"Tonight you have just witnessed the final, collective vote on secession, a decision to make it effective at midnight, and the selection of former Nebraska Senator Bryce Hamilton to serve as the interim President of the new nation. If you have been following the situation closely, you will know that Senator Hamilton told me in an interview earlier today that he will not run for election to that office, once the election process has been established.

"Right now, our producer is trying to secure an interview with Allison Webster, the Oklahoma delegate who made the motion to make secession official. And it looks like… yes he is bringing her over here." The young woman joined the reporter and stood nervously beside her.

"Allison… could you tell us where you are from?"

The flustered woman laughed and took a deep breath. "I live just outside of Tulsa. I own a flower shop there with my mother."

"And what started you on this journey, from operating a flower shop to making a motion to secede from the United States?"

"I remember specifically, it was in February, 2016. I was really not paying much attention to politics. I was in my late twenties, paying off college loans and living in a tiny studio apartment over the flower shop my mother and I had just bought. My father had died a couple of years earlier and things were tough.

"Mom and I were just barely getting by, and the shop almost went under. We were literally budgeting our personal money and the business down to the penny. One evening I was on the sofa nursing a cold, so I turned on a news channel, something I never did usually.

"They were talking about the national debt being over sixteen trillion dollars, then they quoted a couple of members of Congress … They were both saying that the country wasn't spending too much, but instead it was a problem with being able to pay the bills.

"That was the first time I ever paid attention to politics. I even got on the internet and looked those comments up, because I thought I had to have misunderstood what they said. But it turns out, that's what they had really said. I just got intrigued by that.

"So I started watching more, and following how the government spent our money. I voted, and I wrote letters. But I got so frustrated, and became convinced that it wasn't going to change. I even ended up testifying about taxes in front of our state Senate. I suppose you could say I became an activist. And that's how I ended up here tonight.

"Then we had a new President in Trump, and he got Congress to lower taxes. But then Malcolm comes in and first thing he wants to do is raise taxes again".

The reporter nodded to her guest. "Thank you, Allison Webster of Oklahoma, for speaking with us tonight." The producer led the delegate away.

"Now as you heard earlier, due to security concerns, we don't know where, but the delegates are going to reconvene somewhere tomorrow to begin conducting the business of a new nation. At risk of editorializing, I will add that I have been in this building all day, and after seeing firebombs thrown in and the vicinity being besieged by large groups of very violent protesters, I can understand the precautionary steps they are taking until permanent, secure arrangements can be made.

"It appears right now that police are asking non—delegates to clear the building, so we are going to be terminating our broadcast from here at the Scott Conference Center in Omaha, Nebraska. This is Marsha Bentley reporting, and now we will turn coverage over to regular programming."

Chapter 16

Ben Stirling sat in the moderator's seat at the conference table at the NewsNet studio in New York. He was joined by Cynthia Warren and Mike Silver.

"Well, about three hours from now, fifteen American states will become foreign territory. The implications of all this are staggering."

Cynthia Warren appeared pale and devastated. "When I go back to Dallas to visit my parents… I won't even be in the United States. It all seems like a bad dream."

Mike Silver's eyes appeared red rimmed. "Decades from now, historians will still be struggling to understand how a nation could've sacrificed hundreds of thousands of people in the 1860's to preserve the union and quell a secession, only to have it happen again, but successfully, several generations later. And except for the ugliness that took place in Austin and Omaha, it would have taken place totally absent of any bloodshed."

Cynthia Warren spoke again. "I'm sure that in the 1860's, Lincoln was being advised by some to simply write off the South and let them go their own way. But I think that when all this is sorted out, a key role will have been played by those adhering to what we have been referring to recently as the 'good riddance' movement. There were enough members of the Democratic Party, joined by those in the media, to make John Malcolm feel convinced there was no mandate for him to take strong measures to prevent the secession."

Mike Silver responded. "I agree. The discord became so great, letting the secession happen became the path of least resistance. There was no stomach for bloodshed or force, and therefore, no real means to stop it."

Ben Stirling leaned forward toward his colleagues. "The White House has been strangely silent today. Do you think that is simply a means to allow all this to play out? I suppose there's nothing really they can say or do at 1600 Pennsylvania Avenue to actually change anything."

Cynthia Warren shook her head. "A White House staffer who will remain nameless, told me today that President Malcolm is fighting a stomach disorder, and has simply been monitoring events from the living chambers in the executive mansion. However, at the White House briefing earlier today, no illness was mentioned."

Ben Stirling shrugged. "I think the President would be entitled to an ulcer on a day like this. And now he will be losing Howard Litton, not only as his Vice President, but also as a close advisor."

Cynthia Warren chimed in: "Also, this takes out the Speaker of the House and the President of the Senate. I would assume that the Republican minority leader Melanie Brackett is busy as we speak arranging to call the House into session for tomorrow. Of course, now Democrats will vastly outnumber Republicans in the United States House of Representatives. These vacancies present some very urgent business to be taken care of to avoid the nation being put into an even more precarious state of affairs."

Mike Silver spoke next. "This is going to be fascinating, to see who President Malcolm picks as a new Vice President. It's going to say a lot about what the Administration has in mind philosophically on the heels of these unbelievable events. He may wish to pick someone who has a centrist reputation, to keep from alienating states like Ohio, Indiana and Kentucky. On the other hand, the far – left of the Democratic Party may really be feeling its oats right now, seeing so many Western, Southern and Midwestern Republicans exiting Congress."

Cynthia Warren nodded. "One thing we have not talked much about is the prospect of other states eventually joining the CSA. There are some very conservative states that never made a move in that direction. But if the Democrats take the United States too far to the left, and states like Kentucky and Indiana see a booming prosperity in the breakaway country, all bets could be off. It's not inconceivable that every major food producing state except for California could end up on the other side. That could be very problematic."

Ben Stirling held up a piece of paper. "As industries go, we may not be talking General Motors here, but we just got a joint press release telling us that every firearms manufacturer in the United States is moving its operations to locations in Texas, Missouri and Oklahoma. Now many of these jobs have been located in New England among other places, but they will now be free of all the manufacturing restrictions on the weapons themselves, types of ammunition and magazine capacity.

"Now the United States government, and the individual states remaining in the union will have to determine what they will and will not allow to be imported from CSA states. But think of this... for a very wide swath of what I guess we can still call America, the federal authority of the United States of America to regulate guns and ammunition will be totally nonexistent. What will be the fallout from that?"

Cynthia Warren spoke up first. "My first reaction is a rather flippant one... I am tempted to say that perhaps places like Chicago and Baltimore may turn violent. But in all seriousness, considering how freely firearms already flow around the country, I don't see how the states remaining in the union are going to stop the importation of guns and magazines they would like to ban. For that matter, I can't help but wonder if this is when the Malcolm Administration may go for the gold in terms of gun registration and that outright banning of many types of firearms."

Stirling arched his eyebrows as he glanced at his guests. "But what about the Second Amendment?"

Mike Silver laughed. "I know that there will still be a lot of gun advocates in Ohio, Florida, Kentucky, Pennsylvania and Georgia. But a lot of the heart and soul of Second Amendment advocacy left the nation this evening. Things may not happen overnight, but future Supreme Court appointments are going to result in the court going very far to the left. Gun ownership in the United States may soon face some very serious peril."

~~~

Just after midnight, Marjorie Malcolm sat on a chair outside the Oval Office, the President's secretary next to her with her arm around her. Jim Walters and Howard Litton stood ashen face in the doorway to the fabled room, watching the President's physician go through his motions.

Litton walked over to the crying woman and crouched down to speak to her. "Marjorie... when was the last time you saw him?"

The woman raised her tear stained face. "When we were all together earlier today, when I was trying to... sober him up. He told me he was going to be all right, but that he wanted to stay on the job… until midnight. I didn't catch on to what he meant by that… until midnight."

A Secret Service agent walked over and knelt down. "Mrs. Malcolm… is there any chance you may have missed seeing a note in your living quarters?"

She shook her head. "No… but feel free to go and look around."

The agent rubbed his forehead. "Had he ever before attempted suicide?"

Marjorie nodded. "Four years ago, when we were skiing in Aspen. Our daughter was involved in drugs, and he tried to cope by drinking too much…. again. He took an overdose of my antidepressants. He vomited them all up, though. He never went to the hospital, and no one else knew about it."

The doctor came out into the hallway. "There was an empty flask in his suit coat pocket." He held up a small brown plastic bottle. "Xanax… I don't know where he got these. There's no prescription authorization on the bottle. I'm going to guess he was dead for half an hour before Jim found him."

The tearful Chief of Staff took his phone from his holster, and then walked slowly down the hallway.

~~~

Calista Myers had just settled into an overstuffed chair in the library of the main lodge at Camp David. She could hear a rapid but hushed conversation being conducted by the Secret Service agents outside the room, but she was concentrating more on waiting for the aspirin to kick in and relieve her headache, the one that had discouraged her from trying to go to bed.

Suddenly, the conversation stopped, and she heard a knock on the door. Before she could respond, the two agents somberly approached before the more veteran of the two spoke. "Ms. Myers... a Frederick County judge is on his way here. You need to be sworn in. We think you are now the President of the United States."

Calista Myers had never cared for helicopter rides, and at age fifty, the slender brunette had no intentions of changing that. Now she was on Marine One, clad in a black dress, being sworn in as President by a Maryland judge as the chopper began to descend to take her to the White House, her new residence.

As the helicopter landed on the White House grounds, she was relieved to see that the mansion was not surrounded by colored flashing lights. She was briskly escorted inside, and then taken to the Library. She was immediately joined by two Marines who stood guard at the door.

Jim Walters momentarily appeared, then walked in and sat down in the chair next to her. "We've put off a public announcement... I don't think we can wait any longer."

The newly sworn President was reeling at the turn of events. "Okay… have Margolis start calling… I mean by phone, all the networks and the wire services. We will announce that President Malcolm has died. It has to be emphasized that you found him deceased in his office, and that there is no reason to suspect foul play. Then finish it up by announcing that I have been sworn in.

"Jim… everybody went to bed with their minds full of the secession. Can you imagine the conspiracy theories that are going to be starting around… right now?

"And Jim… get General Adams on the line for me." The new President walked to the door of the Library and closed it.

Within a minute, the phone on the desk buzzed. "President Myers."

"General Adams."

"General… I want you to immediately mobilize the military forces and stop the secession."

For a moment, there was no response. "Madame President… I will not do so."

"General… I am your Commander in Chief. That is an order."

"And I am not going to initiate an action that could result in a loss of tens of thousands of Americans."

"I can relieve you of your command."

"President Myers… in ten minutes I can have loyal Marines swarming the White House. I may face a firing squad or spend the rest of my life in prison for it, but with God as my witness, I will take over the government and declare martial law before I shed that much blood in such a futile effort."

The President went quiet. "Go to Def Con 2. Please."

"Consider it done."

~~~

At 6:00 AM, a room full of sleep deprived and exhausted delegates joined the President of the Constitutional States of America to sit in front of the television in the same room in which they had met the previous evening. Disheveled from sleeping in their clothes on cots provided by the National Guard, they sipped coffee in an attempt to rouse themselves from a surreal night of cell phone calls, tweets, emails and text messages.

Tom Edelstein walked into the room yawning and placing his phone back in his pocket. He walked back to stand next to Bryce Hamilton, who then placed his hand on the younger man's shoulder. "Remember… I told you we would be blamed for all kinds of things. I just wasn't expecting this."

They all watched in quiet sadness and amazement as Mike Silver reported for NewsNet.

"All of America is waking to the startling news of the passing of President John Malcolm last night. The President was found dead at his desk in the Oval Office a little after midnight by his Chief of Staff Jim Walters.

"An investigation into the President's death is being conducted by the Secret Service and Federal Bureau of Investigation with the assistance of the Capitol Police. The Secret Service is not releasing many details at this time, but wishes to assure the public that there is no indication of foul play, and noted that the President had not been feeling well the previous day.

"Due to the fact that the Vice President, Speaker of the House and the Senate President were all elected from states that are now part of the Constitutional States of America, the line of presidential succession resulted in former Secretary of State Calista Myers being sworn in as President at approximately 1:00 AM this morning at Camp David, where she had been taken as a precautionary measure. She now is serving as the Chief Executive of a nation of thirty-six states.

"We are expecting President Myers to address the nation at any moment, in spite of the early hour on this Saturday morning, but taking into account the extraordinary events that have taken place during the past twelve hours.

"I am getting word now that we are ready to go to the White House for an address from President Calista Myers."

The camera feed went to the scene of the new President sitting behind a desk in the White House Library. "Good morning, ladies and gentlemen. I come to you this morning with the heavy heart we all share at the loss of a great man, and our President, John Malcolm. It was my great honor to serve alongside President Malcolm in his Administration.

"I am speaking to you from the White House Library, as the Oval Office is still the scene of an investigation into the circumstances surrounding the President's death. However, I wish to reassure all of you, there are no signs of foul play. However, the family of President Malcolm is entitled to the same closure and explanation of an unexpected death as any other family. Therefore, the family and friends, and fellow countrymen of John Malcolm will receive a full explanation of this tragedy once all medical data is evaluated.

"It appears that the President's death occurred just shortly after another tragedy, that being the secession of fifteen states, and the resulting founding of the Constitutional States of America. As a result, during the past hours, America has suffered two devastating blows to our national stability.

"The world is a dangerous place under the best of circumstances, and there may be unfriendly nations and groups viewing us right now as weakened and distracted. To ensure that there is no misunderstanding of our resolve to maintain our vigilance, at 3:00 AM this morning I ordered that our global military readiness status be raised to Def Con 2. That means that our military readiness is one step below a state of war. We will remain in that status until our military leaders advise me that we can stand down. The status of the military bases and personnel located in the CSA is complicating the matter.

"During the night, I spoke with Congressional leaders who will be bringing both houses of Congress into special session today to address the selection of a new Speaker of the House and Senate President. In addition, I will ask Congress for expedited action on my selection for Vice President, and that nominee will be named before the day is out.

"I ask for your patience, but most of all your prayers, as we struggle through these difficult days together. May God bless America... all of America."

~~~

The delegates hovered near a cargo delivery door at the rear of the Scott Conference Center. The first of a series of armored vans intended to carry riot police was being readied for their transport to the National Guard Armory. There they would reconvene and set about to select a Vice President, and pass a series of resolutions.

Staying behind to step onto the final truck, Bryce Hamilton was busy with his cell phone. He made several calls, then reached into his wallet and pulled out a small slip of paper. It was a telephone number he had been given by John Malcolm at the beginning of their meeting at the small college in Ohio. Recalling a childhood game he had played with his neighbor, he had written the number in a special code he had never forgotten.

He punched the number into his phone, took a deep breath and waited. Finally, a male voice answered. "May I ask who's calling?"

"This is Bryce Hamilton."

"Can you please give me a verification code?" Hamilton read aloud a combination of numbers and letters he had been given by John Malcolm.

"Please hold."

"This is Calista Myers."

"Madam President… I'm sorry to speak to you under such conditions."

"Thank you… Mister… President."

"Did President Malcolm ever make you aware of a document called Transition of Military Forces?"

"I'm not aware of it at all."

"I must confess to a lie. I have left the impression, at least publicly, that there were no concrete plans for transitioning bases and forces after a withdrawal of states. The truth is, a very detailed and elaborate plan was finished several months ago. Do you know retired General Lawrence Martin?"

"Of course I do."

"For the most part, he wrote it. A copy was sent to President Malcolm. We attempted several times to follow up with him about it, but to no avail. He never mentioned it at the Urbana meeting, so I'm assuming his staff made sure it never reached him. For security concerns, and I mean for all of America, it was never mentioned publicly. So a certain, sympathetic member of Congress from Georgia will be dropping off a parcel this morning. I think you may find it helpful. It provides for an immediate joint defense arrangement. I assure you it will give pause to any foreign entity that thinks that America has its guard down."

"If I do like it… what then?"

"Then I will ask the CSA delegates for immediate ratification of our defense pact. That can be accomplished before lunchtime."

"What if I don't like it?"

"Then you can enjoy Def Con 2 for a long, long time."

"I'll be back in touch with you. Have a good day, Mister President."

"And you as well… Madam President."

~~~

Marie Howard stepped to the podium in the Senate chamber, then picked up the gavel and banged it down to bring the body to order. She was the second ranking Democrat in the Senate, and it fell to her to attempt to bring order out of chaos.

All present knew that the first and only order of business on the mind of Senator Howard was to elect the new Senate President. She guided the grief stricken body through the process, and when it was finished, she had assumed the position that had been held by her chief rival within the party.

The only business required of the morning having been accomplished, she gazed out over the gathering, now interspersed with many empty chairs. Just as she was about to adjourn the Senate for the day, she heard a familiar voice call out to be recognized.

Senator Elaine Ford from Pennsylvania strolled to the microphone. "Madam President... I rise on this sad day to offer words of hope for our future. While we spend the next days mourning together, coping with the grief we all feel at the loss of our President and the loss of fifteen states, we will find ourselves calling forth the strength that makes us Americans.

"There are now thirty-six United States of America. We must now stand behind and support President Myers as she deals with an unfathomable crisis.

"President Myers must now lead a nation different in content from any of her predecessors. At the same time, citizens of the United States of America are now presented with an opportunity to summon the spirit of innovation and imagination that leaves us, still, a nation of great power and influence.

"There is no question that fifteen states with a different vision of America are now free to chart their own course. But the United States of America will now take on a new and unexpected challenge... a challenge to seize this moment to take bold initiatives to allow us to press forward and achieve the full potential for equality, justice and equity of opportunity we have long yearned for.

"For years now, we have been coming slowly to the realization that the founding of our nation, while unique in its circumstances and legendary in its own sense of appeal, is not really timeless. America in 1776 bears no resemblance to America in 2021. It is no way similar in landmass, demographics, and most of all, an understanding of the needs and dreams of today's citizens.

"The founders of our nation... those who wrote the Constitution, did not include any women. There were no people of color included. And at that moment of the very founding of our nation, slavery was a flourishing enterprise, and even some of those white men were slave owners themselves. And there was not even a universal right for women to vote. Even to achieve that modest right, the nation had to go through a tedious process of amending the Constitution.

"To this day, however, we are asked to follow a Constitution that a growing number of esteemed scholars and historians have come to question as a legitimate guideline for governing a modern United States of America.

"Blind devotion to this aged document makes it unnecessarily difficult to protect our citizens from unnecessary gun violence. It protects the right of the wealthy to disproportionately influence elections.

"And it should not be lost on us, that an almost cult-like devotion to a document written on decaying parchment played no small role in the breakaway of fifteen states. And our Supreme Court should only be asked to judge whether an action is in accordance with our own, carefully deliberated statutes, rather than trying to conduct a judicial séance to determine what a group of exclusively white men from the eighteenth century may have wanted them to do.

"I ask for President Myers to establish a commission to examine whether our nation is best served by a relic of a document deserving of a special little corner of the Smithsonian Institute, or simply a code of statutes written by and voted on by two houses of Congress, the members of which are elected by a modern people of all genders, colors and beliefs.

"Madam President... I thank the Senate for its indulgence."

A single Democratic Senator stood and began applauding. A few seconds later two more stood. One by one, Senators rose and joined in the ovation.

THE END

Made in the USA
Columbia, SC
03 December 2022

72316539R00202